The Bismarck Folly

Part 2

Retribution

The Minstrel boy to the war is gone,
In the ranks of death you'll find him;
His father's sword he has girded on,
And his wild harp slung behind him;
"Land of Song!" said the warrior bard,
"Though all the world betrays thee,
One sword, at least, thy rights shall guard,
One faithful harp shall praise thee!"

The Minstrel fell! But the foeman's chains
Could not bring his proud soul under;
The harp he loved ne'er spoke again,
For he tore its chords asunder;
And said "No chains shall sully thee,
Thou soul of love and bravery!
Thy songs were made for the pure and free
They shall never sound in slavery!"

Thomas Moore

Folly [noun]:
1. Lack of good sense; foolishness
2. A costly ornamental building with no practical purpose

Acknowledgements

My thanks to my wife Catherine, without whose encouragement this book would never have had the resurrection it needed. My gratitude to all those who withstood the barrage of questions necessary in the search for technical accuracy, all those years ago. There were many. In addition, and recently, I've mercilessly pestered both my youngest sons who are now at sea themselves as officers in the merchant marine but who were not yet born when this story was first written.

Thanks to a more recent endless source of info to someone who has forgotten so much of how things were, the crew of the Navy-net –albeit unknowingly.

A further note. I hope for the early release of the six British ex-soldiers held unjustly in an Indian prison for doing their job. These men were some of the brave souls who risk their lives to guard merchant ships at sea. Being on anti-piracy patrols protecting merchant sailors from the scum who steal and murder for personal gain should not be a criminal offence.

Terminology and Acronyms.

AWO: Advanced Warfare Officer, basically controls a battle usually a LtCdr.

Bandit: identified hostile aircraft.

Bikini Amber: Heightened security state for terrorist alerts

BOST: Basic Operational Sea Training. First of a series of ship work-up courses.

Bogey: Presumed hostile aircraft.

Bootneck/ Bootie: Slang. Royal Marines

BMMP: Russian designed tracked armoured amphibious personnel carrier. UK equiv Warrior

BTR80: As above but wheeled

Buzz: Slang for Service Rumour.

Crab- Navy slang for RAF personnel, any kind

ECM: Electronic countermeasures. Jamming enemy emissions

ECCM: Electronic counter countermeasures. Anti-Jamming.

ESM: Electronic Support Measures, a passive means for the detection of enemy transmissions

FLASH: Highest priority signal, jumps the queue to the top every time.

FLIR: Forward Looking Infra-Red. Advanced digitised system using heat generated by objects to detect them.

Gulf two: Reference to the second Gulf war in 2003

ICABA: International Compressed Air Breathing Apparatus

Jungly helicopter: Slang. One which is painted olive green drab.

Jungly Pilot: Slang. RN pilot who has served with the Royal marines

LSM: Landing Ship Medium

LST: Landing Ship Tank

MEM: Marine Engineering Mechanic

MMSI: Maritime Mobile Service Identity. Series of nine digits which are sent in digital form over a radio channel in order to uniquely identify ship

MGCC: Main Gunnery Control Centre.

Muppet: Slang. Most Useless Person Pusser Ever Trained

Pusser: Slang. The Navy as derived from Pursers issue or Pusser's Issue

Pusser's War Canoe: Slang. Any RN ship. From 1975. Idi Amin offered to lend RN his Royal Barge to fight Cod war

PFDHEC: Pre-Fragmented Directional High Explosive Canister. A new shotgun like AA shell.

RHIB or RIB: Rigid Hulled Inflatable Boat. Fast light craft which are used by marines and for boarding operations.

SAM: Surface to air Missile

SART: Search and rescue transponder

SIC: Subject Indicator Code. A formalised prefix on signals for routing/security purposes.

Sitrep: Abbreviation, Situation Report

SSM: Surface to surface missile

Stonk: Salvo of shells from either naval or shore based artillery, upwards of four and more.

WAFU: Slang. Wet And fuck-all Use. Derogatory/familiar term for fleet air arm ratings and officers.

".....and the Minister is doing what he can but he thinks that he's in the shit as well, so..."

Andy Evans broke in impatiently.

"What fucking Minister Winston? What the hell are you babbling on about? Hold on lad, you'd better start from the beginning."

Andy sitting in the security room on *Bismarck* sighed in confusion, Christ almighty what a complete balls-up.

He listened as Winston related events since their arrival in Haiti, cursing himself for not checking things out personally and for Christ's sake, not knowing that his boss's wife was staying with a blasted government minister of the country they were technically at war with. Still, he calmed himself, everybody has sniper hindsight.

Winston got to the part about his reconnaissance of the police station and Andy's concentration narrowed, trying to visualize the ex SBS marine's description of the terrain, the buildings themselves and the locale.

"OK Winston, I think I've got the picture. Now let me tell you what's happened here. Andy quickly brought Winston up to speed on events at the other end of the Caribbean, finishing with a short exposition on how they'd extract the fugitives once they were away from the police station. Andy explained why they couldn't 'jack up' a helo extraction -distances to nearest refuge, availability of suitable aircraft, covering forces etcetera. He went on to explain that *Bismarck* would be the extraction vehicle as soon as she could get there, say in about thirty six hours or so, they'd refine it nearer the time.

Winston sat back and switched off the power. He carefully re-stowed the antenna on the phone and turned to look at Tetsunari.

"Fucking wonderful. Just fucking wonderful. All he wants us to do is to break Mrs 'K' out of the jug, lug her to the West coast and hide for a day or so whilst *Bismarck* trots across the pond and lifts us off a beach. Not much to ask is it? I've got a large penknife Tettas, what have you got?"

Tetsunari smiled for the first time since Mrs König had been taken that morning. He had actually understood some of Winston's sarcasm, but two things puzzled him.

"Winston why did you say we had to get her out of a jug? And what is a lug?"

They were sitting in Louis D'Orville's rose arbour about thirty yards from the rear of the house, the best place they'd found for satellite reception, and privacy.

"Sorry Tettas, 'Jug' is slang for prison and 'to Lug someone' is to carry them. What we really need to find out," he began to pace the small rose arbour "is how many of the bastards are in that police station. It'd be no good going and getting ourselves 'malletted' 'cos there's fifty of the buggers in there when we walk in."

Tetsunari nodded in agreement, pleased that he understood 'being malletted' was military for being killed.

He caught a movement out of the corner of his eye and immediately he became alert. He signalled to Winston to keep talking and moved quietly around to the rear entrance of the arbour and circled it. Then he walked back in the front, signalling a worried Winston to carry on, having spotted that it was only old Marc, the minister's gardener.

Then he had an idea. Five minutes, a bit of sign language and some pidgin later, they had a good enough answer and Old Marc had a new $20 bill carefully secreted away.

Apparently at night there were only five men and a Sergeant on duty said old Marc, two of them patrolled the streets most of the time and the Sergeant held court in the bar Marc used most often. They made their plans and went back to the Minister to see if he could help with one or two items.

Louis D'Orville was upstairs busy packing some cases with his wife, clothes and personal effects strewn all over.

The two bodyguards were a little taken aback at the sight, until the Minister explained that he and his wife were going to try to make a break for the Dominican border that evening. Since things were looking decidedly unhealthy for him in Port Au Prince he'd decided to pre-empt his arrest. He knew a few people in the Dominican Republic and would get somewhere safe just as long as they managed to cross the border before the alarm was sounded.

Winston sympathized, it wasn't easy just to up and bug out, would be far easier to stay and hope things would blow over.

He explained that they would release Mrs 'K' that evening if all went well. The soon to be 'ex-minister', agreed to help as much as he could. Both Tetsunari and Winston hoped that it would be soon enough for Sophie König.

*

Similar thoughts but on a global scale were meandering through Andy Evans' mind as he made his way back to Reiner and the Supply Officer, Lt Marchello Vitali, in the OPS room.

Apart from supervising, however distantly, the rescue of Mrs 'K', he also to think about preparing the islands for defence, bringing in additional manpower and weapons. There was also the stark prospect of evacuation, if the defence proved inadequate or peace didn't suddenly break out.

Andy had no idea whether there was any possibility of averting an invasion but he was too good a soldier to tackle the job half-heartedly. As he arrived in the OPS room Reiner and Marchello were conferring on the stowage of the extra ammunition that might be needed and Andy sat down to wait for his turn, only half listening to the conversation.

Reiner was pleased with the quantities of extra shells they could stow, it nearly doubled *Bismarck*'s normal loading of 1000, 130mm and 1800, 76mm rounds.

The only problem, of course, would be loading them into the ready use magazines as they were needed. Unlike most warships, *Bismarck* only possessed ready use magazines with no shell hoists to load individual rounds from a deeper magazine.

This had been an essential space saving compromise necessary in order to fit everything into a hull much smaller than usual for its armament and purpose. It meant that any individual turret would have to cease fire whilst the ready use magazine was re-stocked, a definite disadvantage in a prolonged conflict.

Reiner was not particularly concerned with the dangers of having spare ammunition lying around since they would be packed in special cases and the PBX type explosives in them were less sensitive to both thermal and mechanical insult.

He smiled as he recalled the salesman talking about 'insulting' explosives, something he tried to avoid –the thought popping irreverently into his mind. Why didn't the fellow just say they were less temperature sensitive and less likely to go off by being dropped or bounced!

Besides which, most cases would be placed in empty storerooms since if *Bismarck* had to fight again, it would be from its home port and they would only need stores for a couple of days at most.

Andy waited until they'd wound up the discussion before passing on his hastily prepared list of requirements.

Reiner frowned and then whistled softly as he read down the list.

"You don't mean to play footy, do you Andy?" He said at last.

"It's 'footsy' Reiner, and no I don't."

Andy was of the Royal Marine school of thought that said 'why bother to storm a hill or building when you can flatten it and save lives'?

The Royal Marines had pioneered the use of use of light anti-tank weapons and the like when assaulting dug-in machine guns and occupied buildings which had helped reduce Marine casualties in the Falklands campaign. Since then everyone had jumped on the bandwagon.

"Reiner, if half a dozen thugs broke into my house I can assure you that I'd happily use anything that came to hand, if they start it, it's their problem. It's the same here with these bastards, except I've got a bit of warning. If I'm forced to fight, for whatever reason, then they'd best not be expecting me to play fair.

I can assure you that any of the bastards I come up against are going to wish they'd stayed at home –those that live that is. If they take us, then they'll have paid for each and every inch they gain."

That was a long speech for Andy and Reiner knew it, he looked away from the grim faced ex-Marine and perused the list. As he took in the inventory of anti-personnel mines, M18A1 Claymores, grenade launchers and sniper gear Andy wanted, he felt a moment of sympathy for those who might contest the islands, but it was only a moment.

The extra men and materials would be flown into the main island the next evening, hopefully. Reiner wished he knew if it would be soon enough.

An hour later he had answers to some of the questions that had plagued him since that morning. The call from Jake had lasted just five minutes and had left Reiner with much to do and not long to do it.

Firstly, as a precaution, Jake had ordered that all families should now be evacuated to Grand Cayman in preparation for a charter flight back to Bermuda on the following day.

Secondly, *Bismarck* was to sail as soon as possible for the main island, bringing all the Haitian wounded and prisoners with them -a separate flight by government helo would lift out their own casualties in about two hours' time. Finally he wanted an update on when Little Cayman's radar, and weapons systems would be on line.

Apparently the latest satellite info showed the Haitian task force on the same course and heading. They were upping the stakes and seemed hell bent on invasion regardless.

17:00 Thursday May 24th 2018
George Town, Grand Cayman

Jake stood on the jetty near to the point where *Bismarck* would shortly berth, and watched intently as his ship slowly covered the last hundred yards or so. He jumped slightly as someone in the fleet of ambulances that waited behind him, accidentally touched a siren button.

Beyond the line of trucks and ambulances he was surprised to see that a large crowd had now gathered to await *Bismarck*'s arrival and that the heavily armed Ministry Protection Police were hard put to keep them off the jetty.

Word of *Bismarck*'s morning battle was widespread and he supposed that the presence of the uniforms and trucks had announced that something was in the wind, hence the large expectant crowd which appeared to spread in both directions along the sea front.

As big Trev Kent expertly cast the first line, Jake wondered at the reception his men would receive. Good as his word this morning, Sandiford Roche had commenced his campaign to discredit the Haitian propaganda with radio broadcasts one of which Jake had caught.

It had sounded utterly convincing to Jake but then he knew the truth anyway and now it would be a good test to see if the crowd had appreciated *Bismarck*'s timely intervention this morning.

He looked again at the men that lined the ship's upperdeck, all dressed in their tropical whites and standing to attention as *Bismarck* finally came to rest alongside.

The bosun's pipe shrilled again and a voice boomed out from the Tannoy.

"Attention on the upper deck. Face for'ard and salute."

Everyone on the upperdeck faced the bow and saluted the Caymans flag as it rose up the Jack staff.

The roar of approval from the crowd made the fine hairs on Jake's neck prickle and he felt a surge of emotion swell inside.

The cheering went on for what seemed like ages and finally degenerated into a disjointed attempt to sing their national anthem which grew louder and more confident as it went on.

Jake stood to attention as did everyone else in uniform, so it was some moments before the men could be dismissed and the work of transporting the wounded and the prisoners could commence.

*

Back on board again he studied each man as they filed into the wardroom for the briefing, particularly Ian Halshaw. Ian's face displayed no obvious emotions and Jake fervently hoped that the Weapons Electrical Officer could manage to put a lid on his tragedy until this conflict was resolved.

He knew it was an utterly selfish 'ask' but balanced that with his need to have the ship in fighting trim for the coming conflict.

He'd waited until 18:00 to call the meeting in order that he could have a long chat with Andy Evans regarding the rescue OP for his wife.

Andy had gone through all the options again adding only that it was just possible that they could get a small team into Haiti by HALO parachute drop (High Altitude Low Opening) to help cover the three on their way to the coastal rendezvous.

But of course, he added, the more people to hunt for; the more likely a capture. Jake had just nodded and confirmed in a pain filled voice that *Bismarck* couldn't go until the Islands were safe.

Andy knew this anyway but had hoped that McTeal would release them from their obligations. Finally Jake asked that, if worst came to worst and *Bismarck* did not survive, then he wanted to be sure that Andy would continue with Sophie's rescue by other means.

When everyone was present and drinks had been served, he commenced the briefing by handing over to Miles Carlson who gave the background to the events of the day.

When Miles had finished, Jake thanked him and activated a small blue tooth projector, displaying shots of the satellite photos.

He led them through the chronologically arranged photos explaining how the Haitians had sailed in three groups, obviously trying for a little deception, which had now joined together.

Given the timing of that manoeuvre Jake suspected that it was in response to *Bismarck*'s attack that morning. Finally he left a slide up which displayed the make-up of the Haitian task force and handed out a sheet which gave the specifications for those same ships.

The wardroom was silent for a few moments whilst everyone absorbed the information. Leaving the slide on the screen Jake pointed out where their information was deficient, they didn't, he said, know what the weapons load-out of the enemy ships were.

For example, was the *Sovremenny* class destroyer fitted with the deadly SSN-22 Sunburn missiles, or for export, had they been fitted with an older outfit of say, SSN-9 Siren missiles?

Lieutenant Commander Scotnikov had interrogated the two surviving Ukrainian adviser/trainers and took up the story. One of them he said, a Captain second class, had been more than willing to talk about his erstwhile employers, expressing the desire to pull the trigger himself on those 'child murdering bastards'.

Jake shot a quick look at Ian Halshaw after that accidental gaff of Scotnikov's, but he seemed not to have been affected by it.

Scotnikov continued. It appeared that in general, Haitian training was at a level whereby they could carry out their tasks, if not expertly, then at least adequately. There were a number of Eastern European and Chinese advisers on each ship and the flagship carried a Haitian Rear Admiral and an Ukrainian one too, who seemed to get on reasonably well.

Scotnikov finished with the point that the advisers were kept ignorant of operations for as long as possible and so they knew nothing of the fleet's plans. Their Ukrainian Captain had not known until last night what was planned for today and was disgusted when it happened.

He was sure that the *Slava* had P-500 Bazalt missiles which were NATO code SSN-12 Sandbox, ship killers. He didn't know what the former Chinese ships had loaded but had discussed it briefly with his Chinese counterpart on the *Dessalines*. He seemed to think they had the export versions of the C802, the AK variant but knew nothing of the guidance packages.

Mr Sandiford Roche rose to give an appreciation of where they stood on the world stage. In simple terms he explained that it was an uphill struggle to counter the continuing Haitian rhetoric but that both Britain and America had been made aware of the true situation and its origins.

As for assistance, unfortunately America did not seem inclined to step in militarily despite the fact that their own intelligence community had confirmed the Haitian aggression.

Britain, he said, appeared to be dithering. The Prime Minister would consult the military chiefs to see what, if anything could be done and would then consult the cabinet. Other Caribbean nations were for the most part standing on the side lines encouraging a 'dialogue' -as if it was the newest word they'd learned.

"So Gentlemen," he summarized, "we appear to be on our own for the present, and, I suspect that any assistance, if offered, will arrive too late. The burden, it would seem, rests on you and your ship. The Prime Minister recognizes that you are not mercenaries, also that your roots are not yet grown here. And so, he has reconsidered his position on *Bismarck*'s obligation to fight. He formally thanks you for your brave actions this morning, but removes from you any further obligation to continue the fight. I would like..."

"Nooo!" It was a shout from the depths of his soul.

All eyes swivelled towards the source. Ian Halshaw stood at the back shaking with emotion.

"I'll not quit now. No Sir, not a chance. I'm staying even if everyone else goes. I'll fight ashore or afloat, I don't care. I've unfinished business with those bastards."

And he sat down, in complete silence. Now Jake knew why Ian was here and not mourning his daughter. He thought that he would be the same too. He would not rest, would crush any objector, and would do anything to make sure those responsible didn't get what they wanted.

It was the only meaningful thing left for a father, for Ian to do. If in some way he could help prevent those accountable for his daughter's death from profiting, or prevent them murdering more people, then he could let her lie in peace. Aye, and maybe gain a measure of peace for himself and his wife.

Yes, Jake well understood that kind of obligation. It wasn't as simple as revenge; it had many more facets than that. He stood slowly in the gathering silence.

"Thank you Ian, for reminding us of what we are about. And thank you Minister for releasing us from our obligation. But I too will stay." He looked around at everyone.

"I will however, put it to my men, that if any should wish to leave they may do so without shame."

He looked around the faces of his officers and his eyes came to rest on the one representative of the lower deck. Kipper sat with a look of grim determination etched on his craggy features.

"I'll put it to the men Sir." Was his only comment.

Jake looked askance for any further comments and then carried on.

"Right. Now it's obvious that we can't just simply up anchor and sail off to fight them, despite our armour I suspect that we wouldn't be able to go it toe to toe against this lot with much chance of success. What we require gentlemen is a subterfuge, some form of deception tactic that will give us a degree of surprise or an edge of some kind. Now look here."

He changed the PowerPoint and a chart of the Caribbean appeared on screen.

"I've drawn some projections based on the likely course of the enemy task force. As you can see, up until they reach a point some hundred and fifty miles south east of us, we can fairly well predict their course and if nothing changes, their time of arrival at that point."

He moved the laser dot to the 150 mile point on the map.

"Then they have a number of options. Firstly, they can turn north west and land on the south coast of the island at either Great Pedro point or Ironshore point."

He swept his pointer from the south coast round to where they sat now.

"Or, secondly, they could come in on a slightly north of westerly course and turn to attack the east coast here at George Town or Seven Mile beach."

He moved the dot to the huge open mouth on the north side of the main island.

Thirdly, they could take the risk and sail their landing ships through the Main Channel and into North Sound. Finally, they may do any of these and split off a group to take the outer islands at some point."

He looked around the room.

"Anyone think of any other ways to get at us?"

He waited a moment looking at the shaking heads. "Right. Now here's the tricky bit. What can we do to put a spanner in his works? That is without trying a 'Custer's last stand' approach, as I've heard suggested." He turned to look at a smiling Miles Carlson.

"Any proposals will be welcome."

Ian suggested mining the approaches, a good idea but unfortunately given the time scale not practical, as were under water obstructions and the like, although blocking the North sound might be done.

The sighting of machine guns and entrenchments covering the landing areas was of course the province of the quiet gentleman sitting with Andy Evans. Steve Robinson, the Chief of the MPP had said nothing but listened with obvious interest.

Kipper kept quiet until he was fit to burst, then could stand it no longer.

"Sir. What about the 'Snakey Blake' trick, you know, the one we pulled on the Yanks, begging your pardon Mr Carlson, when we attacked *Nimitz* and *Carolina* in the channel."

Jake looked up with interest sparking in his eyes, now here was a possibility.

"Go on Kipper explain to everyone."

Kipper just managed to prevent an irreverent 'unaccustomed as I am to public speaking' from slipping out, and launched into his account.

"My dad told me this sea story ages ago. Well it was like this. He was on the old *Blake* -a kind of half-baked cruiser left over from the good old days; back in '75' I think it was, and they were tasked to attack the Yank's latest carrier and her escorts."

He paused to let them consider that.

"Well of course he said, they all fell about laughing at the thought of little old *Snakey Blakey* at around 15,000 tons taking on that 93,000 ton monster and a brand new nuclear powered missile cruiser with a shed-load of frigates and destroyers."

He had their attention now.

"Anyway the skipper who was a former submariner, obviously took it seriously and they proceeded down Channel towards where they thought the American task force could be."

"Come nightfall, the skipper had ordered a course change into the main shipping channel and the lights on the dirty great hangar at the arse end, turned on. Apparently not satisfied with that he ordered more lights took up to the hangar roof."

He had them all hooked now even the taciturn Miles Carlson was waiting for the punch line.

"Then he says not a chink of light was to show for'ard of the hangar. And so they sailed along at a stately fifteen knots all thinking the skipper had gone mad."

Kipper was a renowned story teller and he was in his element now as he painted them a picture.

"The search radar was off and only the short range nav radar going which seemed sensible as there's always plenty of traffic down there."

Everyone was listening with rapt attention as Kipper re-told his father's story describing the approach to the giant carrier.

"He said. 'There we were lit up like a bloody Christmas tree and just chugging along, until we were close enough for not only the 6 inch guns but the 3 inchers to engage as well."

"Then he said, all hell let loose, off went the lights on comes the search and fire control radar and bang went the guns. He says they emptied a theoretical 3 inch magazine, using blanks of course, into the *Carolina* and most of the sixers into the *Nimitz* and then legged it for Portland and a safe haven."

He sat back in his chair as the story came to an end.

"The war games computers had put *Nimitz's* flight deck out of action for thirty two hours and they'd sunk the bloody *Carolina*. Dad said the Yanks really were pissed off with them having come sneaking up in the crowded Channel looking like any other small tanker. He said the American aircraft caught them just before they made it safely to Portland Bill, thirty two hours and thirty five minutes after they were hit."

"He finished off saying everyone was deaf for a week and the old PMO was worried about smoke inhalation from all the smoke floats they dropped all around us indicating hits. He said there was so many planes in the sky he reckoned they must have had the whole ships company up there flying, including the NAAFI manager."

Any tension that had remained after Ian's outburst and Roche's little speech disappeared in a gale of laughter, Carlson laughing as loud as the rest.

Eventually Jake brought some order back to the meeting.

"Despite the laughter Kipper, you've got a good point there, that's the kind of thing we need. I'm not saying that that won't work, it's just that Sandy here tells me there are spies on the island, so as soon as we sail they'll know we're out and about and this sea isn't as busy as the Channel."

The meeting continued for a while but with no firm proposals on the table as it broke up. Jake went away feeling that he'd missed something in what had been said, something important, but he couldn't for the life of him work out what it was.

As he started to relax, images of his wife began to stream through his mind. God I hope she's all right, he thought and then savagely shunted her out of his conscious, I can't do anything about it and worry is a pointless exercise, he admonished himself.

19:55 Thursday 24th May 2018
Petionville Police Station, Haiti

Sophie bit back a scream as she felt something tear inside, the second policeman was obviously enjoying his work, she thought, as he buggered her furiously.

Watching from one side, with a smile of both anticipation and enjoyment, was the man she knew as Major Mercier. She could tell by the bulging front of his trousers that he obviously couldn't wait for his turn again.

The day had passed with agonizing slowness since she'd been dumped in the cell that morning. It was a larger room than she'd imagined for a cell, about twenty feet square she reckoned, with one small slit-like window high up the wall.

There was nothing much else in the room, no bed, no chair just a few ring bolts in the floor at the centre of the room and a bucket in the corner.

She had spent the day trying to suppress a growing feeling that not just her days were numbered but her hours too. A knot of fear had tightened in her chest as the day wore on. She knew he was coming back, he'd said so, he had to go to the capital and collect a few things then he'd be back.

She waited. No food and no water, the cell was thankfully cool but she couldn't find a comfortable way to sit on the hard concrete, no matter what she tried her buttocks became numbed after a few minutes.

That she would be abused she had no doubts, she'd seen the looks on the soldiers faces and the superior smile of acknowledgement on Mercier's features. She watched the shadows move around the walls until finally dusk and then darkness.

She'd almost convinced herself that he'd forgotten her when the recessed light in the ceiling snapped on and she heard voices and movement in the corridor. Then the horror began.

First Mercier entered with two policemen carrying an odd looking bench-like contraption which they fastened to the ring bolts in the floor. Then she was ordered to strip.

She told him what to do with himself. When she woke up her head was buzzing and there was blood in her mouth, she tried to move her arms but discovered that she was naked and fastened to Mercier's contraption.

She became aware that she was in a head low kneeling position with arms and legs fastened in place. Then it began.

She had screamed out loud when the first policeman stuck a lubricated finger in her bottom and then had roughly taken her. Mercier had laughed aloud at the sound and then proceeded to talk his way through her pain and humiliation.

"Mrs König, you will never leave here alive, unless you are very good, that is, then I might keep you for a while for my personal use. But I must warn you, I think that unlikely."

He chuckled loudly and she blinked as a camera flash went off. Turning her head she saw another policeman taking pictures and recording events on a mobile phone.

"Yes Mrs König, your humiliation is not to be a private affair, unless you tell me all you know of your husband and his unusual ship, copies of these will be expertly added to a hotel bedroom scene and of course my special chair will be deleted."

He leered at her and began unzipping his fly.

"When they are distributed it will look to all the world like you're having fun in Haiti. Now open your mouth there's another picture I want taken for my own collection before I take you properly myself."

God let it end soon, she thought.

It was very quiet up in the duty room and constable Artou sat impatiently waiting for one of the other two to come up and relieve him at the desk. He had spent most of the time since he'd come on duty at eighteen hundred, thinking of nothing but the white woman down in the holding cell. Yes she was a little older than he preferred but she appeared to be ten years younger than she was.

Everyone was afraid of Major Mercier, sure, but he'd seemed in a good mood earlier when he'd promised the duty staff that they'd get their turn with the female spy he'd caught earlier.

He impatiently checked the clock over the entrance door for the umpteenth time and rubbed his groin. The small waiting area in front of the chest high counter was empty as usual since few dared come in unbidden.

His thoughts strayed back to the white woman and what he was going to do to her if he got chance, he looked down the corridor which led to the cells, damn, where was Henri, he said about eight o'clock didn't he, the greedy bastard.

He turned and saw a scruffy local standing in front of him, the man was smiling for some reason, probably drunk he thought, his anger starting to rise.

"*Kimoun ou ye*?" Who are you?

Winston had quickly looked through the dirty glass of the police station door and scanned the reception area. One man not looking this way, no noises, nobody else in sight, time to go. He'd carefully opened the door and walked up to the counter in front of the policeman, making sure he kept his makeshift blackjack out of sight as he moved.

Actually it was a foot long piece of lead pipe wrapped in a dirty cloth that Marc the gardener had given him earlier.

The policeman turned to face Winston, a look of surprise then anger on his face. He gabbled something at Winston in Creole and Winston just gave his biggest toothy grin. The man's expression went back to surprise when Winston swung the blackjack and belted him on the temple, being careful to reach out with his left arm to grab the falling man.

Holding on to his collar with one hand, he rolled over the counter top and laid the unconscious policeman on the floor. He looked up to see Tetsunari vault over the counter and land quietly on Winston's side of it.

Without speaking he moved swiftly to cover the corridor and Winston searched the unconscious man. Finding a large key ring, he got up quickly and scanned the room again, nope, nothing in here that looks like an arms cabinet, he thought, as he moved silently over and joined Tetsunari by the corridor entrance.

Moving swiftly but quietly they advanced down the dimly lit corridor listening intently and checking each side door they came to. The third one was of heavier construction than the others and Winston quickly examined the lock.

Selecting a well-used key he inserted it and twisted. The tumblers inside the lock dropped noisily and the door moved slightly as the deadbolt slid back.

Winston entered the dark room with hands searching the walls for a light switch, he found it and the room was bathed in light. Three cheers for the good guys, he thought to himself as he surveyed the weapons and equipment lining the room.

Quickly he passed Tetsunari a Colt automatic and a box of shells, grabbing the same himself. He earmarked an old but well-oiled Remington assault shotgun and an old M1 carbine to take on the way out.

Tetsunari quickly filled a magazine for the .45 automatic, snapped it into place, chambered a round then refilled the magazine. A smile touched the corner of his mouth as he watched the corridor, it was time to diminish, but not erase, the stain on his honour.

Back in the passage both Winston and Tetsunari quickly ensured the safeties was off and with greater confidence but equal stealth they moved along the corridor to the head of a concrete staircase.

Stopping to listen at the top they could hear a slightly muffled voice, both men instantly knew who that was despite the muting of the doors. They moved swiftly and silently down the staircase.

They approached a door which was slightly ajar and both men quickly got low down and bobbed their heads to look into the room. Tetsunari lunged for the door, a killing madness on him as his brain registered what the quick glance had shown him.

Winston quickly restrained him and took a couple of slow deep breaths to force down the rage that burned just as brightly inside him. Seeing this, Tetsunari understood and mimicked Winston, thankful that his friend had restrained him. To go into a close quarters killing room in a rage would either get themselves killed or the person they were supposed to be rescuing.

Winston indicated that Tetsunari should go left and he would go right, gripping the edge of the door he mouthed a countdown from three.

Sophie could feel that the man inside her was about to climax, his thrusts were becoming more rapid, he gripped her hips tighter and his breathing became harsher.

Suddenly the world exploded around her, the noise was deafening and she felt something heavy and wet slap down onto her back.

The man pulled out of her and she felt him slowly slide off. Her ears were ringing and she looked up at Mercier, his face was a mask of shock, he was frozen in place with one hand just resting on the holster flap of his service automatic and the other holding his now shrinking member, then she heard a voice she knew so well and began to cry.

Tetsunari waited until Winston ripped open the door and then stormed in, automatic levelled and searching for targets.

He saw a uniformed man against the left wall and shot him once in the chest and once in the head, spinning quickly he lined up on the Major standing by Sophie's head and began to squeeze the trigger.

He stopped himself as the Major froze in place, his penis going instantly limp. Winston had charged through the door immediately after Tetsunari and breaking right, shot the man who was busily raping his boss's wife. A quick double tap, two shots in rapid succession from the side, and the bastard had slumped over Sophie and slid to the floor. Then he lined up on the frozen Major.

"As Clint Eastwood would say Major. Please move. Go ahead and make my day." The promise in his voice was enough. The man didn't move a muscle.

Winston nodded to Tetsunari, who rapidly set about releasing Sophie, then he advanced on Major Mercier with the Colt automatic unwaveringly pointed at his head.

Thrusting the muzzle viciously into the man's mouth, snapping teeth in the process, Winston pushed him against the back wall and removed the holstered weapon with his left hand.

Tetsunari went over to where Sophie squatted on that obscene contraption. Gently he released her hands and legs speaking softly to her all the while in Japanese.

Sophie stood and put her arms around Tetsunari letting out a grief stricken sob of self-disgust, fear, relief and a hundred other fleeting feelings. Easing away, Tetsunari quickly retrieved her clothes and handed her a grubby towel to clean herself.

He turned away while the sobbing, pain wracked woman dressed, and his eyes locked with the 'Mad Major'.

Mercier was terror stricken, the swiftness of the attack, the pain of his broken teeth and the look in the eyes of the two men he faced told him he was a dead man. His sphincters relaxed, he felt the warm trickle of urine down his legs and smelt his own fear.

Winston turned his nose up in disgust.

"He's pissed and shit himself Tettas."

He removed his gun from the bloody ruin of Mercier's mouth and turned to Tetsunari.

"You can have him if you want, he just disgusts me."

Sophie gave a screech of rage and pushed Winston out of the way. She stood in front of Mercier, eyes alight with a maniacal gleam, shaking with an all-consuming anger. Her voice was like the cut of a lash and not much more than a low sibilant hiss.

"You couldn't break me pig. You can rape my body but not my mind, you are unfit to live and therefore you shall not!"

She summoned her strength, remembered the lessons Jake and Tetsunari had painstakingly given her, gathered her power and focussed it. With a titanic 'kiaii' shout, she launched a kick at Mercier's groin.

Smaller by at least a foot than Mercier, she had the snap kick perfectly angled, bent knee pointing at Mercier's groin before the leg straightened at super speed with her hips adding power.

Tetsunari, feeling the pride of a master watching a very promising student, assumed Mercier's testicles had disintegrated such was the power in that kick.

Winston quickly took charge, she obviously needed that release, he thought, but it's time to 'bog off' before the patrols come back in.

Gently he placed a hand on Sophie's trembling shoulders.

"Ma'am we have to go. I'm sure you'd like to spend half the night kicking that bastard's groin but we've got to get going."

He tugged slightly at her arm and suddenly she relaxed and turned to face him.

"Thank you Winston, and you Tetsunari. Yes, let's get out of here I need a drink and some fresh air."

She promptly retched.

"I also want that camera." She said, standing weakly and pointing to the floor next to a policeman's body.

Winston led her out into the dim corridor, motioning for her to wait he silently climbed the steps and peered around the corner. Tetsunari waited until Winston and Sophie had left. Then he reached down and lifted the big Major with ease, sitting him on the instrument of Sophie's torture.

Tetsunari ripped the uniform shirt open exposing Mercier's chest and abdomen.

Then he slapped some sense into the pain wracked man until the light of intelligence again shone in Mercier's eyes.

Tetsunari spoke slowly, his voice laden with solemnity.

"Yes, you are about to die Major. You have been sentenced to death by Mrs Sophia Helene König, and I have the great honour and privilege of carrying out that sentence."

He drew back his right arm curling his fingers very slightly. His eyes locked with the frightened major's and he inhaled slowly and deeply, building the power.

With a spine chilling shout, his stiffened fingers raced forward to meet Mercier's taut gut. Such was the power of the *Nukite* stab that his rigid fingers passed through skin and muscle.

He looked into Mercier's eyes, saw the recognition, his hands encircled their target organs and then, still locked with the Major's eyes, he ripped down and out.

Tetsunari stepped away from the dying man and calmly wiped his hands on the towel, picking up his automatic he left Mercier trying to stuff his guts back inside.

Winston paused at the armoury and stepped in to select the weapons he'd spotted earlier. As he picked the shotgun up his eyes strayed to the end of the rack and he noticed that one of the weapons was chained in place, he couldn't quite make it out and walked closer.

Whistling silently to himself he surveyed what must surely be the personal weapon of someone important. He quickly examined the padlock on the *Snayperskaya Vintovka Dragunova*, or more commonly the famous Russian Dragunov sniper rifle.

Now what the hell was one of these doing here, he thought as he broke open the padlock with a bayonet. The weapon had in fact been presented as a gift to the Defence Minister, who lived nearby, from his happy Ukrainian counterpart, after the signing of the contracts for the new Haitian fleet.

Slinging the Dragunov over his shoulder and quickly grabbing a box of shells for it, Winston made his way towards the door and then stopped. Like a child in a sweet shop he couldn't stop himself from grabbing another M1, a cleaning kit and then a couple of bayonets before relocking the door behind him.

Switching off the light above the outside of the door to the police station, Winston quickly moved Sophie toward the waiting Ford pick-up.

Over the tail gate and under the sacking he gently placed her apologizing as he did so. Leaving the shotgun for Tetsunari, he dumped the rest of the weapons on the front seat and waited by the passenger door for Tettas to appear. Marc, behind the wheel, said he hadn't heard a thing and Winston silently gave thanks for the thick walls.

Quickly exiting the police station Tetsunari was pleased to note that the poorly lit street was as deserted as before and nodding to Winston he picked up the shotgun and joined Sophie under the sacking. The pick-up moved off sedately down the road, old Marc driving as if he hadn't a care in the world.

23:30 Thursday 24th May 2018
Bismarck, George Town, Grand Cayman

Jake sighed with relief and closed the door to his cabin. He wandered over to his bed, debated whether to have a nightcap then decided it was too much effort and flopped down on his front. The next difficult question was 'could he be assed to take his steaming bats off?' Odd that he still used the old navy name for his work boots, his mind drifted. This day had been the longest he'd ever known. Looking back on it, he had the strangest feeling that when he woke up he would find that it had all been a particularly bad dream.

So Winston and Tetsunari had got her out. No wonder Andy hadn't been able to keep the grin off his face a moment ago. Thank the Lord for Marines of any kind, Japanese or Royal, he thought. At least she was safe for the moment.

He had no doubt at all that there would be a tremendous hoo-hah from the Haitians to follow but he was confident that given a reasonable amount of luck, Winston and Tetsunari would make their eventual rendezvous on the West coast.

As he drifted down to sleep, his mind re-ran the early morning battle and again he thanked a God, that he wasn't sure existed, for allowing him to make the correct decisions and avoid catastrophe.

Hot on the heels of this morning's battle were thoughts of what will surely come in the next day or so and so tired as he was, it took a long time for him to settle.

There was something that nagged him in what had been said early this evening, he couldn't quite bring it to mind, something about the date. At last he drifted off.

Winston sat deep in thought as he munched on breakfast of hard bread and dried bacon with a little cheese. They were bivouacked in a grove of trees and through gaps in them he could look down the steep hillsides towards the port of Les Cayes.

He consulted an old tourist map, the best that the minister could come up with such notice, as he sipped his cold coffee. Old wasn't the word for it, patches of terrain were so worn that they had no names or features except that of an indistinct coastal outline.

From what he had seen of Haiti he wasn't surprised that it was no longer on the tourist tracks of the world with most of its trees gone. And if the police and those funny sods with the blue uniforms were anything to go by, he wouldn't want to get picked up even for dropping litter or farting in public.

Still, he thought, Mrs K is bearing up surprisingly well after what those bastards had done to her. He smiled in grim recollection of Mercier's face when they'd burst in. Tettas hadn't been particularly forthcoming about what he'd done to Mercier, just to say that the man wouldn't be amongst any pursuing party for sure.

Winston knew how deeply Tettas was committed to his own ideas of honour and duty and had been saddened to learn that he still felt himself tainted despite the rescue. Ah well, different strokes, he mused and turned his mind back to the problem of supplies.

Tetsunari was at that moment, about a hundred feet above and to the right of Winston having picked a place to stand his watch where the track that they'd followed, passed through a relatively clear area.

It also jinked to the left at this point which meant that Tetsunari could look down over the last half mile or so of it. Sitting as still as Buddha with an M1 across his knees he gazed back down the track half hoping that a pursuing force would appear so that some of the stain on his honour could be erased.

He reflected that had he been true Samurai, then he would have asked Sophie's permission to kill himself after the rescue last night. One has to note how pointless that would be he decided, a clear giving up, rather than making amends. Obviously he was still needed by his charge which meant that he still had many opportunities to remove some of these barbaric Haitians from this life.

Tetsunari like many older Japanese, whether they cared to admit it or not, was by western politically correct standards, deeply racist. They would be wrong of course, seriously xenophobic would be more accurate, since it wasn't just the colour or the race, it was simply that anyone not born in Japan was clearly uncultured, a gaijin, and therefore inferior.

The irony that he didn't see was that he was in service to a gaijin, all be it one who deserved as much respect as he could give to any non-Japanese. With typical far eastern mental duplicity, he ignored inconvenient contradictions in his reasoning. He also worked closely with Winston of course, another gaijin, and enjoyed working with him though he'd given up trying to civilize him a long time ago.

Musing didn't affect his reflexes and the M1 was at his shoulder ready to fire before the movement down the path truly registered in his brain. Lowering the carbine he watched as a hen partridge and four chicks began pecking at something next to the path fifty yards away. All the other sounds about him were natural, a part of his brain told him, and he relaxed again.

Sophie sat next to the pick-up with old Marc and ate her breakfast. Five days of this at least, what the hell was Jake playing at starting a war with her in the enemy camp? She munched irritably, despite recalling his frantic pleas for her to leave.

She was pleased that Mercier was dead and that really surprised her. She had the feeling she had not been his first female victim and so his demise would prevent him killing and raping more women, so yes she genuinely was relieved, more than pleased. Of all the people she'd ever met he was the biggest oxygen thief of all, the who least deserved to live, may he fry in hell forever.

She reflected that knowing Tetsunari, Mercier's death would have been particularly painful. She understood to some small extent how dishonoured he'd felt, letting her get captured in the first place. The previous day's events had already grown a scab of unreality around them, except of course for the occasional stab of pain down below and a painful cut on her lip.

Apart from the obvious she'd come out of it pretty well physically intact, a natural protection she thought, a kind of shock. The mind busily fuzzing up the outlines of traumatic events so as to reduce their ability to affect the organism, she rationalised. She also had no doubts that she would suffer a kind of post-traumatic stress for some time to come.

Finally she considered the plight of Louis and Francesca and wondered whether she was the 'Jonah' of their fortunes or simply the catalyst to Louis's eventual downfall. Well there was stuff-all she could do about it anyway, stuck out in the middle of nowhere.

Marc Bellard erstwhile gardener to Minister D'Orville, considered his future. He had never left Haiti in his life and didn't relish the thought of doing so now.

Old Marc was only fifty five but that was a good age for a Haitian whose life-span averaged 61 and for females 64, unlike their counterparts in the Caymans who could look forward to another twenty years or so.

He knew much of the land over which they would travel in the next few days, the two soldiers -he could tell what they were by the familiar way they handled weapons- wanted to be high up and in the treeline all the way to the west coast but he'd told them much of the timber had been cut, and that meant using back paths and tracks he hadn't crossed for years.

Still, they had enough diesel to ride for today at least, after that well, we'll see how tough these soldier boys are, he thought and then remembered the woman.

Miles Carlson stabbed the disconnect on the screen of his mobile phone and sat fuming. Well, he'd been getting really good at predictions recently so he had no right to expect his career forecast to be off base, and it wasn't.

Vern Weathers and Nate King had run interference for him as much as possible, but at the end of the day he'd pissed off too many people, too high up the food chain. The only thing that had saved his ass at all, was the personal intervention of Mr McTeal and that in itself had 'rubbed' his bosses the wrong way.

Thailand here I come. A demotion and a posting to the Far East was better than he could have expected. Of course it had been all tied up in a neat bow of political bullshit and so publicly Mr Miles Carlson accepted a temporary demotion in order to fit in with the Far East setup and not tread on any toes there.

Ha ha, the laugh is on me. They'd dressed it up for public consumption, an experimental situation of course. The return of senior officers to foreign duties for a refresher on a err, rotational basis is under consideration' blah, blah, blah! Re-connect with field operatives.

Still it could have been much worse and only four more years for pension hopefully he would get his grade back before then. He suddenly sat forward thinking about the phone call he'd have to make to his wife. *'Hi hon, fancy a couple of years out east, no not Boston'*.

Thailand`. Boy oh boy, am I in for some shit from Ilene and the boys. He leaned back in the chair and surveyed his oak panelled temporary office in Government house, not bad, not bad at all for an outcast.

He went back to work, sealing the latest sat-eval and photos in an envelope; he decided to pay König a visit and deliver them personally.

A half mile or so away, down alongside the jetty at the small harbour, *Bismarck* basked under a baking hot sun. She looked rather like a prodded 'termite mound` as her people swarmed all over removing artificial deck guns, lifeboats and dummy turrets. Down on the jetty itself, a line of crewmen and off duty MPP gradually filled truck after truck with furniture, fixtures and fittings. All checked and double checked against Lt Marchello Vitali's master list.

A large refrigerator truck stood to one side awaiting the perishable stores and still another truck was being loaded with the crewmen's personal belongings. It would be apparent to anyone with just a little brain power, that *Bismarck* was slimming down to fighting trim in a figurative and literal sense.

The crew meeting at 07:00 that morning had been chaired by Kipper in the dining room used by senior and junior rates. He began by explaining the background to what had happened and why, as far as was known. There'd been angry mutterings about the fact that it was basically down to a bunch of 'druggies'.

Most servicemen from *wherever*, had an instinctive loathing of anything drug related and *Bismarck*'s people were probably a bit more radical than most crews. These men were different to any he'd served with except perhaps at FOST. They were all 'oldies' the youngest in mid-late 20's with two just knocking on fifty. The majority were in their thirties and forties and of course they'd heard it all before, seen it, got the T shirt and starred in the movie. The '*dits*', sailor-speak for ditties or stories they told over a beer or two, showed they'd been around the block a few times as their American cousins would say.

Kipper knew there was so much real life and real service experience in this room that BS was not an option, they'd see straight through it, not that he would have tried anyway. Not only that, but they deserved better.

So he went on to point out that the latest satellite info showed the Haitian task force still on its way and issued a paper assessment of it listing all that was present. He also informed them that there was little likelihood of any help from Britain or America.

Then Kipper had come to Andrew McTeal's thanks and his offer, to forget the agreement.

"Look lads, it's not up to me to wipe your arses. You're all big boys now you can make your own minds up about this."

He paused to take stock of the mood and then continued.

"If you're asking 'why us' then the only answer I've got is this. Remember Zulu? Yeah the film."

He waited until he got nods from most and explained to some of their non-British messmates the background.

"Anyway, I always remember this bit just as they're waiting for the hoard of Zulus to come an' wipe them out."

He checked to make sure everyone was paying attention and not farting around with smart phones. People seemed to be listening so he decided to continue.

"There they were, all stood to, bayonets fixed, watching some four thousand of Inonu's cousins, big lads," he smiled at the man he'd named, and Inonu grinned back, "coming up fast, then this young soldier turns to his big Colour Sergeant and says 'Why us Sarge, why us'? Well, the big Sergeant turns round with a slightly surprised look on his chops and says 'cos we're 'ere lad, 'cos we're 'ere'. There ain't no one else, just us.'"

Kipper waved for quiet as everyone chuckled at his impersonation of the Sergeant.

"Now then, it's the same here I reckon but for real. There isn't anyone else to help these poor buggers but us."

He waited a moment for that to sink in before continuing.

"You all saw what the sods did to our people and those on Cayman Brac without any warning."

Again he paused searching for a way forward.

"I'm staying. All the officers are staying even Mr Halshaw. Mind you, I should really say especially Mr Halshaw, he's got it in his mind to sort the buggers out one-on-one I think, anyhow never mind that."

He gave them his firm but friendly look and summed up their choices.

"It's up to you lads, no one is going to call you chicken or any of that shit. If you don't want to stay, come and see me in my office and I'll get you paid off and on your way before turn-to today. That's all for now, those that's detailed off already, get your breakfast and get to work."

Kipper had sat in his office from then until turn-to at 08:00. Nobody came to see him and strangely, he felt a just little ashamed. Maybe he'd laid it on a bit thick or maybe it was just the same as it had always been, in the trenches or at sea? You didn't want to let your mates down. Christ, he wondered to himself, how many millions had died in the past because of that simple loyalty?

There was an understandable grim urgency about her people as they worked on *Bismarck*'s deck, in sharp contrast to the happy camera toting tourists that frequently paused to snap the unusual warship whilst making the most of their last day. They had been told by the government that all tourists should leave and that the country would go to a state of emergency, but no explanation why.

There was also an obvious tension in the normally relaxed friendly manner of the locals. They did their best to keep cheerful but when the laughing tourists turned away, the shopkeepers switched off their artificial smiles and sat down pondering the rumours and their future.

The big naval battle the morning before had come as a shock and the subsequent announcement had suggested that it wasn't over yet. The richer ones didn't ponder too long and many decided to visit long forgotten relatives and friends abroad. Oddly enough they seemed to transfer rather a lot of money and take more than just a couple of suitcases as well. Most of the six hundred or so off-shore banks stayed closed too.

Up and down Seven Mile Beach, groups of government workers dropped their usual casual approach to labour and set to with a will. When asked by strangers what was the purpose of the odd concrete creations, they simply shrugged and muttered about a new waste collection system whilst they discreetly covered the machine gun slits of the low lying bunkers.

Engineers carefully took bearings from the known reef gaps deep enough for the enemy's landing ships and the bunkers were sited to interlock fire.

Less obvious preparations were being made elsewhere. A small pilot boat lingered in the marked channel entrance to North Sound, a diver's location buoy nearby. Underwater the diver was busy anchoring his fifth homemade mine in the shallow waters. A crude but efficient touch detonation system, he thought grimly, as he attached insulated wires to the exposed detonators on the oil drums full of explosive, the first ship to try to come through this bit is just going to cease to exist and probably block the entrance, since the vessel will likely be going slow any way.

At Great Pedro Point and Ironshore Point along the south coast, parties of MPP and labourers were busy constructing more strong points along the vulnerable stretches unprotected by reefs.

The bare backs of the sweating men glistened under the glare of the noonday sun, every now and then one would stop to rest and cast thoughtful glances at the empty sea to the south.

Armand Bennot did the same, but he knew what was coming and mapping these sites would help his friends get safely ashore. Getting on the labour gangs had been easy and no one had been vetted in the least, just names taken for the lists to spread the workers out around the island and so they could get paid.

Down at the airport, the runway, in between departing flights, was having bore-holes drilled across the concrete, one third and two thirds down its five thousand foot length.

The airport manager gave out the story that the holes were being drilled for the placement of seismic sensors to test the stress load for larger aircraft.

In fact charges would be placed later then capped and when fired they should in theory break up the runway into three parts making it unusable to most aircraft -if it became necessary.

All these preparations went ahead quietly and without a fuss, but there was an understandable moodiness apparent on the island. In quiet moments, those of them who knew of the Haitian task force, had time for worry and introspection.

When they did, there appeared the menacing vision of a group of ships that drew eight and a half miles closer with each passing hour.

16:00 Friday 25th May 2018
Haitian Flagship *General Farache*, ex Ukrainian *Slava* Class Missile Cruiser

Rear Admiral Ramade controlled his anger with great difficulty, this was the third *Bismarck* sighting since dawn and there had been four more the night before.

He ordered his Flag Captain to cancel the action stations alarms and get the task force back in formation and on course. He then ordered a Captains conference on the flagship.

Later he addressed the assembled Captains with barely concealed contempt. It had taken nearly four hours to muster them in the wardroom, but what he had to say needed face to face contact.

The delay had been occasioned by the dispersed nature of the task force and several of the fleet's helicopters had 'declined to work' necessitating the flagship to send its own to pick the Captains up.

"Listen very carefully gentlemen."

He began in a quietly ominous voice.

"None of you are to so much as activate a pen light without my prior and express permission, and the next one to activate their radar without it, will be relieved of his command instantly."

His voice rose as his fist fell hard on the wooden table top. His breathing was loud in the attentive silence that followed the opening comment and he noted with satisfaction that several of his commanders had jumped slightly. Good, he thought, I don't care if they fear me as long as I am obeyed.

He counted off on his fingers the four alarms the night before, two of which had occasioned ships firing 37mm automatic cannon in the general direction of a yacht.

It had been fired upon first by the leading frigate on the starboard wing of the task force and then again by the trailing frigate on the same side. Worse still they hadn't even hit the fucking yacht!

The other two alarms had been utterly without any reason he could discern, as no vessels were detected when the entire task force lit up the airwaves with millions of watts of radar energy and probably fried all the flying birds for forty miles around.

He knew that it had been some time since he had served at sea and therefore some time since he'd suffered disturbed sleep, but this was ridiculous. Even the day time alarms hadn't been much better, with two helicopters searching ahead nearly all the time he didn't think it necessary for frigates to sound action stations for contacts which had been classified 'merchant' by those self-same helicopters ten minutes before, but some of his Captains did.

He continued in a less aggressive tone, again patiently explaining his EMCON, or Emission Control Orders. They were not to emit radar unless the flagship so ordered or if the enemy was sighted and the sighting confirmed by the flagship.

They were not to spend endless hours on the radios passing messages or gossiping. Communication was to be restricted to sighting reports unless initiated by the flagship.

He went on to reassure them that the enemy ship could not see any further than they could and that it would only detect them at long range if they switched on their radar or were lax in their use of communication equipment. The helicopters would see the enemy long before they could see our ships.

Yes, they did need to keep a sharp lookout and a good listening watch on their own ESM systems. Dammit, he thought, looking at the sceptical faces, that hasn't changed anything. They'll still go on thinking they've sighted that cursed mercenary ship every time a piece of flotsam appears over the horizon. A small revelation was necessary he decided.

"Look I know for certain, that as of 15:00 today the enemy ship was still alongside at George Town. Gentlemen, I will be informed within twenty minutes of its sailing so don't bother about it."

He looked at their surprised faces.

"For heaven's sake, we have spies on the island. Did you think I was a *Hounan* (voodoo priest) casting spells? When the time comes to deal with that damn ship, we will.

He toned things down again now he could see they were happier.

"Make no mistake about it, the ships in this task force comprise the largest and most capable fleet in the whole Caribbean basin. Nothing can beat us."

He decided on an inspiring, incentive filled close.

"And you my friends are the cutting edge of it. This is the start of a new era of Haitian prosperity. Now go away and don't give those army crapauds anything else to laugh at."

The last was a reference to the derogatory comments, received from the Major General commanding the ground forces, regarding the false alarms which had incommoded him as much as his soldiers.

Ramade held the mask of a benevolent father in place until the last had filed out of his cabin, then he allowed it to slip. Turning to his Ukrainian adviser he spat.

"Those damned idiots will advertise to everyone where we are. Even if we knew for certain that the Caymaners were receiving American information we still don't want to advertise, do we?"

Rear Admiral Dmitri Venkov shook his head in agreement and wondered how this man would act if things didn't go quite as planned in a little over thirty eight hours, when the main landings were due to commence.

20:00 Friday 25th May 2018
MacDill Air Force Base, Tampa, Florida. USA

The duty Senior Controller, Captain Sean Harman, looked up from the radar plot and shielded his eyes against the glow from the nearly setting sun. In the distance he could see the strobe of the RAF plane approaching the threshold of the active runway.

The RAF C-17ER transport touched down neatly, taxied off the main runway at the first exit and began the long run in towards the hangars and base facilities specially allocated for their clandestine overnight stay.

The controller shrugged and turned back to the radar plot, everyone in the tower had been speculating about the unusual request for overnight facilities and fuel for an RAF flight, endorsed by US Northern Command.

He'd spoken to a Supply Officer friend earlier at supper and learned that he was to provide food for between a hundred and a hundred and fifty personnel.

Looking down at the plot he discovered that the next arrival was on finals, a Euro-fighter Typhoon. What the hell is going down, and where?

Boredom was the overriding reason for his curiosity -it would help pass a long night duty.

The secrecy bullshit was common enough at MacDill since apart from being the home of the 6th Air Mobility Wing it was headquarters of the Special Operations Command and half a dozen other major commands.

His brain juggled the possibilities, was it the Falklands again? All the aircraft due in had come direct from a UK base so that meant in-flight refuelling for the four fighters. He checked down the list and sure enough one of the new A330 Airbus two-point tankers was listed.

He watched the next two Typhoons land and ruminated some more. They all had advance flight plans filed for Belize City in the morning, but that didn't mean that Belize was the final destination.

But something was going down in South America for sure, maybe it was just the Guatemalans getting frisky again?　He tried to recall any notices in briefings he'd received but couldn't.

He paced over to the coffee pot and poured himself another.　There were four more aircraft due in over the next few minutes or so to complete the first package, more due in via Goose bay in Canada tomorrow.　He turned back to look at the runway and noticed that his next visitor was the Airbus tanker aircraft.

Speculation was fun but he had no idea really what was happening.　Interesting, he thought focussing on the hangar; troops.　He scanned his binoculars across the reserved area more carefully as two lines of men, all laden with seemingly huge back packs disembarked from the C-17, at least a company, and went straight into the hangar.

Jake rubbed his eyes, acknowledged the message on the com-unit and sat back in his chair fiddling with his night cap of Lagavulin whisky.

At least the additional stores were starting to arrive. Marchello Vitali had explained that it had been hell's own job to get the stuff air freighted out so quickly. Very few commercial carriers would take explosives, certainly in the quantities they needed.

They'd had to use two different commercial freight carriers because of the runway limitations at Grand Cayman as the first company didn't use the kind of aircraft needed.

Fortunately, with Miles Carlson, Nate King and Vern Weathers running interference, there had been no customs difficulties in the US during the cargo swap to the second commercial carrier.

Jake finished his drink and toyed with the idea of turning in. He sat staring at his desk whilst he played absently with five linked paper clips and a ballpoint pen.

He noted that the paper clips, when joined together, were exactly the same length as the ballpoint. A thought formed and worked around the edges and then surged its way to the surface of his mind.

He stopped moving the paper clips around and laid them alongside the ballpoint again, carefully making sure the ends were exactly in line. That's it!

Galvanised, he touched his mike and spoke.

"Captain, McClelland, Halshaw." Click. Once the system had opened a link to all three he spoke again.

"Gentlemen I have an idea to even the odds a little."

He sat back again, this time with a broad smile on his face. So, the great dictator has spies on the islands does he?

Well let's make sure they have something to report, he thought as he waited for the three officers. Unable to remain still and mind racing he began to pour himself another whisky then stopped and began to pace the cabin deep in thought.

Winston sat rubbing his feet, must be getting soft, he thought as he powdered them and put on a clean pair of socks.

Whilst he had no blisters, his feet and shins ached from the constant climbing as the path had meandered up and down the hills through sparse forest and dense brush.

They'd had to abandon the old pick-up the previous afternoon after it had finally stuttered to a halt out of petrol, about an hour after they'd passed through Neretteo having left the Route Nationale 2 at Vieux-Bourg-D'Aquin.

Winston had decided take the route to Bonne Finn and then cut across into the hills to the West since they didn't want to reach any major towns where a blocking force could be mustered and they had several days to burn.

They'd pushed the pickup into an arroyo and covered it with foliage, which hopefully would keep their pursuers – and he was sure they had them- guessing when they'd arrive at Aquin or even Quartier just down the Route Nationale 2 from where they left it.

The fact was though that once their wheeled pursuit had met with the blockers, the cat would be out of the bag and they'd begin backtracking for them.

Having left route 204 they'd moved up into the low foothills hills heading as close to due west as contouring allowed. The temperature wasn't too bad at this altitude Winston decided, about 1500 feet above sea level if the View-Ranger app on his smartphone was as smart as it thought it was. Still, they'd all been sweating quite heavily by the time it was time to camp at six the previous evening, all except old Marc that is.

They hadn't seen a soul since leaving Neretteo and Marc had assured them that they could light a cooking fire in the small arroyo they had found next to where they'd sleep the night. Tettas had provided the meat course, snaring a pair of partridges with looped fishing line, having lured them with some stale bread crumbs just before nightfall.

Old Marc had furnished the rest of the meal with a local kind of bean that grew on the mesquite bushes and some fresh grapefruit and avocados that grew wild in Haiti. Water wasn't a problem and they had puritabs to make it clean. Winston had climbed above their position and carefully watched their backtrack until the meal was ready.

Sophie reflected that she'd had worse dinners and that while the partridge was nice it would have been better gently braised in a red wine, garlic and onion sauce.

She nearly giggled out loud at the thought as she followed Winston's instructions on foot care. She did have a blister on each heel, but she was glad that Winston or Tetsunari had thought to bring her some jeans and her walking boots.

The thought of marching around the mountains wearing even the comfy low heeled shoes she normally wore, made her shudder. Sleeping on the ground with a padded blanket under her hips and one of their makeshift back packs for a pillow had been damned uncomfortable but she'd been so tired she'd been asleep in seconds.

Damn! If it's like this after just one afternoon walking what....she pushed away thoughts of the upcoming four days or so of trekking and concentrated on her feet and then carefully stretching the kinks out of her back and hamstrings.

Old Marc watched with silent amusement as the soldiers and white woman tended their feet and began stretching. He had discarded the old cast off shoes the Minister had given him, as soon as they left the pick-up.

His feet and soles were as hard and callused as that of any eighteenth century sailor, having been almost fifteen before he'd first worn anything on his feet.

He smiled at the recollection of the beating his father had given him for slitting the sides of his first pair of shoes to give his toes more room. Ah, those days are long past, he sighed.

Throwing the dregs of his coffee away he began packing up ready for the days' hike, carefully brushing away all trace of the fire and their meal.

They were carrying most things in primitive backpacks fashioned from tied blankets with knotted cloth straps and Winston longed for his old Bergen. Still beggars couldn't be choosers and it could be worse, he consoled himself as he packed his meagre supplies and hefted his weapons and equipment.

He looked up at the clear blue sky with the threatening clouds in the west and wondered what was happening at the other end of the Caribbean and when the shit was going to hit the fan over there.

He also worried that the ship would be destroyed or too badly damaged to come for them but kept that thought to himself. He guessed that contingencies had been made in case *Bismarck* didn't make it.

He checked the fancy sat-phone was off and slid it into the leg pocket of his olive drab fatigues, he would only communicate in emergency or once every two days to conserve battery power and limit the outside chance that the Haitians had access to intercept or satellite signal tracking ability.

Tetsunari watched everything and everyone but spoke little. He was pleased to see Winston and Ma'am Sophie do their morning stretches. He had belaboured the necessity the evening before until realising that she had fallen asleep. He was pleased he had taken the first watch until 01:00 and then when Winston took over he had fallen quickly into a deep sleep, something he could only do when he trusted the person watching over him.

He knew he'd need every ounce of strength and cunning for the days ahead and would of course prefer if they were rescued as planned. He was, however, prepared to sell his life at the highest possible price to protect Winston and Ma'am Sophie. As was his way, he felt no obligation to the old gardener.

07:00 Saturday 26th May 2018
Punta Gorda airport, Belize

Thunder filled the morning skies above the small town in southern Belize, and early risers looked upwards in apprehension thinking of an early season storm, but it quickly became apparent that it was aircraft noise.

Those who were paid by neighbouring Guatemala to keep an eye on things and to report unusual activity darted outside and made their way as quickly, but discreetly, as possible towards the airport.

All through the night at the airport base which housed the small military wing of the Belize Defence forces, recently arrived Gurkha engineers had been extending the runway and renewing the razor wire perimeter. The Belize government was more than happy to allow the changes as it saved them a small fortune.

New sand-bagged machine gun nests had appeared along this perimeter which now boasted six off runway hard standings, alert Gurkha riflemen manned the nests and patrolled the inside of the wire.

The thunder approached the town and became the deafening scream of high performance jet engines, as one by one, four Typhoons, a C-17 and an Airbus 330 took turns to land and taxi to the new positions. Tankers immediately began the long task of refuelling them all.

As the scream of jet engines died away to a whine and the smell of burnt aviation spirit gradually dispersed, the watchers rushed to warn their masters, very pleased to have something more to report after the arrival of the engineer unit two days ago.

Never had there been so much air power concentrated in Belize, even in the days when Harriers had been stationed there. None of the watchers were able to identify the sleek looking fighter planes but the photos would quickly tell their masters that there was something here that was more powerful and dangerous than anything that Guatemala could put in the air.

Within hours of the aircraft landing, discrete unofficial enquiries were being made by the worried Guatemalans and equally discrete -but secretly amused- officials in Belize, said nothing and heightened their old enemy's worry.

Well, they thought, it was nice every now and then to remind the neighbours that 'Big Brother' was still watching closely and visited occasionally.

A similar but smaller scale stir was being created at Philip S. W. Goldson International Airport near Belize City up in the north of the country, as an RAF E3D 'Sentry' aircraft direct out of RAF Waddington, came in on finals. Only the recent extensions and improvements to Belize's largest airport had given the plane the runway length it needed.

Waiting on the ground were a small contingent of Belize Police, Belize Defence force soldiers and Gurkhas from 1 GR, or 1st battalion The Royal Gurkha Rifles, detached from the unit at Punta Gorda. These would ensure any local snooping was done from a significant distance.

Andy Evans looked around the community centre bar and regarded the newcomers. All of them without exception had been fine soldiers or marines. The fact that one came from Canada, three from Russia, two from South Africa, three from Holland, four from Germany, two from France, two Aussies, one Kiwi and eight from Britain, didn't matter a damn.

What he saw when he looked at them was a cross section of the world's military elite who'd done their time and turned to more peaceful work as security experts, but now were back to soldiering again. Everyone a volunteer, which as anyone knew, made for a better motivated and more determined fighting force.

He briefed them quickly and efficiently on the situation as he saw it, and explained that their role would be in the defence of this base alone. If the situation and tactical circumstances permitted, then possibly they'd be airlifted to the main island to help there.

A detailed map of the island's installations and topography flashed onto the screen. He listed the equipment that they would have available for its defence, at which there were a few wolf whistles of appreciation, then Andy told them how he wanted them deployed. They were to be split into six four man teams with two spare numbers, under command of Captain 'Buck' Tayler, late of the 22nd SAS. The rest of today would be spent divided between getting to know each other, walking over the ground and checking their equipment and making sure their comms worked all around the place.

Much later, but before dark, they would set up their prepared fields of fire, lay their claymores and generally prepare nasty surprises for any unwanted guests. Andy left the briefing feeling that it would take an awful lot of well-trained troops -the majority of whom wouldn't live to gloat- to tackle this small but specialist unit.

He'd already been to the other end of the island to speak with the permanent staff member of the resorts there and warned them to stay away from this end of the island until the current problems were resolved.

These people were justifiably unhappy anyway given that tourism was really their primary income and all the tourists had been sent home; Andy wanted no accidents caused by people getting bored and wandering down their way.

His next stop was down at the seaward end of the right-hand harbour wall where he met up with one of the weapons engineers assigned to the island's defence systems.

"How's Quasimodo?"

Andy opened the conversation referring to the aptly nicknamed, rather hunched looking Dardo turret. The engineer smiled at the nickname and turned to face his charge.

"It's all set to go Andy, the remote system is all set-up and we've done all the tests we can without firing it. Just watch this."

Activating a hand held controller, rather like an X-box controller, he watched with pride as the turret responded with incredible speed to his elevation and bearing commands.

"Are you sure you don't want me to try a live test, just to be on the safe side. I mean if we're going to need that thing and it doesn't work then I won't be alive long enough to feel stupid, I expect."

"No Pete, the boss was adamant. There are definitely spies on the islands, I know they've tagged a couple, but Mr Roche reckons there's more about. The last thing we want to do is to give away what few surprises we've got up our sleeves."

He paused to pat the humped turret which was cleverly painted to look like it was part of a large rock. The two spindly barrels poking out of it were only visible when it began to elevate and train prior to firing.

"And this baby, is one of the better ones. How many rounds a minute did you say it can kick out?"

"Ah, now let me see, you knew that it's basically an anti-missile defence gun didn't you? Andy nodded.

"So yeah?   Right, well it's just two 40mm cannon slaved to a multi-function radar system and it can fire over 600 rounds a minute either surface or aerial targets and can be operated manually or totally independently."

He beamed a proud last look at his charge. "Anything that gets within five clicks on the surface or in the air is going to get a very wicked surprise."

Andy glanced back at the turret as they walked, damn good camouflage, he thought, from just a short distance away it really does look like just part of the harbour wall with the muzzles pointed inwards and down.

"And the bad-ass over there?"

He pointed to the position where he thought the camouflaged AK630M2 occupying the end of the other prong of the harbour wall was sited."

"Ah that's ready to go now. All set up. The only snag will be if used and the ready use ammo is exhausted, it's a long run from the dry land out along the wall to cycle the drums for the next load."

Andy nodded. The guys manning this base defences had drawn lots for the job, not because no one wanted it but because they all did. Mad as a box of frogs, he thought.

The techy was fidgeting.

"I'd best be getting back up the hill," he said, "they're still getting a few glitches with the passive tracking systems."

"I'll join you." said Andy. "The boss wants them up and running soonest and he'll blow a fuse if they aren't."

They piled into Andy's little electric golf cart and whirred along the five hundred yards or so of the outer sea wall and headed up the main road towards Weary Hill, where the nerve centre of the base's defences was located.

Bismarck, alongside at George Town, Grand Cayman

Erich Hertz sipped the smooth phenolic whisky and regarded his host over the top of the glass. He was a German ex-pat who owned a pair of large motor cruisers, one he rented out for fishing and the other he lived on. Erich was in his 70's but still spritely with a mischievous glint in his eyes.

Well it had been mischievous until Commodore König had explained his need for both of Erich's boats and also partly because of what König to do with them.

"I will do as you ask Herr König ...Jake," the word was unfamiliar on his tongue, "Poor *Wanda*." He added, referring to the name of the boat he lived on. He shook his head once more in disbelief

"I do know how much she means to you Erich and although your new boat will not be *Wanda*, we will make every effort to give you a suitable replacement, that stands even if the Cayman government doesn't.

I've made arrangements in Bermuda for you if things go badly for us."

Jake smiled, a genuine smile, Erich thought, though tinged with a deep sadness.

"You know I wouldn't ask unless it was vital. There are few we can totally trust to keep quiet and if the ruse should fail then our chances are even slimmer."

Erich noted the use of the word 'slimmer' rather than slim and assumed that it was deliberate. They don't stand much of a chance at all, he suddenly realized, and he knows it but still carries on.

Jake's eyes reminded him of his own father's, the last time he had seen him on the day he'd returned to the Eastern Front. The tears his mother tried to hide, the look of sadness on his father's face. The young Erich did not know what was happening then but knew it was important.

He shook himself slightly and looked into equally compelling and sad grey eyes of the man before him and tuned back in.

"...we must gain the time for the others by doing as much damage as we can to the assault ships. Perhaps Mr McTeal can get someone to help us if he has that time."

Jake shrugged and Erich wondered if the man really believed it himself.

At last, agreement reached, Jake escorted him over the brow and shook his hand firmly as he reminded Erich of the radio frequency to use when he was in place. Erich nodded and stepped down on to the jetty.

He walked a few yards and turned back to look at the ship and the men hastily loading supplies and working on the upperdecks. He felt his eyes begin to brim so he shook himself and walked briskly back towards the Barcadere Marina where his *Wanda* was currently moored, there was plenty to do before nightfall.

Back in his cabin Jake checked the time and moved to the chart stuck on the bulkhead. With Erich on side for the deception, the last piece of the plan was in place. One of the other yacht owners had been more difficult to persuade but had accepted the compensation package eventually.

He picked a pair of dividers from his desk, set them and made a note on the chart. The enemy task force would now be only a hundred and fifty three miles south east and they would alter course very soon if they were to attack the north or south shore. If they held their current course, which was his guess, then given the timings, he expected an attempt at a dawn landing along seven mile beach.

Someone knocked on the door and he shouted 'enter'. Kipper walked in and Jake waved him to a seat while he tried to articulate in his own mind why he believed that there would be only one landing area rather than several. He gave up and turned to Kipper.

"I've a special job for you this afternoon Kipper, and it's no exaggeration to say that it could be vital to our success and survival. Now this is what I want you to do..."

Down on the messdecks, *Bismarck*'s men occupied themselves in various ways as they passed their 'make-and-mend', navy-speak for afternoon off.

In some ways, Reiner thought as he wandered through the ship sticking his head round the corner of offices and messdecks alike, it could be a mistake to give the men too much time to sit around and think about tonight.

They all knew that they'd need their wits about them later so it seemed that many had opted to remain on board rather than face the multiple temptations of drink and women.

Some had stayed on in their work places, catching up on paperwork or tackling faults that had niggled but never been at the top of the priority list. He made his conversation light and few pressed him for information or speculation about the evening.

They were quieter than usual except in the Senior Rates Mess. Reiner knocked and was invited in. The place looked bare now that the mock black oak beams had been removed, even the sign outside the door had been carted ashore and the bar dismantled.

Reiner accepted a soda water and lime juice from Brendan Coultard doing duty behind the bar which was now a foldaway table and a load of crates, and nodded towards the corner where a heated argument was in progress.

"What's the argument about." He asked, sitting on an upturned PVC ammunition case which now doubled as a bar stool.

Bren looked over to where the Captain was indicating.

"Just the usual 'Uckkers' dispute sir. They decided to have a postponed league match this afternoon and PO Rautsch still insists on taking every piece he can whenever he can.

At that moment there was a tremendous ruction and painted drafts pieces flew in all directions as Granny Smith threw a wobbly.

"You fucking six throwing, ludo playing bastard."

He put his hand under the board and launched it across the mess, leaving Verner Rautsch with a puzzled look on his face not knowing whether to be offended, angry or just laugh.

Granny stormed over to the bar and asked for a Tom Collins without the 'alky bits' as he put it. The apparently angry senior steward turned to Reiner.

"All right sir?" And then winked and lowered his voice.

"Yon bugger was beating me all hands down, I was just about to 'mixyblob' but he couldn't resist a bit of Ludo so he gave me an excuse to 'up table'."

Reiner laughed out loud, although he did not fully understand the nuances of Uckkers which appeared to be a complicated game of ludo, he realized that Granny had pulled a flanker.

His countryman was still sitting at the table, surrounded by Uckkers pieces, hurt look on his face, appealing for support from any of the laughing watchers who would listen.

Reiner thanked Bren for the drink and left the Senior Rates Mess much heartened. The Senior Rates were like the bones of the ship's company, everything really hung on their ability and professionalism. He was pleased that there didn't seem to be any problems with the ship's company's skeleton.

16:00 Saturday 26th May 2018
'Bar Crudo', near the sea front, George Town, Grand Cayman

Kipper, followed by Taff Elias and Trev Kent, pushed their way gently through the people on the pavement and into the bar. He stood just inside the entrance unable to see through the gloom for a few seconds after the brightness outside. He let his eyes wander around the tables until he saw one that 'fit the bill'.

Crudo's was close to the ship, just down Merrendale drive and was a pleasant and always busy place where the drinks were good and the company didn't include children.

Well that was in normal times, now there weren't so many folks, no tourists and not much trade. When at last they could see where to go, they headed for the table Kipper had spotted and the three of them sat down.

Even lightweight tropical uniforms were hot to walk around in and they gratefully opened the white jackets and fanned themselves. A young barman sauntered over and asked for their orders. With a nonchalance he didn't feel, Kipper ordered beers for the three of them and they continued a discussion they'd apparently started outside.

"Anyway, what do you know about strategy and tactics Taff? All you do is sit there and watch a TV and push buttons."

Taff made a show of looking around before replying and Kipper thought he was overacting just a bit.

"You don't need to be a bleeding admiral to know what's right and what's wrong with a plan, do you?"

The barman returned with the beer and Taff paused for a sip before continuing. Kipper noted that the young man had decided to polish glasses this end of the bar now, he ignored the lad and turned back to Elias and Kent.

"Well I still say the skipper knows more than you, not only that but the Commodore wouldn't have made him skipper unless he was one of the best. You both know I've known him for years, he was always top of the class on those warfare courses an' the like and so was the skipper."

He paused for another draught of the cold beer.

"Boy did I need this. Anyway if anyone can give those buggers a run for their money, he's the man."

He emphasized his point by stabbing the table top with his index finger, his voice betrayed the beginnings of anger and was raised slightly. A few of the half dozen or so patrons looked up briefly and then returned to their rum or whatever.

"All I'm saying Kipper, is that it don't make much sense to me to just sail around to Rum Point and anchor there when a bloody great bunch of Haitian ships are tearing towards the island. Why don't we go out after them since we know where they are?"

Kipper took another sip of beer before replying and noted that the bar lad had been polishing the same glass now for nearly five minutes.

"That shows all you know then don't it. We aren't getting the satellite shit anymore 'cos the yanks have come over all coy suddenly, I overheard that the CIA bloke has been called back to the states, seems like he was passing us info that wasn't approved by his bosses."

"That don't change a thing..." He was cut off as Kent interrupted him.

"Ah but it does Mr Smartarse. Since we can only guess where the buggers are now, we'll have to rely on coast watchers to tell us when they sight the invasion force."

Kent's voice was getting louder as his anger built.

"So what should we do then sit in George Town until we get word? No fear. The boss told me that there was people watching the ship so he wants to get away from prying eyes if you get my meaning."

He turned and looked suddenly at the bar lad, who with his back to them, had been watching surreptitiously through the bar mirror. He immediately moved a little way down the bar and made a show of re-stacking the bar shelves.

Kipper nodded to Elias and Kent and they drained their beers.

"Come on Admiral, let's be off. We better get back on board if we're sailing at seven-ish."

The young barman left a minute later after making excuses to the old owner. One of Sandiford Roche's men immediately began to follow.

17:30 [Local] Saturday 26th May 2018
HMS *Dorsetshire*, fifty miles South West of the
Yucatan Channel, heading towards Jamaica

"Flash signal Sir, the SIC is 'eyes only Captain' Sir."

The RS, or radio supervisor, could barely keep the excitement out of his voice, Jon Roby noted, still 'eyes only' stuff was quite rare. He acknowledged the message and made his way down to the MSO to collect the signal and the appropriate code cards.

Twenty minutes later he sat in his cabin with the signal before him in clear text and read it again.

26Z230ZMAY18 ZZZZZZZZZZZZZZZZZZZZ
From: CINCFLT
To: DORSETSHIRE
Info: MODUK(N)
BT. SECRET

1. INTEL REPORTS SUGGEST MILITARY CONFLICT HAITI/CAYMANS IMMINENT. UK GOVT HAS NOT YET ESTABLISHED DIPLOMATIC POSITION REGARDING POSS CONFLICT.
2. DORSETSHIRE T0 PROCEED BEST CRUISING SPEED GRAND CAYMAN. IMMEDIATE. SIGNAL ETA.
3. HAITIAN T/F AT SEA. LATEST POSITION AND FORCE STRENGTH TO FOLLOW.
4. EXERCISE EXTREME CAUTION VICINITY CAYMANS. OBSERVE & REPORT ONLY.
5. CAPTAIN J ROBY RN PROMOTED ACTING COMMODORE CENTRAL AMERICA & CARIBBEAN (COMCENTAMCARIB) DESIGNATED THEATRE COMMANDER THIS DTG. ASSET LIST T0 FOLLOW.
6. ROE WARNING: YELLOW. WEAPONS TIGHT. ENGAGE ONLY AFTER
DEMONSTRATED HOSTILE INTENT.

ET.
NNNN

Roby finished reading that and the follow on signals and sat back in his chair to consider the message, by now it would be all over the ship that he'd received an 'eyes only'. He picked the telephone off the cradle on the bulkhead.

"Captain speaking.   Ask the First Lieutenant, the Navigating Officer and the AWO to come down to my cabin please.   Tell the 'Jimmy' to bring Jane's with him and the pilot to bring large scale Caribbean charts."

Well, well, well.   I wonder if Jake's got his fingers in this little turd pie, he mused to himself.   Ever since that slugging match on the 24th with the Haitians Roby had been wondering if that was it, finished, done.   Maybe it had just been the starting gun?

Commodore Roby.   He rolled the words over in his mind knowing that it was only temporary, but it still sounded nice.   He read the follow on signals again and whistled softly as he read the list of RAF assets available.

Someone saw this one coming, he decided.   When they'd left Belize two weeks ago it had been deserted, now he had strike and support aircraft at his disposal and even AWAACS at some point, very nice.

He shouted 'enter' at the knock on his cabin door.   One of the drawbacks with this sudden promotion lark, he ruminated, was that it provided the powers that be with a tailor-made scapegoat if things didn't go at all well.

He gestured for the three officers to sit and without comment passed the signal to John Hayden his First Lieutenant.   Hayden was fairly young for his position and took himself very seriously.   Roby had seen his type come and go.   Hard chargers, 'high speed-low drag Jimmy' he'd heard someone call them, 'In the zone' was another.

Roby detected the gleam that came into his eyes as he read through the text.   In peace time especially, it did a young officer's career prospects no harm at all to be in on a bit of active service, providing that things went as planned.

Especially so given that successive governments seemed determined to shrink the Navy down to just the Gosport ferry and a Trinity House lifeboat, and one of them mothballed too, he laughed inwardly at his own wit.

Roby indicated that Hayden should pass the signal to the AWO and the Navigating Officer and waited for that young man to finish before he spoke.

"Comments?"

Hayden was in quick.

"Congratulations on your promotion Sir, I'll have a broad pennant run up immediately." He was referring to a Commodore's swallow tailed St George's flag.

"That's not quite what I had in mind number one, but never mind."

Roby nodded non-committedly and wondered if Hayden actually had a lower 'smarm' threshold. The AWO, Berry Reeves, said nothing immediately, just nodded thoughtfully for a second or two before putting in his two penneth.

"Odd how half the Air Force has suddenly descended on Belize Sir, seems someone up top had an inkling that all was not well even before that shindig on the 24th, this clearly wasn't an ad-hoc deployment. I take it you noted the company of Gurkhas as well Sir."

Berry was what Roby considered an outstanding officer but was likely to be passed over at the next promotion board unless he had influence because there just weren't the senior jobs any more. Probably his last shot in zone too, Roby added to himself. Silly bloody system for a small navy.

"Yes Berry I did and it caused me to wonder what the hell is going on in someone's mind up at MOD."

He deliberately used Reeves first name and saw it noted by all three.

"That task force is well structured Sir. Some of their kit may be relatively old but I'd not want to go up against it even with our air assets. Do you think *Bismarck* intends to attack?"

"I'm bloody sure it will Berry. Jonathan König is a man of his word and one of the best Warfare Officers I ever met, he was my boss actually on a couple of my previous Pusser's war canoes. Right now he'll be working out a way to level the odds. Still you're right about the nasties. *Bismarck* won't stand a chance even with all its guns and armour. Damned shame really, they seemed a good bunch."

The navigator was still a little abashed in this august company and just stuttered about passage time at current speed and fuel state, which was all Roby wanted anyway.

"Right gentlemen, we have work to do, the first thing being a new course and speed. Pilot work out our ETA based on a direct course to George Town leaving us twenty miles short for now and arriving no later than 04:00 on the 27th , and send it off soonest. Next. What time is morning Astrological Twilight hereabouts Pilot?"

Roby was referring to the three stages of false dawn before the sun actually crested the horizon. Astrological Twilight was when there was light in the sky but not enough to see the horizon. The next stage was Nautical Twilight where the horizon was visible and at this time of year it would be visible first in the north east, not due east as most would expect. It made a difference to ships at sea and not emitting any radar or radio transmissions because it meant they were back to lookouts using the old 'mark 1 eyeball'.

The Navigating Officer quickly whipped out a pocket nautical Almanac from his jacket. It was his constant companion because it was small enough to fit unlike the larger official Admiralty book. After a few seconds of pregnant silence he answered his Captain.

"04:26 until 04:55 Sir"

Berry Reeves nodded to himself then looked up and added.

"Want hands to flying stations on arrival Sir?"

"You've read my mind. Yes I want to have a snoop around using our Merlin's FLIR before we go flouncing into the harbour and find it occupied by nasties. Call the hands 03:00, we'll go to EMCON silent from about 03:30 and action stations for 04:00 number one, everyone breakfasted and full of strong tea. I suppose I'll also need to send a sitrep to our RAF brethren in Belize."

"Aye Sir." They chorused and got up to leave.

18:30 Saturday 26th May 2018
George Town, Grand Cayman

The concrete jetty in front of *Bismarck*'s berth was crowded with uniforms, civil dignitaries, scarlet clad bandsmen and even a choir. Placed apart from the rest stood an honour guard from the MPP. Twenty men in their white tropical uniform and black leather webbing, each man carried an SA80A2 rifle with a bayonet attached.

Two steps in front of them stood an officer with a sword, they all waited patiently for the Prime Minister to make his appearance. Portable floodlights lit the *Bismarck* from various angles and overhead lights kept the presentation area bathed in bright light.

The large noisy crowd was confined behind barriers which left a passage through which vehicles could pass one way in on the north side and out again at the south end. It extended beyond even 'Rackham's Bar and Grill' looking north on Church street and along the waterfront as well as south beyond the Paradise restaurant.

Black staff cars had been coming and going for the last ten minutes, depositing senior officials and their guests. Sailors in working rig were visible on the warship, some gathered in small groups at bow and stern wearing leather gauntlets and hi-vis jackets ready to take in the lines, it was obvious that she would be sailing soon.

The crowds were all locals, the tourists having left a day ago, most wondered what was going on, why the ceremony? Those 'in the know' or who thought they were 'in the know', excitedly gossiped and relished the sudden nervousness their speculation engendered. Most was rumour but it was quite apparent to the listeners that something serious was going on.

The most cheerful people that evening were the reporters who had decided to stay on a couple of days after the battle on the 24th when the others had left. The only cloud on their horizon however was the dictum of the newly appointed Security Minister, a certain Sandiford Roche, who had clamped down on communications and had set aside a government office for the press.

He'd assured them that they could say whatever they wanted, to whomever, but, they would do so only when he judged it safe to allow the information out. He was certain that they would understand and why didn't they come down to the jetty to see the now famous *Bismarck* that was preparing to sail off and fight against great odds?

A few of the less scrupulous tried to get the scoop on the others but the international lines were disconnected and all the satellite gear was guarded so they had no access to the internet or mobile phone networks and had to content themselves with following the minister to the pier; most wished they'd brought a sat-phone which could have circumvented the problem.

Roche knew they'd find a way around his block at some point but didn't care. If he could appear to hold the line, as it were, for the next few hours then the job would be done. It was all about what people thought rather than what was actually happening.

The journalists had just taken their places next to the VIP's and began to make notes, take stills or film as the Prime Minister arrived and the band had struck up with the national anthem and everyone stood to attention on the ship and the shore.

Whilst the Prime Minister inspected the guard, the band played selected melodies for all the nationalities that made up *Bismarck*'s crew. It was a long list. From the sombre Russian folk tunes hummed by a male voice choir they heard the cheerful Hearts of Oak played by the brass band.

Taff Elias managed to get someone to sing the 1862 version of Men of Harlech, he was forever telling anyone who'd listen that it was the best version and included the immortal words '*Men of Harlech, on to glory! See, your banner famed in story, wave these burning words before ye "Britain scorns to yield*!"

Then a rousing Waltzing Matilda and finally the melancholic and chillingly appropriate '*Je ne regrette rien*' for the Frenchmen present, sung by a stunningly attractive local French singer, who, as Trev Kent put it irreverently later, could really roll her 'R's.

Andrew McTeal made a stirring speech about the islands and their newly acquired freedom, about the mistruths spouted by Haiti and that their freedom was now threatened because of greed.

He thanked *Bismarck* and her crew awarding an embarrassed Captain Krull the island's highest award, the 'Cross of Valour' for the action on the 24th and a posthumous 'Medal of Valour' to George Gulobovich, killed on Cayman Brac the same day.

Lastly, as the sun set behind *Bismarck* throwing it into golden relief, a lone MPP bugler stood atop turret Anton and accompanied by the band on the jetty, played the Royal Navy's version of 'Sunset'.

As the final haunting notes of the last post died away the Guard presented arms and the Caymans flag national flag was lowered from the Jack staff at the same time as the naval ensign was lowered from the flagstaff on the quarterdeck down aft.

With everyone back on board, the shouted orders to slip the mooring lines could be heard and the whine of the big gas turbines briefly rose above all other sounds.

A bosun's pipe pierced the silence to bring the sailors on the upperdeck to attention again and they stood silently and ramrod straight as *Bismarck* backed away from the jetty and a gap appeared between ship and the land.

A short hum of feedback was heard and then over *Bismarck's* main Tannoy system came the clearly identifiable sound of drums starting a slow repetitive beat and joined by a fiddle after a few bars.

Then the voice of Joe Strummer and his version of the 'Minstrel Boy', made famous by the film 'Blackhawk Down', started. The haunting words to that old Irish ballad seemed most appropriate.

> *The Minstrel boy to the war is gone,*
> *In the ranks of death you'll find him;*
> *His father's sword he has girded on,*
> *And his wild harp slung behind him;*
> *"Land of Song!" said the warrior bard,*
> *"Though all the world betrays thee,*

One sword, at least, thy rights shall guard,
  One faithful harp shall praise thee!"

The Minstrel fell! But the foeman's chains
  Could not bring his proud soul under;
The harp he loved ne'er spoke again,
  For he tore its chords asunder;
And said "No chains shall sully thee,
  Thou soul of love and bravery!
Thy songs were made for the pure and free
They shall never sound in slavery!"

It was such a moving rendition that there was nary a dry eye and the crowd was silent as they listened and *Bismarck* slowly retreated into the glowing after-sun. They knew they were watching men and a ship sailing out to fight for them; and most likely die for them.

Finally in the gathering night with the afterglow only to light her, *Bismarck* , turned her graceful bows South and sailed into the coming night. The ship's fog horn blared forlornly as a parting word, haunting because she was no longer visible, having doused all but her running lights and slipped into the shadows. The time was 20:15, nearly the end of nautical twilight. The press were having a field day, as the ship moved out on what would likely be its final voyage.

Jake pushed the viewer away and turned to Reiner sitting in the command chair, but spoke to the bridge at large.

"Thank God that's over, Hollywood eat your heart out. I nearly shed a tear myself. Still, I think the show was necessary, there's no way any spy is going to doubt that we're going out to fight."

He considered the line in the Minstrel Boy, 'One sword, at least, thy rights shall guard' and thought to himself, sadly too true.

Reiner nodded at his remarks about Hollywood as he took in the receding lights along seven mile beach and noted they too started to disappear in blocks as Roche started the process of bringing the Islands to war readiness including a declaration of martial law and a black out.

"Captain Krull." Jake said formally. "Please carry out the next phase as planned."

"Aye, aye Commodore." Reiner answered equally formally then turned to Buller on the helm.

"Buller, starboard twenty, course 005 until we clear the point and give us revolutions for fifteen knots, we don't want to go too fast so that the watchers lose sight of us do we? They should still be able to just make us out in the very last glow of after light and our green starboard light should give us away."

"Bridge, OPs. Just received Mr Hertz's signal sir, he's in position now and confirms the fourth motor cruiser is too."

Reiner answered.

"Good, thanks. What's the latest from Mr Carlson Robby?"

Pete Robinson who was the other member of the OPs team and doubled as RS most of the time, was a Tyneside Geordie and proud of it, his voice with it's strange, to the uninitiated sing-song accent.

He reminded Jake of a sleeping England so many thousands of miles away. They would wake up there in the morning and watch their breakfast TV and perhaps hear about a battle fought thousands of miles away over a tiny island in the Caribbean.

It would mean stuff-all to most of them. They wouldn't give a toss as long as it didn't interfere with 'Lorraine' or Philip what's-his-name'. It would be of passing interest if some of those killed were British. Robby's voice came back with the answer.

"Just had him on the secure net Sir, time of sat run was 19.48 local, enemy on same course except they increased speed to sixteen knots between the last one and this. He also mentioned that the formation appeared to be changing."

"OK Robby, keep me posted, bridge out."

He turned back to Jake

"I wonder why the increase of speed?"

Jake nodded and said.

"I think it's time for another chat with Simon, come on Reiner."

Reiner turned to the Gunnery Officer.

"Julius you have the bridge."

"Aye, aye, Captain. Gunnery Officer has the bridge."

Replied Julius Kopf, moving to the vacant chair as Jake and Reiner disappeared down the ladder.

They sat and stood around the central holo display in the OPS room, Simon McClelland, Reiner and Jake. On the display was the 3D computer generated chart which showed the islands and two hundred miles of water around them in a faint hemispherical dome.

The enemy's track was marked up to the last known point where the time was also included, several dotted lines splayed out from it marking possible Haitian routes. If they wanted they could have zoomed in to check the make-up of the approaching task force but they already knew what was coming.

Jake slapped his forehead.

"Damn Reiner! How are our new crew members? I'm sorry I forget to ask earlier."

Jake referred to the twenty volunteers drawn from the MPP and the ordinary police, who had come aboard to help with hauling of the ammunition crates during the action to come.

"They're settling in quite well Jake, Kipper, Kent and Dettweiler are showing them what to do now."

He changed his tone.

"I don't really think they've any idea of what they have let themselves in for."

Jake considered his reply carefully.

"I'm not sure any of us do really, there aren't many alive who've gone 'toe-to-toe' in a naval slugging match, not since the Second World War I think."

He paused a second before continuing.

"One thing we can't have is a breakdown in the ammunition supply, we must make sure that they are supervised when the shells start hitting us and that any sign of panic is stamped on immediately. Who have you got as loaders and supervisors?"

"Well, Kiwi McClean down aft and Kent is in charge for'ard...."

Jake interrupted. "Say no more. There won't be a problem with them there. Now Simon, what do you make of this speed alteration and the changing of the formation?"

"Difficult to say really. It might simply be because they are aware of possible satellite surveillance and are trying to coordinate movements for maximum effect between satellite passes. I still think they'll go for a dawn landing because the troops and assault ship crews will not be greatly experienced in night ops."

He stroked his chin.

"If I was their commander, no way would I consider a night landing especially without the channels between the reefs being marked now. But we really need some hard intelligence on the formation changes and the next sat run will not be for another seventy minutes or so."

He pushed a couple of keys on his datapad.

"Their current course and speed would put them off George Town anywhere between 03:00 and sunrise depending on whether they cut the corner or not. Of course this may only be part of the task force and we may see a breakaway group if they take our bait and the rest plodding on at their previous speed."

Jake turned to Reiner. "Anything Reiner?"

"I agree with Simon about the dawn landing, everything is too confusing at night to take the chance and they've only got one shot at it."

Jake sat quietly for a moment.

"Can we launch an Arado without our spectators noticing, do you think?" They both considered silently for a moment before Reiner answered.

"With shaded torches and as long as we get it off before we turn for Rum point, I think we can. They'll have difficulty seeing even with NVG if we launch to Port, since for a while at least, we'll be heading almost parallel to our observers."

Jake stood up. "OK let's get a recon drone up and have it head towards the last known position gentlemen."

Reiner nodded and spoke into his mike.

"Shipwide." Click. "Hands to flying stations. Prepare to launch a reconnaissance RPV."

Then he turned to Simon.

"If they've split, it will clearly suggest they've taken the bait. I expect we'll begin getting ESM data pretty quickly."

"OPs, drone control. We'll be ready to launch in five minutes Captain, just uploading the nav package now."

CPO Kempfe and his team were clearly on the ball thought Jake.

"Right." said Jake "I'm going to get back up top. Everything ready for the next phase Reiner?"

"Yes Sir, everyone standing by."

Five minutes later the Arado 196 RPV hissed into the night sky and was quickly lost to sight. Another five minutes passed and *Bismarck* slowly turned almost 90 degrees to starboard, bringing her on to a course which would take them three miles north of Rum Point.

21:50 Saturday 26th May 2018. Missile Cruiser
General Farache, Flagship Haitian Task Force, 80 Miles South of Grand Cayman

Ramade stood next to his Flag Captain, Guyon, peering through his night glasses. He turned at the polite cough and read a proffered message. Good. The signal from the *Jacmel*, an ex-Chinese *Luda* class DDG, reported that she and the *Cap Haitien*, an ex-Chinese Type 53H2G frigate were in position approximately fifty miles East South East of Grand Cayman.

The radio message from their man near the harbour had reported *Bismarck* sailing at 20:15. As expected it had sailed a deception course southwards initially and then turned north when, he presumed, it thought it was out of sight. The other watcher near Rum Point had just reported a sighting as it now came into view east of Conch Point.

Captain Guyon lowered his own glasses and turned to the signalman standing at his left elbow.

"Acknowledge, and send 'Good hunting' to them."

He looked around at Ramade.

"Anything else Admiral?"

A shake of the head was his only reply as the Admiral left the bridge and returned to the chart room.

Guyon sighed quietly in relief; he looked around the bridge and observed that his men also relaxed their stiff backs now that the Admiral had gone.

Ramade pored over the chart, noting the neatly drawn lines and timings. He traced his fingers along the lines of the two extra tracks as they had turned away from the main task force.

One *Yunshu* class Landing Ship, another of the *Luda* class destroyers paired with a Type 53H2G frigate and one Type 37 corvette made up the eastern track.

They were heading for the two outer islands and would now slow down, timing their arrival to coincide with the main attack just after dawn.

The first two, the *Jacmel* and *Cap Haitien* were almost in firing position and hopefully at or before 22:30 eight C802 Chinese surface to surface missiles from the *Jacmel* and six more from the *Cap Haitien* would put paid to that bastard mercenary ship, he mused to himself. They were just waiting for the news that it appeared to have anchored.

Yes it was overkill but the damned thing had to be destroyed utterly, after which the *Cap Haitien* would re-join the main force and the *Jacmel* with its four 130mm guns would join the outer islands force.

He recalled General Farache's ice cold stare as he had personally explained the catastrophe of the 24th. That memory was worth another shudder.

Moving his fingers to the track of the main force he checked the pencilled calculations. They had speeded up and then turned due west an hour before sunset and would now hold this course until 00:01 when they would turn North West again. He nodded his satisfaction to the Navigating Officer and walked out of the chartroom.

"I'm going to my cabin now. Tell Captain Guyon to call me ten minutes before the helicopter launches." He smiled a secret smile as he contemplated the destruction of the mercenary ship, he couldn't bring himself to give it a name.

His flagship's Ka-25K helicopter would provide the terminal guidance for the missiles as they sped in towards their target and that would be his only obstacle out of the way.

What a blessing it was to have up to date and accurate intelligence reports.

22:00 Saturday 26th May 2018
Bismarck, off Rum Point, Grand Cayman

"Revolutions for five knots, port five steer O90." Said Reiner. "What range to our friends now?" Reiner moved out onto the port bridge wing and spoke into his mike while waiting for an answer.

"McClelland." Click. "Simon you'd better get down aft and supervise there, we can't afford any mistakes."

Simon left the OPs room and quickly made his way towards the stern.

"Range is 300 yards Sir, our speed coming down to five knots now."

"Thank you Buller, take us in to lie exactly abreast of them and put the agreed limited deck lighting on when we completely shadow them."

"Aye, aye Sir."

Jake stood on the fo'c'sle with a pair of night binoculars and stared towards Rum Point, aware of the slap of waves against his ship's side as it slowly moved into position. He was wondering whether the shore-side operation would come off, lots could go wrong. He shoved those doubts out of his head. Nothing he could do about it ergo no point in worrying. If it didn't work they had other options.

Reiner looked out into the night, he could see nothing even though he knew there were vessels close by. After a few seconds he thought he could hear something else apart from the gentle 'flop' of waves on the hull and the low whine of the engines. Yes, he was sure now, the gentle thrum of idling diesels reached him through the darkness and suddenly there were vague shapes as well.

A few moments later with *Bismarck* station keeping using the bow thrusters and the Steerpods, Erich Hertz left his beloved *Wanda* for the last time to climb aboard her. He timed his step with the swell and climbed up onto the *Bismarck*'s main deck from the deployed boarding platform like the old pro he was. He turned back to look at the sixty foot motorcruiser now moored fore and aft parallel to the shore.

She'd been his home since he retired ten years before and emigrated from Germany, and he'd miss her. Seeing Jake up in the bows he went to stand next to him.

"Good evening Herr Commodore, it goes well, ja?"

Jake jumped and turned quickly.

"Hell Erich, you nearly scared the... err yes, it looks like it should be OK to move in few minutes or so. Who else did you get to help?"

Well I think I could have got about forty *alter folk* like me, if I'd wanted, but I settled for Jason Sims over on Cayman Brac and...."

"He's the one that sent us the light signal the other morning isn't he?" Jake interrupted. "We really owe him."

"On the contrary Jake, we are all in your debt and will be more so before this night is over I think. Jason sends his best, he's manning the boat we shall use to return to Governor's quay, he wants a tour of your battleship after the action."

"It will be my pleasure."

Jake looked away, slightly embarrassed. He didn't feel in the least bit heroic, only by keeping busy was he able to push aside worrying thoughts of the forthcoming battle.

It was worse, he decided, being the Commodore rather than the Captain; the Captain had endless details to deal with and occupy him but the Commodore operated on the strategic wavelength looking at the big picture and had plenty of time to second guess himself.

Erich could see he was preoccupied so he stuck out his hand.

"Anyway I shall have to leave now. I wish you good hunting Commodore and thank you."

Jake nodded, shook the proffered hand and turned back to watch the manoeuvrings below. He looked down at his hands and saw a tremor and gazing out into the balmy night he gripped the guardrail fiercely. 'Sophie, I wish to God I knew where you were and that you were safe', he whispered to the night. All these loose ends swinging in the breeze and me desperately needing to focus on the battle to come.

Moments later with the four motor cruisers moored end to end alongside *Bismarck,* the false masts with their lights and the radar reflectors were raised.

At around 22:15 the watcher at Rum Point blinked, or thought he had. Just for a fraction of a second the lights on the warship seemed to go out.

No, it's still there he decided, and settled back against the bole of a palm tree watching the lights in the distance, it was easy money this and no danger either.

A hundred yards to his left, two anti-terrorist MPP officers lay silently watching the man, covered head to foot in black they stayed just off the beach within the line of the palms quietly observing. They had been there since late afternoon having checked along the coast each way for the best possible position an intruder could view *Bismarck's* demise without being seen themselves. They were careful. They took their time and narrowed the options to just two, then took up a watch which covered both.

Their orders were simple. After the explosions, wait until the agent had used his radio, sat phone or whatever, to communicate. Then pick up him and 'Bring the bugger to me', were the words of Steve Robinson, boss of the MPP.

Jacmel, Type 51D *Luda* D Class Missile Destroyer.
Twenty Miles East of Grand Cayman

"Weapon activation distance ninety five kilometres, bearing only, eight to launch, commence firing sequence." Intoned the voice of the Warfare Officer. The two ships had turned ninety degrees to their target bearing to allow the missiles tubes to bear. One at a time, gouts of bright yellow and red flame erupted from the *Jacmel*'s eight silos. This was repeated at intervals of ten seconds. At the same time the action was duplicated on *Cap Haitien* but with only six missiles.

As the last fiery trails from the boost stage surged into the night the two ships lamp signalled farewell and separated, one to return to the task force and the other to join the group heading north to the outer islands.

The Ka-25K, NATO code Hormone B helicopter from the flagship was flying a slow racetrack course at about two thousand feet and fifteen miles north of the eastern tip of Grand Cayman.

Tension mounted as the two missile shooters briefly broke their transmission blackout to announce that the deadly missiles were on their way. All was activity now as the pilot swung onto a course which would keep him a mile or so north of the missile tracks but generally pointing south.

In the rear cabin the systems operators prepared to switch the surface search radar from standby to active. The total flight time of the missiles would be approximately six minutes as they sped through the darkness at over six hundred miles an hour.

Up in the Ka-25 helicopter, sweat dribbled down the face of the Haitian operator as he switched the radar to active, the flying suit, helmet and the tension combined to make him most uncomfortable.

As the radar stabilized he picked up the incoming missiles to his left and there over on his right at a range of about twenty miles was the enemy ship. There were several other contacts within seventy or eighty miles but there was only one that really interested him.

His colleague activated the unit to send command guidance course corrections in short bursts to each of the missiles as well as telling them where to look for their target.

Six miles from the target they activated their own radar for the terminal phase and locked on. Another half mile later all fourteen of them, each carrying a 350lb SAP warhead, rose up suddenly to three thousand feet to begin their terminal approach. The idea being that a sudden pop-up and dive would defeat the ship's point defences but also allow the missile to penetrate deeper by diving through the deck.

The operators watched keenly as the missiles all raced toward the bright blip on their screen, one fell away and crashed, a second passed the target and flew on to crash a mile further on, decoyed they wondered? There was a momentary flare and then the blip that was a ship began to fade.

A little saddened, the technician switched back to standby and sent the predetermined code word *Zèklè*, 'Lightning' back to the Flagship. The pilot accepted his instruction to return to base and waited for his new course to intercept the flagship in about an hours' time. He looked thoughtfully at the glow on the western horizon and considered the fate of however many men there had been aboard that ship.

*

On the beach, the watcher concentrated, looking slightly to the east of the ship's lights while he waited for the tell-tale flame trails. He'd had to be extremely careful on his approach to his current hiding place, oddly, because there were no tourists. This area had several guest houses, bars and restaurants which were normally getting busy this time of the year and tourists never took notice of an old ragged black man. But since the tourists had gone, the only people wandering around were locals. Bored locals got curious.

Any time after ten thirty they'd said; he checked his old Timex briefly for the tenth time since half past the hour and this time shook it briefly in case it had stopped. He focussed the binoculars once again on the lights and then swung them a bit to the right. Nothing.

He was looking in the wrong place. The missiles came arcing down out of the night almost in pairs with no flame trails, the flash from the successive explosions nearly blinded him and the concussion made him jump as each plunged into the inferno created by the first.

He sat back and put the binoculars down, he didn't need them now. There were a couple of secondary explosions and burning debris flew high long after the last missile had landed, and what was left of the ship burned brightly for a minute or so before there was darkness again.

He rubbed his eyes but all he could see when he closed them was the flash imprinted on his eyelids. After a moment or so he pulled the sat-phone out of his pocket, dialled a number, waited for the connection and said 'Loraj', the Haitian for 'thunder'.

Then, contemplating the bonus payment he would trouser after the successful attack, he reached into his jacket pocket and pulled out the half bottle of dark rum he'd been saving until after the job was done.

Unscrewing the cap he lifted the bottle in salute to the dark waters and the foreign ship that had died, automatically he wiped the top and put the bottle to his lips. He froze as a cool hardness pressed into the back of his neck, accompanied by a sharp metallic 'snick'.

22:45 Saturday 26th May 2018
Bismarck Eighteen Miles West of Rum Point, Grand Cayman

"Well, they seem to have taken the bait, what have you got in mind now that we're dead Sir?" Asked Simon, as he pushed two keys on his console and spoke into the headset.

"All yours Joachim." He said, handing over control of the Arado RPV that had been launched after their move away from the 'bait' motorcruisers.

The pictures of the missiles striking the four moored motorcruisers had been chillingly good quality and there'd been plenty of 'goofers' in the OPs room watching when it had happened as amazingly, everyone had a good reason to be there. More to the point, the ship's ESM had recorded the entire event completely and it would now be analysed for clues about the guidance packages on the missiles.

The RPV that had filmed the event was now on its way to get initial reports on the northern group which was slowly heading towards Little Cayman and Cayman Brac.

Jake took a moment to ponder Simon's question before answering.

"That depends on how they formate for their approach to the landing grounds, which must certainly be George Town or Seven Mile Beach since they've passed below the island now. What say you Reiner?" Jake studied the softly lit display in front of him and added. "And what do you make of their formation changes?"

Reiner contemplated the holo display, the three of them, Simon, Reiner and Jake, all Warfare Officers at one time, were concentrating seventy or more years total experience in the job, onto this one set of problems.

"I was wishing that a few more escorts had been sent with the outer island assault group but that's a bit unfair on Brac and Little Cayman."

Simon nodded and reached for his coffee cup, he was in his element now.

"The really good news I think is this. We now have a very good idea of the timing for the main landing. By projecting the course and speed of the Northern group we find that they will be in position around the outer islands by dawn and since they are not going at full speed, I think it's fair to assume that this is therefore timed to synchronise with the main landings. So dawn it is in my opinion."

He drew a breath and leaned back against the chair stretching his back.

"Secondly, if we assume that they want to have a coordinated attack then we can reasonably predict the main force's course by where it must be at Nautical Twilight and then dawn. This group we know has a maximum speed of seventeen knots due to the Kunshu class LSMs they're using, but I doubt they'd want to thrash them so sixteen knots is a more likely maximum rate of advance." Simon punched a few keys on his chair arm and used a laser pointer to activate functions on the holo display

"Excuse me gents." He added and a new series of tracks appeared on the holographic display.

"By building in a little time for cock-ups etcetera, this is the course I reckon they'll take. They'll want to do it as simply as possible so I reckon they'll just turn north at some point between 23:30 and 00:30, then stay on that course until they are on the same latitude as the landing grounds, then a final turn on to O90 when they get here at about 03:00," he indicated a point about twenty miles west of the Island with the laser pen "it gives them plenty of time to shake out into the correct formation and be ready for when it begins to get light at 04:26 but the horizon won't be visible until 04:55 at the earliest. Once in formation I believe they will slow to a speed consistent with a dawn arrival at the reefs. They will be OK for final manoeuvring at that time but I'm certain they won't want to cross the reefs until full daylight, and that would be from 05:47 onwards."

He was pointing to the several known reef gaps off Seven Mile beach.

"And then they just steam straight for the beach, not far from Hell." He smiled at his own humour. The village of Hell had a Post Office which was world famous for post cards. 'Having a wonderful time in Hell' etc.

Jake studied the course projections for a moment or two.

"Why not further south or even alongside in George Town?"

"Well they could I suppose but it is much more readily defensible, they also know that the MPP are pretty well trained and won't give in without a fight. If they want the world to automatically condemn them, the best way is to level half of George Town in the invasion and have lots of civilian casualties, I'd have thought. Most importantly though, landing off Seven Mile Beach they'll quickly cut the island in half and take Government House."

"OK. Fair points, I'll go along with that." Jake concurred. "Now, dependant on the final formation he adopts, I think we should try to somehow slip in between the escorts as we approach, then get in close to attack the assault ships before he knows we're there. I think we can become part of the assault force. We might even manage to stay hidden in the pack if he emits because the second we pick up transmissions we could swing on to a course of 090 and look like part of the gang. I suppose that depends on whether he maintains an EMCON silent approach now that he thinks we're not around to bother him. The other controlling factor is the visibility. What's the latest met?"

"The bad news is that we've got a nearly full moon for the night, setting at 04:30 in the west with an increasing overcast though towards full dawn which is 05:47. And then rain likely, courtesy of tropical depression Adele, which is north of Cuba as we speak, winds light to moderate not much of a sea running." He read from a sheet.

"So, not too bad boss just as long as the overcast follows us around."

Reiner said "What about curling around and sliding up behind them as they move towards the beach?" But as soon as he said it, he knew it wasn't practical and Simon quickly confirmed it.

"I thought of that Sir, but we must assume that he'll want to check that everyone is in place before the big moment, the order to commence landings. I think he'll use radar briefly so we couldn't really get closer than twenty miles even though we have the radar cross section of a very small fishing boat."

Jake stared hard at the screen and carried out some mental arithmetic.

"Don't they have tactical data links like NATO forces?

"Well yes but you have to wonder if they are using it and up to scratch, don't forget not all the ships are from the same source Sir."

Reiner thought it time to input.

"Well we have to assume they are using what passes for their equivalent of Link, but it will only be at the most as good as Link-16 probably not that good. So it will be the big picture on the flagship only, the rest will just feed in. It would mean that they don't have to use radar for formation checking though. We will only find out when they turn for their final course I suspect."

Jake came back in.

"If they use radar that would bugger up a stern approach then wouldn't it? We'd have to go flat out to catch them up and probably wouldn't manage it until after they hit the damn beaches. So we have to assume they use radar and not Link because we can't be in two places at once."

He tapped a pencil against the desk, irritated.

"I would really have preferred to have a go just as they were changing formation ready for landing, you know, come at them out of the West, maximum confusion etcetera, but I agree with you Simon, I think he'll use radar to make sure everyone's in their places and we need to be much closer when we expose ourselves. It's the first time I've wished for some of John Roby's missiles" Jake sighed and sat back too. "Let's look at what the bad guys are up to now."

The OPs room already on red light, dimmed even further to project on the aft bulkhead the live feed from the Arado RPV keeping the Haitian task force company.

Flicking between low light TV and digitised infra-red they could see the formation chugging along, still heading West with the flagship leading the gaggle of LSMs all screened by an inner and outer layer of DDGs, FFGs and corvettes. They all watched in silence for a minute before Jake went back to the Holo table.

"What if we just head back towards Rum Point and wait. We know the watcher has been caught and their ship movements indicate they think we're out of it. If we stay a few miles offshore and obviously with no running lights, we'll be in the land shadow of the Caymans if he uses his Nav radar to sort the formation. We should be nigh on undetectable especially if we are bows on at that time." He pointed to the map again. "Maybe go back to Rum Point at speed and then progress slowly towards Conch Point. We know what time he needs to be heading in to the beach. So providing he doesn't cock it up spectacularly we'll be in position to head towards him at high speed, coming in on an almost parallel track with the coast to our port but beyond likely night vision distance. Then, depending on his final dispositions, we can try to pick our way through the outer screen to the assault ships without having to race from behind. We'd have to complete the manoeuvre before Civil twilight -at what time Simon?" he said looking over at him.

"05:23 Sir."

"Seems sound enough." Said Reiner.

"About the best we can do for now." Added Simon.

"Right," said Jake "I'm going back up to the bridge for a while. We could really do with total darkness, let's just hope that the clouds keep rolling in. If anyone has any bright ideas please don't keep them to yourselves."

It's amazing, thought Jake as he climbed the ladder to the bridge, how important weather still is in the warfare of the twenty first century.

Many at home would wonder why the ships didn't have their search radar on all the time but the reality was that doing so would tell your enemy exactly where you are but crucially, before you had a hope of seeing them if they had theirs off!

Carlson waited patiently for the end of Andrew McTeal's call to Downing Street, he knew from the half of the conversation that he could eavesdrop, that McTeal wasn't getting what he needed from the British, simply put, a commitment to come to their aid. He dredged up from memory an image of the British prime Minister, not long in the job since Britain had opted for exit from the EU and she had replaced the facile David Cameron.

As he listened to all the parting platitudes, politicians seem to excel at them, he considered the plight of *Bismarck*'s crew as it drew nearer the time when they would engage the approaching Haitians.

It was a bit of a bum deal, he thought, most of them had given up everything they had all over Europe, to come down here and start a new life and look what happens, they get caught up in someone else's ambitions. The shitty end of the stick. He poured another cup of his favourite Earl Grey which by British traditions he noted, he should have stopped drinking at six, because it is an afternoon tea, however as far as he was concerned it was 6 o'clock somewhere. He sat back in the comfy leather Chesterfield scrutinizing the office's other occupant, Sandiford Roche.

Apparently the little exercise on the beach had gone well, the spy, for want of a better word, had been apprehended after he'd made his transmission.

Under interrogation he had revealed two further names and also that he wasn't expected to report in again that night, all very useful. It wouldn't have been as easy to ensure security if he'd had other contact times.

Dammit! He marvelled at Roche's composure, in another few hours he could be up against a bullet pocked wall and looking at him you'd think that we hadn't got a thing to worry about. A kick in the butt might just get a reaction, he thought. The phone call ended.

McTeal surveyed his two guests. The greying American tried to look uninterested but failed, he looked over to

Sandy, smiling as he saw that Roche had again chosen the least well-lit area to sit, in such a light it was difficult to read a man's face.

"Pull your chair in closer Sandy, I can hardly see you over there." He smiled inwardly at the reluctance with which Roche moved into the light shed by a tall standard lamp, the only illumination in the room.

"Now you both heard one side of the conversation, let me tell you the rest.

The British have asked for a UN Security Council emergency session but since that won't be until it's too late for us, then it's not a lot of use. Given the time zone difference I was quite surprised that I got a civil reply at all at two o'clock in the morning. However, there is a frigate on its way here, should arrive tomorrow morning sometime I gather."

He held up his hand to restrain the interjection that hadn't got past Carlson's lips yet.

"Yes I know Mr Carlson, one frigate isn't going to make a jot of difference if the *Bismarck* doesn't manage a miracle tonight. But I'm certain I detected something in her tone - deliberate I'm sure- that makes me wonder if there isn't something else they may be up to. Miles what else, in the way of a military effort, could the British mount on short notice?"

Carlson, caught in mid sip, quickly put his teacup down before answering.

"Good question Sir. It really does depend on whether it really is short notice to them -if you take my meaning. As I said before, one of their top brass has known that something could be going down out here for longer than you have. It may be that this slight tonal clue that you got refers to something they have in place courtesy of that gentleman."

He got up and walked over to a map on McTeal's wall which showed the whole Caribbean with a good chunk of both North and South America.

"Now there are really only two places within reasonable range that they could mount any sort of operation from and they are Bermuda and Belize. I would discount Bermuda for the simple reason that Cuba lies right across the track from there to here, thus extending the flight time of any aircraft which would have to fly around and it also takes them right past Haiti."

He pointed out the routes on the map before adding.

"And it must be an aerial operation, since we already know they only have one frigate around here, so that just leaves Belize."

He turned to look at them both.

"Well, I know that they quit there in late 93', but the airfield is big enough for any military jets they've got. So it's possible that they could use Belize as a forward base since it's only four hundred and fiftyish miles from here. I'd ask my friend over at the NSA if he knew of any movements but I expect he's been told not to communicate with me unless through channels." He sat back down again.

McTeal appeared to consider heavily for a moment before replying.

"Well I think we'd be stretching the good Lord's generosity by asking for two miracles in the same night. I suggest we forget about the British and pray for a *Bismarck* related miracle. Anything to add Sandy?"

"Yes Prime Minister. What was her reaction when you told her that you were declaring a one hundred mile military exclusion zone?"

"Funny you should mention that Sandy. She didn't seem at all put out, in fact I think she found it rather amusing since we only have one ship and no airforce per se."

They all laughed to release the tension but already the night seemed endless.

23:00 [Local] Saturday 26th May 2018
HMS *Dorsetshire*, 110 Miles West North West of the Cayman Islands

Roby had been half expecting the next signal and when it arrived he was seated in his bridge chair staring out into the Caribbean night as they charged East at nearly thirty knots. Again he had to go down to the MSO and feed the appropriate codes into the decryption printer before he could look at clear text instead of gibberish.

Sitting once again in his cabin with the 'war council' as it now was, he felt a sudden deep sadness as he re-read the text, a part of which could only refer to his old friend Jake.

Covering his momentary distress he passed the signal once more to his First Lieutenant then the navigator and lastly to Berry Reeves. One by one they digested the contents of the signal, all of them realizing the import of the first paragraph and all of them sparing a moment of thought for men whom they knew, who may now be dead or at best, swimming in oil and debris covered water hoping for rescue.

Roby looked hard at his little group and wondered if like him, they thought that this was all beginning to look a little too well planned to be just a lucky dispersal of assets, in the right theatre, at the right time. No, he answered himself, they wouldn't see past the signal and its immediate consequences for themselves. He glanced down at it again.

27Z335ZMAY18 ZZZZZZZZZZZZZZZZZZZZZZZZ
From: CINCFLT
To: COMCENTAMCARIB
Info: MODUK(N)
CBF BELIZE
BT. TOP SECRET
SUBJECT: WAR WARNING
1. AT APPROX 0330Z HAITIAN SURFACE UNITS INITIATED SSM ATTACK ON CAYMAN NAVAL UNIT. UK GOVT HAS SUPPORTED PROTEST TO UN. UN SECURITY COUNCIL EMERGENCY SESSION SCHEDULED AT 1000Z.

2. THEATRE FORCES ARE TO ASSUME CONDITION ONE ALERT.
3. CONSIDER THEATRE NAVAL ASSETS INSUFF FOR INTERDICTION HAITI PHIBUNITS. DORSETSHIRE TO REMAIN ONSTA NO CLOSER THAN 50 MILES. COMCENTAMCARIB LIAISE WITH CBF BELIZE RE OP CROSSHATCH (DETAILS TO FOLLOW).
A. ROE WARNING RED. WEAPONS TIGHT. ENGAGE ONLY AFTER DEMONSTRATED HOSTILE INTENT.
ET. NNNN

Roby perused the follow on signal carefully, I'd love to know the date on which this was drawn up, he mused. It was a very detailed operation order. He looked up at his officers and began to speak. Fifteen minutes later he had outlined his intentions and brought the meeting to a close, slowing their approach to arrive fifty miles off shore.

"Change the time for the Merlin launch to," he consulted the bulkhead clock, calculating distance and speed rapidly "04:00 hours armed for anti-ship."

He hadn't revealed to Jake that his was the first Merlin to be fitted out for carrying the Marte *Sea Killer* anti-ship missiles.

"The rest of us can have a lay in, call the hands 04:30 I think, action stations now at 05:15. I'll speak to the ship's company in five minutes. Any questions at present? Right," he dismissed them "come and see me if you have any snags."

Kipper closed the door to his cabin, quickly changing into his No8's (denim action working dress) he moved across to his bunk and sat down on the edge.

He paused a moment staring curiously at his hands which had a slight tremor, whilst his brain went into a kind of neutral mode. A short while later he reached under the bed, opened one of the pull out drawers and extracted an unlabelled clear glass bottle.

Uncorking it reverently, he sniffed the unmistakable raisony, pungent aroma of 'Pussers' Rum'. Carefully pouring a single shot of the deep brown liquid he reflected that this was what ships used to call into Gibraltar for on the way home.

It was the only place you used to be able to get 'Pussers Rum'. When you consider that the Royal Navy's rum ration had ceased in 1971 it was a wonder that you could still buy it up until the nineties, but only in Gibraltar.

He had been touched when his dad had pressed this bottle into his hands before he flew out to take up his new job. Could it even be the last bottle of Pussers Rum? He briefly mused, nah there'll be Jacks all over who still have a tot tucked away somewhere. Savouring the unique flavour of the 100 proof 57% spirit he sipped the rum reflecting on the changes he'd seen in himself and the Royal Navy since he'd joined as a boy and left as a man. He freely admitted that he'd been a bit 'bolshy' when he'd joined, the eighties had been times of great change in both the Navy and the world at large.

He used to have a poster which dated back from the Vietnam war it showed an American GI in Vietnam at the moment of being shot, arms flung out wide and agony on his face, the caption simply read 'Why'.

He'd tried to rationalize the 'why' of the posters then but it had been many years, in fact during the 'Gulf two', before he'd actually reasoned it out.

He'd wangled a trip to Basra, as much for a jolly as any actual need to go, no one questioned a Warrant Officer when they wanted to do something, everyone assumed they knew what they were doing.

What shocked him was that this was the area of the country supposedly anti-Saddam. Weren't they supposed to be on the same side as us now? From what he heard in the mess and from the people he'd gone to see in camp near the town the British forces were under siege and militias were in charge.

It then became clear for the first time why he'd kept the damned poster through draft after draft, carefully unpicking it from the inside of his locker. The last thing any soldier, sailor or airman wanted to do was to die in a way that had no meaning, served no purpose, or for the wrong side.

The dying GI in the poster had signified Kipper's resentment of politicians who sent so many brave men and women, ordinary people, to die for no discernible gain. They had been sold out by their government.

His dad had said that the Falklands was the last honourable war we'd fought. Cut and dried that, he said, bad guys-good guys, the people that went knew what they were fighting for and why and, the opposition had the courtesy to wear a different uniform rather than hiding in amongst civilians.

He'd then stunned Kipper by saying, ever since then there's always been some doubt that it was right, something would turn up later to make you question why it was necessary for our people to go and die there. It always seemed to be someone else's war. It'll be the same this time, he thought, the common factor being that a lot of good blokes will get the chop and bugger all will really change.

He shook himself, by Christ Kipper, you're getting more bloody cynical by the hour. The best thing, he remembered telling his juniors so often over the years, is to do your duty and hope to hell that the buggers up top know what they're doing.

Yeah, do your duty and hope to fuck it turns out alright, best follow your own advice Kipper me lad. He savoured the last drops of the rum, he didn't normally drink on duty but it might be the last chance he'd ever get to have a 'Pussers tot'.

He had nothing else in his life, no wife and kids just an endless succession of ships and bases over the years not that that was a complaint, he'd always been happy with his lot, hadn't wanted the strings of wife and kids, he'd seen it go wrong so many times.

He replaced the bottle and standing up, squared his uniform off. Stepping out of the cabin he returned to the role that he played so well, the reliable Warrant Officer, the unflappable chunk of granite that those above and below expected him to be.

Bugger the Haitians, he thought as he paced back towards the bridge, bugger the lot of 'em, Jonathan Henry will sort that bunch of 'wannabees' out. He also needed someone to believe in.

23:10 Saturday 26th May 2018
Temporary Operations Room, Punta Gorda, Belize

CRAF Belize, or Commander Royal Air Force detachment Belize, kicked at a stone on the floodlit runway and made a note to have a FOD walk done before they flew out -whenever that was.

He was walking back across the hot and humid airfield towards the operations room having wandered the perimeter. Squadron Leader Nigel Greene was thirty years old that day and what a day.

The stocky, sandy haired, fast jet pilot had landed in the morning, after a buttock numbing total journey of almost five thousand miles from his base at RAF Coningsby in Lincolnshire, to be told that his temporary new title would be CRAF Belize and that he would probably co-ordinate and lead an anti-shipping strike, when given the go ahead. All that and much more had been in a complex and lengthy signal that had been awaiting him on his arrival that morning.

Mounting the steps leading into the OPs room he quickly massaged his lower back making a mental note to go see the Doc when he got back, he didn't think that there was really anything particularly wrong but he'd had this 'sciatic' kind of pain a couple of times recently on longish flights.

Still it was understandable today really, since he'd just flown all that way in an aircraft not designed with comfort as its primary function.

With him on the transatlantic flight had been three more Typhoons, an Airbus tanker and a C-17 Loadmaster. They'd originally been going to split the journey by flying via Canada's Goose Bay and there joining up with an AWACS E3D-Sentry of 8 Sqn out of Waddington also in Lincolnshire but in the end the direct route with tanking was chosen. Three C130J Hercules would join them tomorrow having routed the Goose Bay route.

The night-over at MacDill AFB in Florida had been anything but restful since by then the 'Buzzes' about what was going on, had been flying thick and fast. The legendary hospitality of the US forces had not disappointed them and most had left just before dawn, after a massive breakfast, with an extra tin of this or bottle of that stowed in their personal gear.

By the time they departed MacDill, just about everyone had worked out that it wasn't a routine deployment exercise. So too had the American Air force personnel that were helping out, and with calls like 'Blow 'em away - whoever they are' and 'good luck limey -give 'em hell', echoing in their ears, they'd roared down the runway with burners on and woken up everyone in sleepy Tampa just five miles away.

He entered the room smiling, thinking about the complaints the poor USAF Base Commander would have to field today. The OPS officer, Flt Lieutenant Steve Moscrop, noted the smile and quite reasonably, but mistakenly, thought his boss had returned to good humours, having been pushing everyone since he'd read his orders that morning.

"Well Mozzy, anything from on high yet?"

"No Sir, but I've managed a composite weather sat photo of the Caribbean basin for you."

Greene ignored the proffered satellite photos.

"Bugger it all. This is bloody ridiculous, 'hurry up and wait' again. No doubt they'll warn the Haitians first just to play fair and abide by their human rights, and they'll be sitting there waiting for us when we go in. Half a mile behind them in a row boat will be a load of ambulance chasing lawyers waiting to sue us for shooting at them with nasty intent."

Steve revised his initial interpretation of the smile and put it down to wind.

"Any more news about that nutcase and his funny battleship yet? I expect it's already on the sea bottom by now -silly sods. 'Mozzy', are you going to pass me that weather map?"

Mozzy was having as much trouble keeping pace with the conversation as he was tracking his boss around the room. He watched as the pilot randomly lifted sheets of paper, read them without absorbing the words, and moved on to the next piece, keeping up a continuous stream of chat. Still he's got a lot on his plate at the moment and all this waiting around doesn't help, Mozzy thought sympathetically.

He missed it the first time the squadron leader asked.

"Come on Moscrop," Greene snapped, "don't bugger about, pass the weather photo. I want to get some Zz's in a minute, so don't you keep me hanging around as well. Oh and make a note for a full FOD walk before we fly, there's chunks of stone out there that I could trip over."

Moscrop duly noted that a walk along the runway and taxi areas by the ground personnel looking for foreign object debris was to be carried out as soon as light permitted then a further walk at noon. He wondered whether the Gurkha officers would lend them some of their lads too?

Ex-Captain 'Buck' Taylor, sitting in the underground command post near the top of Weary Hill, received the satellite relayed burst transmission from *Bismarck*, with a professional soldier's equanimity.

He swivelled the office-type chair and looked up at the large scale map of the two outer Cayman islands pinned to the wall and tried to second guess the landing point of the single assault ship that was apparently heading in his direction.

A single '*Yunshu*' class assault ship, probably meant something like two companies of troops, say three hundred men, plus maybe a couple of BMDs/BMPs, he thought, since they're Russian/Chinese equipped. Possibly BMMP or BMD-3s he decided. Even though amphibious they'd want a nice beach to drive up.

There weren't that many landing options. Most of Little Cayman was protected by rocks and reefs but there were a couple of likely points at the other end of the island, he thought.

He scrutinized the South coast near the airstrip at Blossom Village and then dismissed it because whilst they'd get through the gap in the reef, he thought the water got shallow too quickly and although shallow drafted the vessel would ground itself way out from the shore.

No, he decided, he'll go for Anchorage Bay on the North coast about a third of the way along. He could see the offshore reef broke there for nearly half a mile. Better and better for them were the roads. One running north south bisecting the island and the coast road too which ran east west.

Better for us too he decided. They'd have to split their forces three ways to cover everything.

Whistling softly he walked across to the communications console on the other side of the room and contacted his teams, telling them to get up to the command post for a final briefing.

Pacing had always seemed to help focus his mind and he began now as he thought through the arrangements that had been made to receive any unwelcome guests.

The very first thing he'd done was to get as many of the two hundred plus civilians on the island over to Cayman Brac. If there was any shooting, he explained to them, then it would be here on Little Cayman since there were no defenders on Cayman Brac. Most had gone but one or two had said they'd hide in the woods and see what happened.

Next had been the preparation of the likely routes that enemy soldiers would use getting to the base at this end of the island. It didn't matter that he couldn't predict just exactly where the landing would take place, because the defenders could safely assume that both of the two roads on the island were likely approach routes, since the rest of the island was either heavily forested or mangrove swamp.

That is unless they're really thick and try for a landing through our harbour entrance, he mused for a second hopefully whilst imagining the effect of the 40mm camouflaged 'Dardo' gun and the multi-barrelled Gatlings on the thin skinned assault ship.

There were a half dozen pinch points on both the north and south road which they had laid IEDs alongside, having 'borrowed' a dozen or so of *Bismarck*'s 130mm HE main gun rounds. There they would ambush them and force the enemy to move inland to flank them.

Inland on the North side meant an upslope covered with trees but it would take dismounted infantry to work around and discover where they'd also laid claymores. These were backed-up by tiny Wi-Fi video cams in order they could be remotely detonated at exactly the right time. Then they'd move another hundred yards back to the next pinch point and start again.

Same with the south side except the terrain inland was a mixture of mangroves and brackish pools as well as bare rocks and trees. There was one point where the road turned 90 degrees left or eastwards, right next to the coast. Three command detonated 130mm shells had been dug into the land side the road there, one before the corner, one on the corner and one further around.

He hoped they'd bunch there. Unseasoned troops often bunched if their way forward was slowed or they hit resistance. If it played out right, the leading troops would detonate the first charge, the others would take cover then crowd together while someone checked the road, then the next two would go off.

It was nasty stuff but then anyone who thought war was pleasant or civilised was an absolute bloody loon. He reflected that if you want to win in war, you fight hard and dirty and you succeed by killing as many of the other guys as quickly as possible, thereby rapidly instilling fear and demoralising them.

He didn't think the enemy commander would initially deploy dismounted troops to the inland side of either road. But that would change when he took his first casualties.

Having sown both approach roads with anti-tank, anti-personnel and IED devices and the inland areas with the claymore anti-personnel charges he was confident that these, backed by careful sniping would endlessly delay the enemy and also attrite them badly.

One four man team would have overwatch for each road to prevent any remaining locals from blundering into them. These same men would man the first ambushes.

When they retreated, the second team would be waiting for them at the next ambush point. Now the enemy would face twice as much harassing fire. At each pinch point, increasing numbers of soldiers would attack the advancing forces, retreating to the next team along each time an ambush was triggered. This would continue all the way back to the base area.

Having caused as much chaos and as many casualties as possible and with the survivors facing increasingly larger manned ambush sites, they would make the final stand at the Weary Hill base.

Hopefully they'll have had enough by then. He ruefully considered the prospect of the dirty fighting that would erupt in the area of the accommodation and other buildings if the Haitian attack persisted.

If they thought they'd had a hard time at the ambushes in the woods then they had a horrible shock awaiting them in the built up areas. His British and Russian contingents were expert in urban warfare with hard learned techniques galore; they'd be bloody hard to ferret out by even experienced urban fighters, in spite of their large numerical superiority.

The rest of his men would then infiltrate the enemy line and attack his rear areas causing chaos.

He sat down at the desk and considered what the supporting destroyer and the corvette could achieve. Not much, he thought, bearing in mind that his teams would ambush and move, not giving much time for naval suppressive gunfire to have an effect. But if it came to house clearing they could use indirect fire, difficult but not impossible if it was well spotted. But it would have to stop before the troops moved in.

They'd probably come in range of the Dardo and Gatling guns and he'd have to decide whether to use them then or wait for the final attack on Weary Hill where they could each cover the final approach roads.

He looked around as the first team leaders came through the blast proof doors, yeah, he thought, we should be OK if we keep our heads –and they do what I want them to, he added cynically.

"Gather round lads I've got a 'sitrep' for you. The next time you hear from me will be when it hits the fan so listen up." Said the former counter-revolutionary warfare expert.

The hills about twelve miles East of Anse D'Hainhault, Western Haiti

Winston sat down heavily next to Sophie and Tetsunari, old Marc was keeping watch, not that that meant much. The rain continued relentlessly, he could barely see a dozen feet and had to raise his voice to be heard.

"Ma'am..." started Winston.

"Oh hell, now what?" Interrupted Sophie, knowing that it was bad news because Winston had called her Ma'am.

Sod it! thought Winston, why can't I bring good news for a change. He pushed on.

"I've just finished the routine link up..."

"I bloody well know that Winston, since I handed you the bag with the phone in, remember?"

Snapped a soggy Sophie, losing her temper briefly.

It was warm, hot even, but they had had so much rain they'd barely been dry for more than a couple of hours in the last three days. Clothes wouldn't dry, socks stayed soggy and Winston was genuinely bothered about Sophie's ability to keep up now.

Her feet were shredded, the boots she'd started with had fallen apart after the first day much to her annoyance as they were supposedly top of the range. So they'd been bound up with an assortment of string and palm fronds but the rubbing had first blistered and now was just raw where the blisters had rubbed away. She was in pain just sitting there but refused to give up.

"Just tell me what the hell has gone wrong now Winston and cut the crap. I hope it's not another delay, I swear I'm dissolving!"

She finished in a weary voice and laid back on the mushy ground unconcerned by the rain beating down on her like a warm power shower. She just waited for the hammer to fall.

Winston looked helplessly at Tetsunari and got nothing but one of his best 'inscrutable Oriental' specials.

"Well it's like this."

He drew a deep breath and rushed on,

""In about three to four hours' time, *Bismarck* is going to take on the Haitian invasion forces. Jake sends his love and wants you to know that arrangements have been made to get us out if..."

He stumbled badly but then continued.

"If they can't come and get us themselves."

He sat waiting for her reply and the silence stretched on, broken only by the cicadas. When her reply came it was almost too soft to hear.

"He could have said goodbye to me himself."

Winston looked down and guessed that if it weren't for the rain, he'd see the tears tracking down her cheeks. There was nothing he could say, so he said nothing, lay down on his thin soggy blanket and closed his eyes.

"Winston, give me the phone please?"

He sat up, looked at her and just passed it across.

"Just press the recall button and ask them to put you through to him." He smiled. "They won't argue."

Bismarck, 60 miles North, North West of Grand Cayman

Jake rapidly exited the OPs room, his mind in turmoil. He'd desperately wanted to speak to Sophie for one last time, but he'd never been happy displaying emotion even face to face let alone via a satellite link.

It wasn't that he didn't feel the appropriate emotions, it was just that something inside prevented him from showing it, except in very extreme circumstances.

Which was precisely why he had chosen not to speak to Sophie then. He knew that he wouldn't have been able to suppress his feelings and if sharing them with his wife was very difficult, then sharing them with the duty staff in the OPs room was impossible.

I must be nuts, he thought as he abruptly changed direction and headed for an upperdeck door instead of the Bridge. He rapidly climbed the steps up into the aft superstructure and operated the door mechanism. As the hydraulic rams slid the door panel to the right he stepped over the coaming and out onto the quarterdeck next to turret Caesar.

Absently he pushed the button on the bulkhead and the door closed with a short hiss and a solid sounding thunk. Strolling slowly aft he cleared his mind of all the pressing urgency of the current situation and let it wander. Walking to the side rail he leaned against it and looked out over the frothing silvery wake. Just then his earpiece beeped.

"Incoming Sat call." Then he was connected.

"Jake?" Said a soft voice he knew so well.

"Are you there?" He moved quickly back in to the lee of the turret so the noise was lessened and didn't waste time asking why she'd called using precious battery power.

"Yes darling I'm here. Sorry I didn't speak earlier, I was in the OPs room…" He stuttered to a halt.

He heard a throaty chuckle.

"Still hate to let anyone think you've got a heart eh?"

"Got it in one Sophs. How are you holding up?"

Sophie lied through her teeth to protect the man she loved.

"Fine, a few blisters for a start but I'm fitter than you give me credit for. Diet is a bit samey but I could do with losing a couple of pounds. How are things with you?"

Jake lied through his teeth too to protect the woman he loved.

"We've got an excellent plan, a great ship and total surprise, should be a cake walk."

They both knew the other was being seriously economical with the truth, but sometimes it was necessary.

"I love you." He said.

"I love you too." she said quickly before her voice cracked too much.

"We'll be there as soon as we can my love, just hang in there and do what Winston tells you."

"I will. See you soon my love, bye" Another lie.

Jake stood there a moment gazing into the night then shook his head, time to get back to work.

A 'tactical thought' suddenly intruded and he quickly glanced up at the night sky, noting the thickening cloud to the north and west and the still cloud-free near full moon directly above.

He realized that it had been the silvery wake that had caused him to look up, suddenly remembering his earlier pleas for a complete overcast during the approach to attack. Casting aside the errant thought he momentarily lost himself in the beauty of the star studded night sky. It always had a sobering, diminishing effect on him, as if God were showing him just how insignificant he and all his efforts were. He smiled up at the moon and bid it a silent goodnight.

Sheltering in the lee of turret Dora, the aftermost gun turret, Joachim Kempfe watched his Commodore look out over the rail. He didn't move, not wanting to disturb what was obviously a private moment for Jake.

Then he saw Jake touch his left ear to take a call and step swiftly to the lee of the turret. Now he couldn't move again. He heard Jake's side of the conversation and smiled. Good on you boss.

He saw Jake look up at the stars, lost for a time in their enduring beauty and then he saw his commander smile, his face calm and bright in the moonlight, then walk slowly back towards the after superstructure.

For a long moment Kempfe sat still, his earlier mood of melancholy disappearing as he contemplated the Commodore's calm smile. An urgent burning sensation pulled him back to reality; he quickly flicked the cigarette stub over the side and sucked his burnt fingers.

Jake sat in his chair in the OPs room watching the screen as pictures, relayed from one of the Arados, were digitized to show a look-down view of the disposition of the Haitian task force. The time was 00:20 and the enemy vessels had passed the south western tip of Grand Cayman at a range of forty five miles, now on their North West course to cut the corner.

If Simon's prediction was correct, he expected the formation to change as soon as the right hand screen ships reached a point level with, but about twenty miles West of George Town. At this point, he anticipated that the force would wheel through a hundred or so degrees until pointing right at the island and then deploy into assault formation.

As he'd said before, this was the time at which he'd like to attack since there would be the maximum amount of change occurring, making it easier to approach unseen as everyone would be concerned about station keeping, not wanting to be the one who bumped into someone else.

However he suspected that the enemy commander would, as Simon suggested, risk a brief activation of his navigation radar. Without lights showing and with no radar allowed, it was back to the Mark I eyeball and a commander really had to be sure that everyone was heading where he wanted them –unless of course they were using Link of some kind. He also didn't think they'd be confident enough for needless night flying, risking the few helicopters they had.

Therefore the decision to wait until the formation had settled on its new course before attacking still seemed the best. The reality was that *Bismarck*'s only chance for success and survival lay in a close range, surprise onslaught of the most frightening ferocity. In the moments following the attack he hoped that thoughts of 'flight' would predominate over 'fight' in the minds of the enemy commanders.

Their hopes of achieving this surprise were aided by two other factors. One was simply that the enemy must surely believe *Bismarck* had been sunk otherwise, given their proximity to the target, they would now have gone active with their radar, trading secrecy for advance warning of a sneak *Bismarck* attack.

The second factor was based on his knowledge of sailors and human nature in general. Peacetime navies were different to wartime navies. Peacetime sailors in a task force would be more concerned with avoiding an admiral's wrath than anything else, and during complicated evolutions, each ship had to be where it was supposed to be.

Therefore, he reasoned, most eyes would be facing forward towards the landing areas or concentrating on station keeping. Sailors in navies that were at war and had already suffered the shock of sudden attack, spent more time looking all around them, very conscious of their vulnerability.

On the other side of the OPs room, Simon McClelland was immensely pleased with the information that the Arados were supplying. After the initial launch to locate the Haitian force and shadow it, the second Arado had been sent up to monitor the advance of the group which seemed set to attack the outer islands, which it did.

Since then *Bismarck* had launched a replacement for the one watching the main Haitian task force, recovered the original and was waiting for the distant RPV to return now before sending another.

The only slight 'fly' in the ointment was that the ship had to slow right down in order to recover the float planes. In any kind of sea they'd probably cartwheel on landing but with the sea at the moment it was possible for the ship to swing suddenly left or right thus creating a lee, a calm patch of water, for them to land on. Scotnikov was designing a catcher system that used the same cranes that lifted them but that was months away from testing.

Once landed, the RPVs could taxi on their floats towards the crane derrick which was swung out over the side of the much slowed ship. At this point a heavy duty rigid nylon loop would flick up from its upper wing surface, this was hooked on to the crane derrick by a sailor (suspended on a life-line) riding the crane cable down.

Of course in action, the planes would have been launched and not recovered until after the battle. This was what was planned now. Each aircraft had an endurance of about six hours or so and it was hoped that all would be available at the start of the action.

They would be launched immediately before action commenced and when low on fuel all four would recover not to the ship, but to the sheltered area of North Sound, Grand Cayman.

03:15 Sunday 27th May 2018
Bismarck steaming slowly Westward,
North of the Haitian task force

At 03:15 on the morning of the 27th of May 2018, *Bismarck* went to action stations, most people had been at their posts for a while but this formalised it. Raucous alarms momentarily dispelled the torpor that had overcome the men as the evening and night had dragged by. The almost continuous enemy position reports and their proximity to *Bismarck* thereafter, made each minute seem like an hour to the crew.

It is a truism that in war, the worst moments are those spent waiting for something to happen. At these times men begin to doubt themselves and volunteers especially, curse their own stupidity for putting themselves in this position.

In some ways this was worse than usual for *Bismarck*'s crew, since they all knew where the enemy was and that they were themselves swiftly, inexorably and voluntarily steaming towards a vastly superior enemy force. Each man copes with this strain in his own way, there are no guidelines on how to alleviate it, no 'old hands' quick cures. Some read, some write letters, others endlessly check the systems they are responsible for, and others sit quietly waiting, with the fear forming a tight cold knot in their guts.

Only when the action starts does this become irrelevant in the well trained, and overwhelming and self-destructive for the poorly trained.

At 03:50 the Haitian task force began to change shape as ships manoeuvred into their positions for the final run in towards the beaches, just as the clouds finally arrived overhead. *Bismarck*'s ESM picked up a radar transmission from a Nato code 'Palm Frond' navigation radar at 04:00. Only two ships in the Haitian group possessed this radar, one was the *Slava* class cruiser and Flagship *General Farache,* and the other the remaining *Sovremenny* class destroyer.

Two more brief transmissions were noted at 04:15 and 04:20. They could see from the feed sent back by the Arado RPV that the Haitians were now in their attack formation and the landing ships clearly heading towards the reef gaps now slowed to ten knots. Gambling that the Haitians would not use their big search radar now, Jake ordered the approach to begin. Reiner gave the command to turn towards the enemy and to go to full ahead. They were committed.

The drone on station to the east of the enemy task group kept a weather eye out for any final changes as Simon down in the OPs room began to calculate how to thread in between the escorting enemy ships with the minimum risk of visual or NVG detection in order to get at their primary targets, the troop transports. In *Bismarck*, hearts began to beat a little faster and brows became beaded with nervous sweat.

The Haitians had gone for a formation which had the assault ships nearest to the island with a close escort of three Type 37 corvettes and an outer ring of larger DDGs and FFGs plus the flagship.

Bismarck raced down an almost parallel, but reciprocal course to the nearest outer escort of the enemy group, getting no closer than five miles, then turned sharply in behind it, about three miles astern.

With the moon set and the clouds covering the stars, black as night itself, *Bismarck* moved in. They manoeuvred her to the inner ring and turned onto the same course as the enemy. She kept her speed just high enough to overtake the assault ships slowly and approached the northernmost LSM of the strung out line.

They expected the action to start in about another fifteen minutes at around 04:55. Up in the main gunnery control centre (MGCC), Julius Kopf ordered the computer to load illumination rounds for turret Anton and high explosive (HE) shells, flash-less and fused for Semi Armour Piercing (SAP), for the remaining six guns of the main battery.

There was no need to illuminate their target from a gunnery point of view because they would see their targets via radar, infra-red, or TV, but Jake had decided that it would momentarily blind lookouts, cause confusion and demoralize those illuminated by the star shells.

There had been some tense moments at about 04.35 when they'd come closest to the nearest escort as they passed going in opposite directions. Everyone knew that if they were spotted they'd never get near to the transports and that would be that as far as stopping them went.

Kopf had sat, left hand ready to flick off the safety the other with fingers resting on the trigger as his guns using infrared had tracked the unsuspecting Type 53 frigate, out of sight but only five miles away.

Now they were set. The four turret selector lights glowed a soft green on the panel in front and he turned to Carl Dettweiler his number two.

"All set Carl. I hope to heaven that they manage the re-loading of the ready use magazines. We'll be fucked if the breech clicks empty when we need them most."

"Yes boss, truly fucked." He was only half paying attention to his boss as he reset one of the AK630M2s a second time, the ready light had stayed on amber in the standby mode instead moving to green on activation. He made a note on the computer to replace the switches and fuses then thought how stupid he was since they'd likely be lighting up the sea bed before long.

Carl had ordered the eight 3 inch guns of the secondary armament to load a mix of ordinance on both beams. Some firing shells that would explode and fragment above the target, to wreck the delicate radar antenna and communication equipment, others were firing HE for the landing ships.

Once again the first rounds would be fired using *Bismarck*'s YAG laser rangefinder with a cross check supplied by the Arados above. Satisfied that all was in order, Dettweiler switched his systems to standby and began a computer calibration check on the fire control system, the third that night.

He knew he was just doing things for the sake of occupation but it seemed that it was the only way to keep the icy worm of fear from overwhelming him. He glanced at his boss and noted the beads of perspiration on his forehead just below the edge of the anti-flash hood.

"What do you think our chances are Sir?"

Kopf jumped slightly, so absorbed had he been in his own system checks.

"Uh, oh err, I think surprise is the big thing and once we set those assault ships alight, we get out quick and they can't continue the invasion."

Dettweiler nodded, it sounded so simple really but it couldn't be that basic could it?

Down in the OPS room Reiner offered a report as his Commodore re-entered the compartment.

"The ship is at action stations Commodore, all guns loaded in accordance with our instructions."

Jake wandered over to his old friend, sensing that it wasn't the end of the conversation since the ship had been at action stations for an hour and a half now.

Reiner debated whether or not to speak again but finally decided he had to.

"Are you aware of the date today Jake?" He asked in a lower voice so the other OPs staff could not hear.

Jake looked quizzically at his long-time friend.

"Of course I'm aware of the date Reiner, what's bothering you? Come on spit it out man you look like you're having problems swallowing something."

Reiner looked as if he wished the deck would open up and swallow him. He squirmed inwardly at his own superstitious nature but determined to carry on.

"Sir, seventy seven years ago today our namesake was sunk." he rushed on "and that ship had sailed on the 18th of May as we did from Bermuda. And on the 24th of May it fought a first and successful battle at almost exactly the same time as we did." He trailed off as he saw Jake's face muscles stiffen.

"Coincidence Reiner. Coincidence. Nothing more, nothing less. Now I'm going to the bridge and let's be about our proper jobs, eh? And quit the soothsaying"

The tone was reasonable but there was a hint of ice. Reiner took the hint and returned his attention to the displays in front of him.

As soon as he arrived on the bridge Jake took the command chair and announced to all by Tannoy he was on the bridge. He brought up the display screens on the bulkhead in the style he preferred, automatically noting their own position in relation to the Haitian screening ships.

He tried to focus his thoughts on the upcoming battle but found he couldn't drag his mind from the conversation with Reiner. It *was* a hell of a coincidence he conceded. He fished back in his memory for significant dates and times. The first *Bismarck* had sailed on her maiden operation on the 18th of May and yes, I suppose we did really, when we left Bermuda after the work-up period.

In the early dawn of the 24th of May, he couldn't remember the exact time six something in the morning he thought, the first *Bismarck* had stunned the world by quickly sinking the Royal Navy's 'Mighty *Hood*' one of the most powerful warships in the world at the time.

We too surprised everyone, he recollected, just after dawn on the 24th, then he dismissed it all.

We haven't been hounded from one end of the Atlantic to the other for the last three days. Still, what would it prove? Was destiny struggling to re-assert itself?

Should the name *Bismarck* have stayed at the bottom of the Atlantic? Or did Reiner think that some grand, godly chess game was being played out in which events were re-cycled with different players? Nonsense!

He dismissed the notion. We all make our own decisions -don't we? He felt a sudden and preternatural urge to turn the ship around onto a safe course. Shivering slightly he shrugged the feeling off.

We Königs always do what is right, regardless of the cost. He remembered his Grandfather's words, explaining why he had left Germany in 1936 with his young English wife but without his own brother Max.

More than a little unsettled Jake turned his mind back to the displays again, the range was closing rapidly now. The last of the Arados were airborne and sending back good pictures and most important the Haitians were clearly not aware that the 'wolf was in the sheep pen' and that the countdown had begun. As the seconds ticked down to zero and the range diminished, the tension built to a crescendo - of silence. Each man expected the enemy to wake up to the danger and unleash a storm of shells at them every second of their approach.

Everyone who had access to a viewer was glued to it, the near perfect pictures of the ships they were approaching, seen of course through low light and infra-red enhanced systems linked to the Arado RPVs and the ship's passive sensors, were all the more alarming because the watchers found it difficult to comprehend that they hadn't themselves been seen.

In the forward magazine Trev Kent waited with his eight MPP officers. Because of space restrictions Anton and Bruno turrets shared a common magazine reloading area, the same with Caesar and Dora in which PO Kiwi McClean awaited his orders.

Outwardly Kent was placid, smiling, joking and asking the nervous policemen about the best bars in George Town because he intended to drink them dry when they got back. Inwardly he was just as frightened as them, more so really because at least he knew what was coming to some degree.

Time and again they'd gone through the drills to load the spare shells into the pair of shell hoists that would take them up into the ready use magazines of Anton and Bruno, now he was satisfied that they could do so quickly and safely. They waited, sharing that false, nervous pre-action bonhomie, in which anything that's said is hilariously funny.

Granny Smith with Lawrence Cribb, the doctor, had finished setting up the emergency operating room in the wardroom and Bren had checked his two first aid parties, one located for'ard in the ratings dining hall beneath the bridge superstructure and the other in the laundry room beneath the after superstructure.

It would be his job to rush to wherever the casualties were and organize their transportation to the wardroom and the doctor, perhaps using some of his medical expertise if necessary but relying mainly on the battlefield first aid of his two groups of chefs, stewards and storemen, to save life.

Just forward of the laundry on 2 deck were the workshop spaces, both electrical and mechanical and now the location of HQ1 the damage control and firefighting centre. Lt Ian Halshaw was the Damage Control Officer, backed up by Kipper and the Buffer with a mixed team of two Leading Seamen, two Marine Engineers and six other seamen and two electricians.

Around them in sports bag sized burlap sacks with carrying straps, were spare softwood wedges with mallets for hammering into splinter holes. On the deck in various locations were strapped packs of pre-cut timber for shoring, others being distributed throughout the ship in small dumps.

Next door to the workshop was Halshaw's office with its monitors, alarms and displays reporting on every function of the ship's electrical and mechanical systems. He sat there watching the various screens but saw nothing. In his mind's eye *Bismarck* was leaping through the water, racing towards the bastards that had killed his daughter and he was pulling the firing trigger. Oh to swap places with Julius Kopf and pull that damned trigger myself, he lamented.

Up in the MGCC Julius Kopf was having his own pre-battle nerves.

A mental shout ringing in his head. Standby! Standby! Not that again, he thought as he wiped the sweat from his face and settled forward into the soft eye-cups of the viewer.

"Standby!" Came Jake's voice over the Tannoy. Kopf had a little snigger, funny you should say that sir, he muttered to himself, checking the alignment and lock of the various targets for his guns.

Each turret had a job and had been given commands to fire 'x' shells at target 'y' and so on. The system would automatically correct the fall of shot leaving the operators' time to select the next targets and ammunition if they desired a change.

Standby! Standby! Fuck off! He thought at the voice in his mind.

The digital clock clicked to 04:56, the range reading to the nearest assault ship fell to 2000 yards and Kopf spoke over the main broadcast.

"Engaging. Standby!" Then.

"SHOOT!" and he gently squeezed the trigger.

A millisecond later so did Dettweiler.

Anton crashed out the illumination rounds.

Bruno hurled its shells at a Type 53 frigate.

Caesar shot at the *General Farache*.

Dora fired on a Type 51D Destroyer.

The port secondary batteries fired at either the *Ropucha* or the *Yunshu* class transports as *Bismarck* stormed across their sterns, the starboard batteries sought out other escorts.

Down in the OPs room Reiner jerked as the opening shots blasted out. Through the viewer he watched the star shells pop above and beyond the line of transports and felt the vulnerability of the men revealed by that stark white light.

The *Bismarck*'s viewers had automatic glare suppressors so they didn't 'white out'. He turned and scanned the screens in front, now filled with information from the newly activated radar. The shit, he decided, has well and truly hit the fan.

*

Eight miles to the east, the seafront along Seven Mile Beach was deserted apart from the odd pair of MPP officers patrolling between the camouflaged gun pits in the still warm pre-dawn quiet.

They stopped suddenly and turned seawards, cupping their ears. Grimly one rushed to the beach front command bunker to report.

Gunfire and light to the west Sir! His officer nodded and equally grimly spoke into his radio and alerted government house.

Andy Evans, Miles Carlson and Andrew McTeal already knew that the battle had been joined. At 04:55 they had received *Bismarck*'s terse message 'Am in action with main task force 8 nm west of GC, will advise as practicable', and had immediately sent back their own 'Our hopes and prayers are with you'.

McTeal calmly watched König's security man Evans, as he paced the office like a caged tiger, the rumble of distant gunfire clearly audible now. It was clear that he considered it his duty to be with his employer and long-time friend and was frustrated that he couldn't be.

Carlson had also noticed and tried to lighten the atmosphere.

"You'd really like to be out there with them, wouldn't you Mr Evans?" He said with a smile of understanding.

Andy turned to the American and glared at him.

"They are my family Mr Carlson, it's my job to make sure no harm comes to them. And now, when they're heading into danger I'm not with them. My boss's wife is wandering around Haiti with two of my lads being hunted and I'm not with them either. I don't seem to be having much success with my job at present, so, yes Mr Carlson I would very much like to be doing something I'm very good at -breaking heads."

Carlson continued smiling. I bet you are too Mr Evans, he thought, I know you should be, because I've seen your service jacket. Royal Marines Commando, then SBS, perhaps even more dangerous than our Navy SEALS. But he just said.

"Sure, it's the waiting around with nothing to do but worry that grips us all Andy."

Yunshu Class Assault Ship Two. Seven miles West of Grand Cayman

Lieutenant Andre Toulin standing on the starboard bridge wing was instantly blinded as the illumination rounds popped high above and ahead of him. Before he could react he heard a massive rolling crash astern and to port, like a giant peel of thunder but right next to him.

Unable to see a damn thing he cursed and lurched backwards just as the first of the 3 inch HE shells smashed into the bridge blowing him back over the guardrail and into the sea.

He bobbed to the surface coughing and spitting seawater and turned round to see what was happening. His ship was moving steadily away unaware of his predicament, more flashes and explosions lit her up.

She was the second in the rough line abreast formation of five which were spaced unevenly and aimed for the breaks in the reefs ahead; he watched as the wheel house and bridge were hit again, then one of the twin 37mm mounts complete with guns, was hurled high in the air by a cataclysmic explosion, it fell with a tremendous splash into the water astern.

Debris splashed all around him as his stunned brain tried to work out what was happening. Moving his head left he found himself staring almost head on at the cause of his nightmare, less than a mile away. It was the damned mercenary ship they'd all been told was sunk! Now it was side lit by the illumination rounds and he could see its great white bow wave heading straight towards him. He began frantically swimming away from the onrushing metal monster.

On his ship no one was left alive on the bridge or in the wheelhouse and when the helmsman had died he'd slumped over the wheel turning it and moving the throttle handle to full as he slowly slid to the deck.

A fire was burning on the after deck and the bridge area was a mass of twisted gaping holes through which flames licked hungrily. The ship had started a swing to starboard and the frightened, milling soldiers in the well-deck forward were starting to panic as they looked aft at the flames rising from the bridge area.

Most of them were ordinary men who were in the army for the simple reason that they got fed regularly, had somewhere to sleep and didn't have to buy their own clothes.

They knew nothing of the sea, and the sudden onslaught in the night had terrified them. Their officers weren't in a much better frame of mind and as shells continued to hit the ship intermittently they started to lose their grip on themselves and their men.

So when she collided with the next in line and the massive shock threw everyone to the deck, it was no surprise they lost it completely. As water began spurting in through the crumpled bow doors it was every man for himself as they kicked, punched, butted and clawed at each other to get on a ladder that led upwards from the tank deck and the rising water.

*

On the *General Farache* Admiral Ramade didn't know yet what was happening. He was halfway back to the OPs room when the action station alarm sounded.

Having just had a twenty minute rest in his cabin because the OPs room displays gave him a headache if he stared at them for too long, he struggled through the whirling mass of sailors rushing to their action stations.

He felt the twelve thousand ton ship shudder several times and could smell smoke. The action stations alarms were still blaring out their strident message when he arrived at the door to the OPs room.

Suddenly he realized what was happening, everything clicked into place with the precision of a Swiss watch. He'd been fooled and would now pay the price for believing that damned mercenary ship had been sunk so easily.

Before opening the door he composed himself. It wasn't fear that coursed through him, it was a boiling, seething rage aimed at the man who commanded the mercenary ship; he had no doubts at all as to who the enemy was. He unclipped the armoured hatch and stepped over the coaming into bedlam. He could see immediately that half the displays were out or flickering and heard frantic voices calling for reports.

His Ukrainian counterpart had already settled himself in the command chair and commenced direction of the battle.

"Dmitri where is he?" Venkov looked slightly surprised that his Haitian counterpart had grasped what was happening so soon.

"He is approximately one mile astern of the assault ships and steering almost south now, they are five and a quarter miles on our bow."

He paused to draw on one of his foul smelling cigarettes.

"He has damaged three of the transports, but only two are in a serious way at present -they collided."

Again he drew on his cigarette before continuing with the catalogue of disaster.

"We have received eight hits." the ship shuddered again. "Make that nine."

Another drag.

"We have lost our helicopter, which had to be pushed overboard as it was on fire, the hangar, the after SAN-4 missile launcher and the starboard after, 30 millimetre Gatling mount. There is damage to some of the starboard Bazalt missile launchers. There is other shell damage but not so serious. Also he seems to be using a mix of fragmentation shells since we're losing a lot of our sensor and communication aerials, we've lost the main search radar, our IFF antenna and one SAM radar."

Ramade made a desperate effort to control his facial muscles, waiting for Venkov to end his report.

"Now the good news. Our gunnery and missile fire control radar -fortunately located forward- are functional. His principal error has been in not neutralizing our main weapons, the ship is still seaworthy and the engines are intact. I have ordered a speed increase and turn away to the north in order to open the range so that we can finish this quickly with our missiles."

The Ukrainian's air of calmness in the face of this disaster annoyed him intensely but he daren't show it since he may need the man's advice soon.

"Why can't we fire them now?"

He said it immediately and without thinking, annoyed that the Ukrainian hadn't helped him by explaining. Venkov hid his annoyance too; impatience had no place in warfare.

"Because Admiral, the transports are too close and he may decoy the missiles towards them or they may acquire the wrong target themselves. At this range there is no command guidance as such. They weren't designed for close-in fighting, picking friend from foe so close together."

Turning quickly away Ramade put on his headset and spoke to the Communications Officer.

"Send this signal to the outer islands task group, 'Surprise lost. Close with targets and commence landings immediately. Do not wait for dawn. Crush any resistance totally.' Send it now."

He swivelled to see Venkov's expression but it was unreadable as usual. Venkov was thinking 'fool you've panicked, we never had strategic surprise just tactical, they knew we were coming', but of course he said nothing, just lit another of his foul smelling cigarettes and nodded encouragement to Ramade.

"Captain Guyon, commence firing. All units to close with and destroy the mercenary ship." Guyon quietly spoke into his headset and their twin 5.1 inch guns opened fire.

*

On *Bismarck*, the collision of the two assault ships had been a welcome bonus, the five enemy troop transports had been steaming a varying distance apart lining up for the reef breaks it seemed. The maximum separation was 400 yards, in a rough line abreast formation and steering due east.

The second one, working north to south, had been hit about the bridge, wheelhouse and superstructure several times and had obviously lost control, since it had then swung to starboard and rammed the third ship which, although quite close, had turned to port probably trying to put distance between *Bismarck* and itself. The two of them were now locked in deadly embrace as flames and explosions from the first transport ignited sympathetic fires on the second.

Dettweiler gave a short whoop as he watched the collision and instantly switched the port batteries, P1 and P3, to fire at the other three assault ships. Two down and three to go, he thought, then we can break out and get lost.

The starboard batteries S1 and S3 were still firing steadily, six shells at each destroyer and frigate alternating, it was hoped that the special PC frag rounds would disastrously affect the enemy radar and comms.

Dettweiler turned as Kopf spoke.

"They've woken up at last, the *Slava* has just opened fire." Even as he watched two bright flashes lit up the enemy ship's stern as another pair of *Bismarck*'s shells impacted and then *Bismarck* herself shuddered under the first impacts.

With surprise gone *Bismarck* went back to using standard shells and she was now lit almost continuously by flashes from her own weapons as they chugged out round after round from every battery. Smoke hazed the sky around her helped by the pre-dawn lack of breeze making it look from a distance like an glimpse of Hades.

He quickly allocated another ten shells from Dora to fire at the *General Farache*, aimed at the for'ard section, and spoke to McClean ordering him to re-load Caesar -adding that he had two minutes to load as many shells as possible before the guns were required again.

The problem with these wonderful fast firing guns, he reflected, is that they can empty the ready-use two hundred and fifty round magazine in just over four minutes at maximum fire rate, and who wants to fire slower than they can do? But he was having to.

Bismarck simply couldn't allow all of her turrets to be out of action at the same time so it was a matter of staggering them to give Kent or Mclean and their teams a chance, so they all fired at differing rates.

OPs room, HMS *Dorsetshire* 52 Miles North West of Grand Cayman

Roby was suddenly alert. The AWO, Berry Reeves, was gently shaking him. He gathered himself and sat up straighter in his chair taking in the increased activity around the OPs room as his brain began to function.

"Sir, we have active transmissions on multiple bearings, a large group to the south and east of us with a smaller group further to the east. The bridge lookouts can hear gunfire, confirmed by the officer of the watch." Fully awake now he glanced at his watch, set to local time, and then at the plot to see where they were.

"Sound action stations. Bring all weapons to immediate readiness. Have the Merlin pre-flighted."

He paused a second searching his mind for anything else then went on.

"Have you classified any of the transmissions yet?"

"Yes Sir. We have class 'A' bearings on all emissions as follows. In the south eastern group we have seventeen different locations for a variety of Chinese and Russian origin radars. We have ten different surface search sets on various bearings, 'Top plate', 'Front Door' and 'Kite Screech', but no 'Top Steer' or 'Top Pair', a bit queer that, not using their main search radar. We think they're from the *Slava* and *Sovremenny*. 'Square Tie', Type 360 and Type 345 from the Chinese origin Type 53's, 51's and 37's." He paused a moment to let it sink in.

Roby was thinking fast. What the hell are they shooting at? Panic maybe? The landings perhaps?

Reeves continued with a slight smile.

"Finally Sir, more or less in the centre of that group, is a signature that we've only recorded once before." He paused as Roby looked up.

"Near Gib Sir."

Roby's face lit up. He knew Reeves was referring to *Bismarck*. When she had left Gibraltar they'd got a good recording of that Swedish Saab radar system that Jake had bragged about, now the computer had matched it.

"Bugger me, they're alive then. That crafty sod must have ....arranged his own demise earlier."

Then his brain sorted out all the bearings and his smile vanished completely. Jake was right in the middle of the bloody lot of them, he realized suddenly. Must be going for the troop transports, he mused, idly scratching at his beard. Christ though, even in that 'Ironclad' of his he'll never get out, they must be closing in on all sides. I wonder how they're doing.

"Berry, what time did that bloody 'crab' say he was going to get his airborne circus up?" Roby was referring to the RAF strike group at Belize.

Berry checked his watch.

"Should be getting an on-station signal in about twenty five minutes Sir, I believe they were due off at 04:30 so that they would be on scene just after daybreak."

"Right, we'll stay out of surface detection range at present and just hope they don't put a Helix or Harbin up. I'll have to get in touch with MOD. Seems like one of our 'allies' is being attacked, I'll have to ask for a change in the rules of engagement if we're going to help at all. Oh and I think I'll make a quick satellite call to Commodore König just to see if he needs a hand."

Berry nodded. Troubled he walked back to his own chair, seems like the old man wants to get us into this damn scrap, he thought, not a good idea with the odds stacked as they are, even if we've lots of friends over there, this isn't an 'ironclad' it's just a bloody cling film covered frigate.

05:04 Sunday 27th May 2018
Bismarck West of Grand Cayman

Jake, up on the bridge, felt rather than heard yet another hit on *Bismarck*'s starboard side, somewhere near S1 he thought, level with the bridge but low on the superstructure. He glanced at the bulkhead clock, only seven and a half minutes into the battle but it felt like three lifetimes. A quick glance at the ammunition counters showed they had used more than half of their base load already.

SLAMM, SLAMMM! Another pair of impacts close by.

Checking the displays he noted that the *Sovremenny* had turned south and the *Slava* had turned north east. One of the Type 53s had also turned north east, the other west.

Two of the corvettes were closing rapidly, the one to the south west being closest. Looking at the gunnery order repeater he saw that Kopf had just shifted S1 to cover the nearest enemy corvette. Good.

The sod's going to get a shock any second now. Soon though, he knew, there'd be too many targets to cover satisfactorily, we must finish the transports and get the hell out. The idea of a 'blow through' attack, in one side and out the other seemed possible, if enough confusion was caused.

The damage to them was already mounting though, superficial in terms of the ship's structure, but increasingly serious in terms of fighting ability. The port forward 'AK630M2' was a tangle of useless metal and through the viewer the afterdeck and superstructure looked like a rubbish dump, with splintered deck planking, life-rafts and twisted deck fittings draped everywhere.

More important was the loss, probably just buried, of the starboard after 'AK630M2' and the after radar antenna plus it's mount, not recognizable, but hidden somewhere in the jumble. The funnel had been hit twice.

The searchlight platform, half way up the funnel side and also holding a chaff launcher, was now decorating the port side hangar roof. More seriously though, the port

ECM/jammer was missing from its position on that side of the funnel.

Fortunately there had been no penetration of the hull or decks and the main guns were still cracking out shells. He trained the viewer on the enemy flagship, now about seven miles away, and saw with satisfaction that there were several fires midships, starboard for'ard and perhaps a list to port, but it was difficult to tell even under high magnification.

Moving round to starboard he noted that several frigates and DDGs were still unscathed and ordered Kopf to change that. The remaining *Sovremenny* had lasted longer than her sister ship on the 24th but was still suffering under the highly accurate cannonade from *Bismarck*, several fires were visible on her upperdecks too.

He swung further round just in time to witness a landing ship blossom into a fiery pillar of flame and debris, and that meant fewer soldiers to deal with ashore, he thought without pity.

He switched to the two remaining assault ships and noted with annoyance that they appeared to be heading north easterly. At least there wouldn't be a landing on this side of the island he consoled himself, it was more a problem for them now because of the reefs just about everywhere else.

The assault ships had sensibly turned away from *Bismarck*'s ferocious assault and now, with the range opening and escorts screening them, it seemed possible that they might escape around North West Point.

He pondered this for a moment, they were clearly damaged but still under way. Should we have put more guns on them? Maybe so, maybe not.

But he couldn't ignore the destroyers and frigates any longer. Could the few defenders on Grand Cayman cope with two assault ships loaded full of soldiers? They may have to, he decided.

"Robbo send a signal warning Grand Cayman that the remaining two transports are heading towards the north side of the island."

He paused a second.

"Time for us to disengage if we can I think, Reiner?

Reiner spoke over the open circuit.

"Julius, that one on 285 range 10k, the Type 53, he's turning to launch. Concentrate on him for fifteen or twenty main gun rounds." He turned his attention to Jake.

"Yes Jake, I agree but we have to suppress the missile shooters or they'll have us as we go."

"You have a point Reiner. Robbo, tell them we'll attempt to disengage as soon as we can."

"Aye, aye Commodore." Said Pete Robinson juggling RS duties with his ESM filters and the quadrant he was watching.

Reiner knew exactly why the *General Farache* and the *Sovremenny* were speeding away and that once they deemed the two remaining assault ships and escorts clear, they would turn and fire their deadly missiles.

Damn! Nothing I can do about that without reversing course and chasing the remaining landing ships. Damn too that *Bismarck* had only two of her specialized anti-missile guns left and only the starboard ECM/jammer.

The 3 inch turrets with their special ammunition would have to be reserved for anti-missile work now too he thought. Decision time. The ships were separating at an incredible sixty miles an hour; soon, very soon, the enemy commander would judge it safe to fire without hitting anything of his own.

Forget the remaining transports, he told himself, blow a hole out of the net that's closing around you and disappear, you can always come back later for another go. He spoke his thoughts through his headset to Simon and Jake.

"Type 53 on 285 destroyed Sir." Julius Kopf relayed the message but no longer felt the joy of winning. It wasn't at all like World of Warships after all.

Reiner continued.

"We need a change of tactics gentlemen if we are to survive. Either we turn towards the retreating assault ships and use the clutter to shield us while we reduce the escorts one by one, or we run and discover whether our depleted defences can withstand the onslaught of at least 8 SSN 12s and 8 SSN 22s."

He checked his displays.

"Eight Sandboxes because I think the *Slava* has lost those on the starboard side."

"Distance to nearest escorts around the transports?" Asked Jake.

"3.5 miles Commodore." Answered Inonu monitoring the north to east quadrant.

"With these angles, if we turn now we can put them between us and the *Slava* in about 45 seconds. Chipped in Simon.

"Or we take on their missiles." Added Reiner.

"My call then." Said Jake as Strategic Commander.

"Are the *Slava* and *Sovremenny* still in main gun range Julius?"

"*Sovremenny* is but *Slava* will be out of range in a minute or so Sir." Replied Kopf, listening in whilst still directing the gunnery.

Time slowed whilst Jake's mind raced, all his decision making over the years both in the service and in business had led him to the here and now.

"Left full rudder and full ahead. Execute."

"Aye Sir. Left full rudder and full ahead. Course Sir?" Asked Buller on the helm.

"Put us on a course slightly to starboard of the main group, get us on the island side. Try to keep them between us and the *Slava* as we approach." Said Jake, grateful to the enemy commander for turning north instead of north west.

"Scotty squeeze whatever you can out of the engines. Get us there yesterday."

He smiled to himself.

"I've always wanted to say that Ivan but if you aren't a Star-Trek fan it won't mean anything."

"Next. Julius, hit the *Slava* with the whole main armament, those SSN 12s are massive. I want it dead and fast before they can get a lock on us; we'll have a little more time now they aren't heading directly away. Then shift to the *Sovremenny*." Commanded Jake throwing out the orders like chaff, now that he had made the decision.

He drew a deep breath.

"Dettweiler, use the two forward 3 inch mounts to harass the escorts around the assault ships, we need to get in amongst them again at point blank range. Simon prepare to turn away if we have incoming vampires. Our sides should be virtually immune to shellfire but we're not proofed to plunging fire." He stopped himself. Let them sort out the details, that's what they're paid for.

"OK gentlemen let's get on with it." He sat back and let his breath out slowly. Done it now, he thought to himself. Pushed us right back into the fat and the frying pan. Got two chances Jake, part of his mind said, but the other part said making 50:50 decisions was real bad planning.

Over on the port side Buller took a sneaky look at the boss in the command chair. How the fuck does he do that sort of thing, he thought? It's like them submariners on their 'perisher' exam when there are contacts all over the place and they have to keep them in their heads. Thank fuck I never had those kind of ambitions.

He concentrated on weaving the ship erratically a few yards right and left but maintaining a mean course to the right side of the enemy main group.

Down in the engine room Scotnikov burst out laughing having just had it explained to him about the Star-Trek reference. He checked the gauges and increased the current to both Steerpods by another few dozen amps.

They had been operating at max rated level but he and all engineers, like the ubiquitous Mr Scott, always kept a bit back for the right moment and this was it. Carefully he added in a few more amps every few seconds, watching the temperature readouts like a hawk.

Buller smiled as he noted they'd just passed thirty seven knots. To no one in particular he announced.

"Steady at 37 knots on mean course zero one zero Sir."

Jake looked over and smiled back, he too was amazed at what his ship had achieved.

*

Down below in the forward magazine, Kent and his MPP team were heaving the last of twelve shells onto the hoist that took them up into Anton's ready use magazine They could manage one every ten seconds when they were unpacked and stacked ready.

The sweating men had discarded their shirts and anti-flash gear after the first re-load despite the hurricane force air conditioning. Four unpacked while four took turns to lift and load. Kent watched, panting still as two policemen hauled the over two metre long 5.1 inch shell to the hoist. Not only were they nearly seven and a half feet long they weighed in at about 86kg, around 190lbs in old money! This was because the shell and propellant were in a single unit.

He watched as they released the double handed callipers after positioning the shell in the shallow cup. Then they stepped aside and one shouted 'Clear!' whilst retaining a steadying hand on the upper part of the projectile itself. Kent then punched the button to slide it sideways and hoist it up into the magazine above.

He waited until the shell had disappeared and the buzzer sounded telling him that it was secure, then he mashed another button on the panel which closed the circuits giving turret control back to the Gunnery Officer.

Quickly he ordered the empty shell containers to be ditched in the forward messdeck. He then told Bruno turret's party of four policemen to break into the next of the special plastic cases, which carried individual shells, and to be ready for loading before his small team headed aft to get more shells moving.

Leaning back against the bulkhead he swigged from a water bottle and listened to the almost constant booming percussion as either Anton, Bruno or both fired. Despite the sound proofing and two decks between them and the guns it was still necessary to shout above the noise.

We're doing OK, he told himself as he watched the sweating men, I wonder if we're winning?

*

Ian Halshaw was worried. He and his men had been able to do nothing about the damage so far inflicted on the ship for one simple reason. All of it was outside on the upperdecks and to go out there would be almost certain death.

Jake had made it plain that when the action started, he expected the upperdecks to be swept with fragments and impacting shells. On no account, he said, unless the safety of the ship or its fighting ability are threatened, are there to be external damage control parties.

Very clear. Now however, with growing trepidation he observed the fire sensors in the aircraft hangars on either side of *Bismarck*'s funnel. The port sensor was reporting a fire and the CO_2 drenching system seemed to be malfunctioning -damaged? Kipper had already tried the armoured hatch that opened from the hangar into the main bridge superstructure and was unable to budge it even a millimetre. The eyehole showed fire on the other side anyway.

Worse, there was an aviation spirit outlet in there and it was possible, or even likely, that if the fire took real hold that the whole thing could explode sending a blow back down into the fuel storage tank between the double hull.

He hesitated, thinking it through as calmly as he could. Did the fire have plenty of fuel to burn? Answer yes; from a variety of plastic testing gear and a multitude of lubricants and cleaning materials for the aircraft.

OK. I can't get at it from the inside so a party is going to have to have a go from the outside. Easiest route has to be through the other hangar on the other side of the funnel then round the rear of the funnel sharpish.

Biggest problem, exposure of said deck party to incoming shellfire directly, and via fragments whizzing around.

Shit! I've got to go myself. I can't order anyone else.

"Three volunteers to go with me through the starboard hangar, we'll get at it that way."

Kipper immediately started to protest.

"With respect Sir. I'm i/c of the forward damage control party, it's my job."

"Noted Kipper. However my request stands excluding the Cox'n." He looked around searching the faces of the half dozen or so present.

Waylen remembered his first ever lesson from a senior rating in the Royal Navy. 'Never lad, never ever volunteer for anything, got it'. That had been at Raleigh while the PO had stood over him as he re-painted the white lines around the divisional mustering area.

Fancy falling for the old 'any artists amongst you lot?' trick. Still smiling at the memory he raised his hand. Pete Nuttall, the 'Buffer', he preferred the old title, stepped forward too.

"Can't let two 'pinkies' go outside on their own now can I?" He commented, the reference to air electrical specialists raised a short chuckle. "They'd get bloody lost in their own 'Y' fronts."

Karl Heinz a taciturn seaman from Luneburg raised his hand and completed the group. Duty was duty.

"Right." said Halshaw. "Let's get cracking. Everyone wearing 'fearnaughts', yes?"

Everyone nodded. These fire-fighting suits were unlike the old RN versions, which were bulky, heavy and worn on the outside of normal clothing. These were a compromise, much lighter and worn underneath the heavy denim overalls worn by all the damage control party, with a hood if required.

There just weren't enough people to separate into fire-fighters and damage controllers so everyone wore them. In addition to the under-suit, the men wore a modified 'hard hat', with visor and integral intercom, over their anti-flash hood and had special tight fitting toughened leather gloves.

Leaving a fuming Kipper in charge, Halshaw led the way up to the starboard hangar. They put two 'dogs' or clips on the armoured door behind them to enable a speedy retreat if required, and dragged two hoses from the cradles on the hangar bulkhead clagging them on to a 'Y' fitted fire main.

Waylen and Nuttall grabbed the hose ends and began to unroll them ensuring they weren't twisted, while Ian, carrying a pry bar, cautiously peeked out onto the catapult deck. Heinz waited for a signal then switched on the mains thereby charging the hoses.

Looking aft from the hangar door Ian could see a fire blazing on the portside of the boat cradles of the after superstructure.   Maybe give that a squirt when we're through, he thought. The noise was tremendous, flashes lit the early near dawn sky, and the slamming concussion of their own guns made their ears pop as they quickly worked around the base of the funnel to the other hangar while the acrid smell of burnt propellant filled the night around them.

A shrieking whistle terminated in a bright flash and concussive blast on the port side of the bridge, sending them all diving for the deck as wicked steel splinters droned and whirred past them in the night.

Hastily climbing to their feet the party surveyed the wreckage of the port hangar. Flames were climbing swiftly through a large rent in the roof where the remains of the searchlight platform protruded.

Shit!   Another danger.   The loaded chaff launcher containing nine 3 inch rockets was close to the flames and some pointed down, others up. The hangar door, a sliding roller metal type, was buckled outwards but Ian brandished the pry bar and leapt at it shouting to Nuttall.

"Get some water on that chaff launcher or it'll be like a real November the 5th in a minute." Levering at the side of the roller hangar with the pry bar he grunted as Heinz's weight joined him in the pull. The door started to give and they could see flames roaring inside. "Get the nozzle in here Waylen and stand by with a 'water wall' Buffer once we've got this bastard open."

Another couple of heaves later, the door jumped its track and began to slide open. Waylen leapt back as the Buffer ran forward, with his hose set to 'water wall' the nozzle started spraying water in a circular curtain at almost ninety degrees to the direction in which it pointed, providing Waylen and Heinz with a shield against the flames they faced.

Waylen quickly moved to stand next to Nuttall and pushed the nozzle of his hose, set to jet, through the curtain of water. The fire was swiftly was brought under control, Nuttall then switched his hose over to jet spray as well and played it over the 3 inch rockets again.

SHRIEEKKK! WHOOSH! A pair of shells slammed into the water scant yards from the port side of the ship raising huge white pillars which promptly collapsed over the small band of fire-fighters and fortunately extinguishing the last of the fire in and on the hangar roof.

Halshaw quickly ducked into the burnt out hangar with Nuttall, the other two playing their hoses over the after superstructure. Nuttall located the aviation spirit outlet and stood back whistling. In his torchlight Halshaw could see the hissing, steaming brass and realized that the deck was warm even through his boots.

"Right Buffer lets be…….." SLAAMM! SLAAMM! A blinding flash, a searing pain in his right arm, the sound of metal fragments hitting the funnel, like someone's teeth chattering Ian thought irrelevantly, sliding to the deck, his consciousness fading as he slid down the hangar bulkhead.

Seconds later Nuttall picked himself off the hangar floor ears full of a single high pitched tone, unable to hear anything else. He quickly realized that he was temporarily deaf, at least I hope it's temporary, he thought, looking around for the torch he'd dropped when he'd been thrown across the hangar by the blast. Dizzily he bent to retrieve it.

Light. Oh shit! The boss's down. He quickly checked Halshaw over. Lots of blood, upper arm or right side of chest, don't know which.

"Breathing unobstructed and OK. Pulse present OK. Pupils equal and react to light OK." He repeated his training like a mantra as he lifted Halshaw's eyelid and flashed the torch across it.

He quickly checked for non-visible injuries moving his hands up and down each leg, then using the special scissors they were all issued with, he quickly cut Halshaw's overalls and under suit away from the wound.

"Bugger! Shoulder and upper chest, what a mess, best slap a shell dressing on it and get him down to the Doc."

Talking to himself, he clumsily seated the pad of a shell dressing on top of the wound and then pulled it off remembering to put the inside of the opened-out waterproof wrapper on first in, case it was a sucking wound.

When he'd re-seated the large pad he pulled the ties out and threaded them behind and around before tying them in place, then rolled the officer into the recovery position, injured side down.

Next check outside, he muttered to himself. He moved to the doorway, peeked out and recoiled as if struck. Instant vomit.

"Oh fuck." He muttered as bile splashed his boots.

He staggered back to the unconscious officer trying to wipe away the vision of horror outside the hangar. Oh Christ! Past fucking help they are, poor sods.

He closed his eyes and again saw the bloody ruins of his mates, nothing recognizable of poor Karl Heinz but... he retched again dryly remembering Waylen's head and torso, lit by the flash of guns and a fire by P1 turret.

He'd been propped against the catapult platform, like he was just sitting there grabbing a rest, no sign of his legs though. He shook himself and manoeuvred Halshaw into the position for a fireman's lift then hauled him up.

No time to worry about the wound, just make sure you grab his good arm old son, he told himself. Outside now. Slipping and skidding on...he dared not think what it was, he moved painfully across the torn planking and gore spattered deck.

Just as he rounded the base of the funnel, the ship heeled to port and he lost his balance but managed to fall toward the catapult track saving himself from going all the way down.

Squeezing his eyes shut against a sudden stab of pain in his lower back he groped for the upper edge of the track and pulled himself upright. With a groan of mixed agony and fright he lurched away from the catapult and started for the starboard hangar door again.

Inside quick. Door shutter slammed down. An illusion of safety. He could hear nothing but ringing. Still they should hear me, he thought. With his free hand he double tapped the ear piece in his helmet.

He leaned against the bulkhead with Halshaw still over his shoulder. Unable to hear any reply he simply passed his report into the mike and, feeling faint, lay Halshaw down gently. Pain exploded in his lower back followed by numbness down his right leg as he sat next to Halshaw propping him up, whilst waiting for help.

Down in HQ1 Kipper absorbed the bad news. Shit, two dead and one injured I knew they shouldn't have gone. He acknowledged the transmission then tapped his mike and said "Medic." He waited for the click then spoke.

"Bren, casualty starboard hangar not sure how bad, I'm on the way myself." Then he turned to Richard Page the other damage control specialist with him.

"Page we need to get up there and be ready to lift them once the Doc gets there. Let's go."

Neither bothered that the hangars weren't armoured they had mates needing them and they started moving fast.

Better call in the casualties Kipper thought as he reached the hatch and spoke into his mike.

"Captain." Then click.

"Kipper boss, casualty report. Two dead -Waylen and Heinz, one injured, Lt Halshaw Sir."

"How did it happen Mr Herring?" Kipper noted the formal title but thought, hell we're all 'pushed' at the mo'.

"Lt Halshaw took a party up to sort out a fire in the port hangar sir, seems they got caught as they finished."

"Carry on Mr Herring you're now i/c Damage control."

"Aye, Aye Sir. How's it going up top Sir?"

"We'll be making a break for it in a minute... but be warned, we expect to come under missile attack very soon.

"Aye, aye Sir."

*

Bren jabbed the needle into Nuttall's right buttock and squeezed the morphine syrette dry, pulling it out he automatically jabbed the needle into the deck to blunt it.

Poor bugger, he thought, the Buffer obviously didn't know he was injured himself when he carried Halshaw back here, probably a good job really.

Carefully he covered the gaping hole in Nuttall's lower back, shit that's his spine and a kidney there too, he thought, pouring water over it first then packing it with a big wad of 'Kaltsostat' clotting wool and then applying a shell dressing to the top for good measure.

Standing up he signalled to his stretcher bearers and they fastened the Velcro straps of the modified backboard stretcher before lifting the face down patient and taking him down to Lawrence Cribb.

Bren had a quick glance around outside the hangar noting the dreadful mess he then turned to go back down to the wardroom where, he hoped, Lawrence would already be busy exploring the unconscious Ian Halshaw's wounds.

Fuck it, Bren thought grimly, the price is already too high, why'd the bastards start on us anyway? Why couldn't they be content with their own piece of frigging real estate, eh?

*

Bismarck sliced through the seas, shrugging aside the towers of water that rose all around her, a veritable forest of ever changing waterspouts. Frequently, too frequently, there was no spout just a blossom of flame as shells struck along her length.

Flame jetted from her own guns as she blasted out her reply. She jinked to port and starboard trying to make it that bit harder to get her nailed but apparently careless of the damage she suffered.

Jake watched through the viewer as, almost head to head, his ship and an enemy Type 37corvette charged each other.   Range down to only one mile now.   Poor, stupid/brave fools.

Turrets Anton and Bruno were now both concentrating on her she wouldn't last long....there dammit! The enemy ship disappeared for several seconds, deluged in water as a four gun salvo of *Bismarck*'s shells found the mark.

At least two possibly three hits he thought. Again he saw the ship disappear as another salvo roared in. Smoke, flames and debris erupted from the enemy ship followed by a titanic explosion; he presumed her missiles had just cooked off. Was that two or three down now? He was losing track of things.

What about the *Sovremenny*? He thought. Shifting the viewer over to the enemy destroyer on their port quarter he noted she'd turned beam on so that both her twin 130mm turrets could shoot at the elusive *Bismarck*. Flashes erupted from bow and stern even as he watched and it took all his willpower not to duck as the shells raced towards them over a six mile gap. Same guns as ours he mused.

More to the point where's the big bastard with those ship killer missiles? He spun the viewer to the north to see the *General Farache* beginning to turn. Clearly she'd taken a battering too though and had one raging fire on her upperdeck aft, hangar? The nearest and last corvette was North West at about three miles and shearing away too, probably seen what's happened to her sisters. Simon's voice intruded on the joint command net.

"We just lost P3 and the port after AKM630 mount."

Jake jerked as if he'd been slapped. God almighty!

Now we've only got one specialist anti-missile gun mount left, only one jammer and one chaff launcher. Everything's on the starboard side too. Damn and blast it! He cursed silently.

Ramade was becoming increasingly frustrated that they could not yet safely engage with missiles. That fucking thing is just shrugging off the combined shellfire of nine ships he raged to himself as he sat now in the same chair that Venkov had occupied at the start of the battle.

Many of his own ships were badly damaged but that fucking thing, he could find no other words to describe it, seemed to be still firing from all its turrets.

"Captain, turn us towards them now and order all our ships to clear out of the way or risk damage themselves. I want to use my missiles NOW! While we've still got them." He added dryly.

Venkov off to one side resisted the temptation to counter the order and instead applied his most po-faced look whilst fishing around for another packet of cigarettes.

Ramade observed this and hurumphed to himself whilst waiting for the turn. Up to now only one or two of the enemy guns had been trained on the flagship and that was bad enough.

"Bridge OPs." Said the tinny voice of one of junior officers.

"OPs." Answered Captain Guyon.

One of our corvettes just blew up sir, the *Roseaux* I believe. The enemy appears to be training all turrets on us now sir."

Guyon had read the reports of what had happened to the *Dessalines* the *Sovremenny* class destroyer, when this same enemy had turned all its fire power onto her just three days ago, and he knew fear.

"Sir." He pleaded with his Admiral. "We must turn back to our northerly course, the enemy appears to be singling us out now! We can fire from beyond his range."

"Nonsense Guyon." Ramade dismissed. "Prepare the port missile battery for firing." Seeing Guyon hesitate again he shouted.

"Now Guyon."

The Flag Captain gave up the unequal struggle and issued the necessary orders.

Three decks above, the cap on the end of the tube of the first port battery missile, flipped up in readiness to allow its deadly contents access to the lightening sky. The *General Farache* completed the turn and began to line up for the shot, she needed to be near enough pointed at a target this close, there wouldn't be much time for course corrections.

05:14 Sunday 27th May 2018
Bismarck heading 010 degrees four miles
West of George Town

"Simon what range do you think they'll turn and fire those missiles?" Asked Reiner over the open command net. Simon looked back at his displays. He noted that the enemy flagship had already begun to turn.

"I think the answer is now Sir." Then he spoke to Kopf in the MGCC.

"Julius override all main gun orders, concentrate on the *General Farache* NOW!"

Kopf didn't hesitate, he cancelled all current tasks and allocated the enemy flagship forty rounds, five per barrel, and mashed the trigger.

Range was ten miles now, nearly a twenty second flight time. Already sixteen shells were in the air and as he thought that, eight more joined them. The wait seemed endless. The enemy flagship completed its turn and was lined up perfectly with them now.

The sudden blossom of flames on her starboard bridge area made him think she'd launched her missiles. Then it all changed.

One of the SSN-12s must have cooked off thought Julius as he watched in horror as the entire left side of the ship seemed to sprout crimson and yellow flames, jetting out almost horizontally. He wasn't sure but he thought the right side of the bridge area suddenly had flames shooting out too but then there was a flash and an eruption of flame the like of which he'd never imagined.

His viewer desperately toned down incoming light so he could still see but it was a lost cause. All he could see of anything now was a pale yellow vertical fountain of flame rising from the enemy ship and nothing else.

No one spoke. Julius quickly cancelled the last octet of shells and just stared.

Jake took a deep breath and held it. The armoured screens prevented him from looking outside directly so he too had to wait for his screens and viewer to catch up with events.

There now, he looked and where *General Farache* had been all that was visible appeared to be a disappearing stern section. She'd gone completely just in a flash.

Reiner, mute as the others at first, recovered his composure.

"Good shooting Julius now let's get that *Sovremenny* before he too decides it's time for his missiles."

"It should be a while before he can Captain, we are too close to the others at the moment." Chipped in Simon.

Reiner noted a Type 51D *Luda* class DDG, on fire, begin a roll to starboard that kept going until she was all the way over.

"If we keep this rate up there won't be anything left to cause clutter Simon."

"Oh Lord the *Sovremenny* has already begun to turn. Julius anything you have. *Sovremenny* NOW!"

Jake waited impatiently for *Bismarck*'s reply to this threat to become evident. Suddenly it was.

First two then four then all eight guns of the main battery firing as fast as they could all zeroed in on the big destroyer as it turned towards them.

The *Sovremenny* called *Miragoane* was still turning but now she was wading through the same kind of waterspout forest *Bismarck* had, and as with *Bismarck* many shells were finding their mark. Unlike *Bismarck* though, these shells were penetrating the scanty armour. Grimly, eagerly, Jake and everyone that could, watched *Miragoane* change into a massive coal brazier, willing it to blow up, turn turtle, turn away, do anything but fire those missiles.

No one watching through the viewer could distinguish the flash of the missile ignitions from the flash of impacts on the ship. Inonu Kyne Sam though wasn't looking through a viewer, he was intently monitoring his remaining ESM arrays as he should have been.

"Volcano! Volcano." He roared as he picked up the missile radar signals. He was followed closely by Taff Elias on the radar.

"Vampire! Vampire!" Taff yelled.

"System auto, tracking three... no four... system locked... firing..." He took a deep breath.

"Buller come right to 080, emergency helm." Said Simon.

Then Taff continued his discourse.

"New tracks. Vampires are 015, 016, 017 and 018. Same bearing." He cleared his throat as the tracks appeared on the holo display. "Two more designate 019 and 020." Then sombrely. "Another designated 021."

Simon spoke calmly into his mike.

"Inonu pull the plug on the chaff when I shout, I know we can't make a good pattern but get it off will you." Typical thought Simon, when you want re-loads you can't have them or else I'd punch the damned stuff out now.

Jake sat on his armoured bridge, thought miserably the wind's negligible, our course is wrong, the distance is too short. What a bastard eh? Now I suppose we find out how good the flaming armour is.

"Time to run... 25 seconds." Intoned Taff. They could all hear the BRRRRR stutter of the only surviving AK630M2 as it churned out anything up to 130 heavy rounds a second towards the incoming missiles.

Reiner spoke into his mike. "Shipwide." A click.

"Do you hear there, Captain speaking. Missiles inbound starboard side, clear away to port. Emergency parties standby, if you have a God it's time to pray. Report damage immediately. Good Luck!"

He turned back to the displays in front.

"Splash 015." Shouted a joyous Taff. Good, only six more of the buggers to go, thought Jake in frustration. The remaining starboard 3 inch battery was also pumping out the PFDHEC rounds at 130 per minute, which was fine but that would empty the magazine damned quickly, thought Simon, then again it won't matter if we get zapped.

Taff intoned. "Splash 017, err and 016 too."

Down to four, Simon used a joystick override to edge *Bismarck* to port presenting as small a stern-on target as possible and deliberately giving the missiles a steady aiming point as well.

The idea being to put full starboard helm on in the last fifteen seconds, firing short fused chaff astern, to lengthen the ship's radar image, hoping the incoming missiles would go for the centre of the new large radar target and miss the real ship to port. Not exactly orthodox, he thought, but who knows.

Another missile fell in fiery flames leaving three.

"Helm. Emergency Starboard!" Ordered Simon. "Chaff now Inonu."

The computers instantly responded to the emergency verbal order, both Steerpods rotated almost to ninety degrees and the bow thruster kicked in too.

Three and a half thousand tons of ship pivoted like a ballet dancer and lunged to the right while nine chaff rockets punched into the sky where *Bismarck* had been just seconds before.

Throughout the ship men fell to the deck if they weren't holding on to something, others found something soft to stand on, it was supposed to absorb the shock. Some prayed, some stared at the deckhead numbly waiting for the end, all were on the port side except the OPs and Bridge crews.

The wind was too weak for a decent cloud it wouldn't disperse properly; it had been moderate and steady throughout the night but now had dropped and almost died completely. The chaff rockets, fired astern in three sets of three, popped and deployed their clouds of aluminium strips and magnesium flares. The Aluminium to lure the radar guided missiles and flares to sucker any infra-red guided missiles.

"They're in pop-up mode. Woah! Not all are popping! Zero 19 is turning, going for the chaff. Standby!"

"Eight... seven... six..." Offered Taff.

It nearly worked. The computers in the warheads of the remaining two missiles had just started to adjust to port to cope with the 'longer' ship when they ran out of space.

The explosions, when they came, were so close that they were almost simultaneous. *Bismarck's* last second turn to starboard meant that she heeled over the other way.

In other words more of her starboard side was exposed above the surface than usual. One missile impacted starboard side, three yards from the stern and just a foot above the current waterline. The other followed in its tracks barely a hands breadth lower punching a foot wide hole through the already stressed hull.

The shockwave from the double explosion expanding outwards, ruptured the hydraulic lines on both the port Steerpod rotation control and the variable pitch propeller. This meant the pod could no longer be turned and was locked in 10 degree starboard turn which had been on the wheel as Buller began to straighten up, and the pitch could no longer be altered. The bad news didn't end there.

LtCdr Scotnikov picked himself off the deck in the engine control room. More than anything the shrilling of a dozen alarms which would have woken the dead, and a panel full of red and amber flashing lights in the main control room, brought him back to his senses. He got up from where he'd been thrown and reached across his console to punch the emergency stop button for the Steerpods and the banshee wail of alarms diminished to several low pressure alarms and system failure warnings. He muted them too.

The ship righted itself and the hole which was above the waterline during the turn, was now under it. It got worse. As soon as water entered the compartment it shorted the two motors on the inner bulkhead which controlled the hydraulic power packs for the starboard Steerpod. These, because of their more frequent maintenance requirement were outside the watertight pod compartment; so for a totally different reason the starboard pod was now locked to ten degrees starboard too.

All the cabling carrying the immense amount of current into the electric motor in the pod below the hull, the massive hydraulic motors with their 500 bar feed pipes and their half ton electric motors, were safe inside the pod compartment. The weakest link was outside.

Once again Scotnikov was deafened by another series of alarms and even the quiet competent senior engineer felt a rush of panic as he quickly checked and muted the new series. Fuck, he thought.

The sensors in the starboard compartment auto reset to use their redundant relay, which immediately fried too. In the near silence when all the engineroom alarms were muted Scotnikov could hear a sound dreaded by sailors the world over. Water. Water under pressure forcing its way into the ship and pounding on the bulkhead opposite the wound.

Up in the OPs room everyone was still in their seats, thanks to the lap straps, but since the seats were fixed to the ship, they had felt her lift bodily and slam down much more acutely than most others.

Alarms rang out and were silenced. Power failed then returned. Coloured lights broke out in a rash across Reiner's damage control repeater screen.

Down in HQ1 Chief Braime muted his own alarms and watched as the 3-D schematic of the ship rolled and rotated until it showed a view of the stern from starboard just below the waterline. The camera in 2 Juliet showed water pouring in and he boosted power to the pumps.

He ignored the manic clamour around him and concentrated on the display. Deck two, section Juliet. Through this compartment, the lowest and sternmost, ran the fittings and power supplies to the Steerpod electric motors. It also housed the sub-compartment with the hydraulic motors and electrical motors for them. He hoped and prayed that the seals held because they could replace the control motors but not the big electric motor inside the sub compartment.

The pumps were helping but it would be a short while before they'd know whether they were winning against the water, he doubted it.

More important than that though was the fact that the ship was slowing and still turning to starboard. He desperately wanted to know the status of the generators and the Steerpods so he got the low down from his boss as he organised a shoring party to immediately support the bulkhead with India 2 the next compartment forward.

In the OPs room Reiner waited for information. He resisted the temptation to contact Scotnikov whom he knew would report as soon as he had half a second. There were two other questions in his mind. Why had the *Miragoane* only fired seven missiles? Were they waiting to place the coup-de-grace? Or had the *Bismarck*'s guns silenced them?

And when were the other ships going to fire their missiles? So that was three questions?

Up in main gunnery Kopf had now switched *Bismarck*'s main armament back to a slower rate of fire and was re-allocating targets. Without a conscious thought his brain had absorbed the tactical implications of reduced speed and manoeuvrability. It had then decided on a policy of 'keep them at arm's length', designed to damage or destroy if possible but discourage if not.

"Simon, how soon can you get a high resolution shot of the *Miragoane*'s missile tube areas?" Asked Jake.

Simon spoke with drone control and told Kempfe to focus one of the four airborne cameras on the bows of the *Miragoane*.

"One moment Sir." He replied. Kempfe immediately reset the closest Arado and ordered the re-alignment before hitting the zoom button.

"She's gone sir. Look she's capsized, must have just got off the missiles first, there won't be a number eight."

Jake breathed a sigh of relief, another one down.

Just then Robby Robinson piped up.

"Commodore we have a request for a secure link with *Dorsetshire*, I've verified that it is Captain Roby Sir.

Jake's mind whirled. It was too much of a coincidence for Jon Roby to call up now for a friendly chat, ergo he was probably close by somewhere monitoring all the fireworks. Not likely to be an accidental placement either, perhaps Andrew McTeal's pleas for assistance had fallen on fertile ground after all?

"Jon, what can I do for you? I'm a little busy at the moment." He tried to make his voice flippant but it sounded strained even to himself.

He knew that Roby wouldn't be taken in. He was right.

Roby heard a quiet desperation in the ever so slightly distorted satellite transmission. This was something that he'd never before heard in the voice of his old friend and mentor who always seemed to have an answer. He could also hear a considerable amount of background gunfire, clearly outgoing so they were still fighting.

"Jake, we were just on our way to see you, fancied a spot of R & R in the beautiful, peaceful Cayman Islands."

Then he decided to skip the banter.

"OK Jake, how deep is the 'brown and smelly' around you? We can hear the racket from fifty miles away and our ESM display looks like Oxford Street on Christmas Eve."

"Jon, stay away. We're in action with a Haitian task group that's intent on invading...."

"I know." Came Roby's calm reply.

"I rather guessed your presence wasn't accidental." Jake smiled ruefully.

"We've taken some shell damage and very recently some serious missile damage which has sodded the steering up it seems but we're still afloat and...I hope to get underway pretty soon. We still have most of our main armament and believe me we're knocking shit out of anything in range." He sighed and continued.

"Our biggest immediate problem is the Haitian task group on its way to Little Cayman. I...I don't think we'll be able to get there for a while at least Jon, there's only a couple of dozen men defending the place and there's a pair of *Ludas*, a Type 53 and a Type 37 oh, and an Assault ship moving in on them."

Roby was alarmed at the 'get under way soon' reference and itched to do something to help.

"OK. I hear you. Problem is, I'm waiting for MOD to change the rules of engagement. You know how they are. But listen, the good news is there's a 'crab' strike group on its way here, due on scene about dawn and believe me there's enough of them to take out anything you leave and more.

How do you assess the air threat Jake?" Jake took a deep breath before answering. This was a question that had occupied a considerable amount of time in the planning stages.

"Our opinion is that it's restricted to daylight due to situation clarity and pilot ability. But for all we know they may be on their way here now."

He didn't say that with zero manoeuvrability, only one AK630 and whatever remained of the 3 inchers, *Bismarck* would be nearly helpless against a determined air attack.

"Last thing Jake, the Northern *Ludas*, have they used their SSM's up?"

"We picked up fourteen sets of terminal radar when the *Luda* and the Type 53 fired on our decoy so that's an eight and a six. We've got one of them down here that's playing like he's still got something to shoot. So if the one that went North has re-loaded as well there'll be eight ready on each and four on the Type 37. But we don't know for sure." You'd best stay away from them Jon, they'll shoot first and check ID later is my guess."

"Thanks Jake. Keep in touch if you can and remember, the cavalry arrives at dawn."

"Yeah I'm looking forward to seeing you on a horse again. I'll get the datalink sorted so you can see our picture too."

Roby signed off and sat back thinking. The cavalry's only coming old friend if MOD extracts a digit and approval comes through, if you're still around then. With a considerable amount of venom he contacted the MSO and told them to fire off another flash signal repeating urgent request for instructions and a change to the ROE.

If they don't answer soon I'm going to take independent action, he told himself. The last signal from MOD had indicated that Her Majesty's government totally repudiated the Haitian aggression. But of course they'd be ringing up all their friends worldwide, especially the Americans, to see if they objected to a military intervention.

Haiti was after all in the American's back yard and on and off in their sphere of influence so to speak. He knew from the briefing pack that the attempted assassination of Father Jean Bertrand Aristide, the ousted democratically elected president, in late 94` had incensed the Americans, since he'd been under their protection. The blame had been put, conveniently, on a Haitian group which resented the idea of the Pope running their country through one of his priests.

But everyone knew that Farache had had a finger in that pie. Since Aristide's return from exile in 2011 he had been scrupulously neutral and refused all public speaking. No doubt it would have been explained to him by Farache and his cronies that that was the condition of his return and survival.

He decided to anticipate the MOD approval for intervention. "Come right to 090. Revolutions for fifteen knots. Have the senior pilot come and see me please."

Dorsetshire dutifully turned towards Little Cayman, forty miles to the East. John Hayden, *Dorsetshire's* First Lieutenant, kept his thoughts off his face, but wondered if he'd have the guts to tackle his Captain if he, as Hayden suspected, decided to anticipate approval from MOD, or in other words exceed his current orders.

Have to, he thought, otherwise I'll be tarred with the same brush when the shit hits the fan, if I'm around to face a Courts Martial, he gloomily concluded.

Jake sat up straight; he was down in the OPs room now. His heart hammered at the thought of the information he was about to receive, the kiss of death or a reprieve? He decided to try and keep it light as with Roby. Scotnikov came up on the command circuit so only Jake, Reiner and Simon could automatically hear and comment.

"Yes Scotty. I only want good news and don't give me any of that 'the engines 'cannae take it Captin' stuff."

He said with a mock Scots accent and heard the chuckles behind him at the old 'Star-Trek' joke. The crew had loved having an engineer with the Russian name equivalent of 'Scotty'.

Scotnikov, however did not respond in kind, he was utterly exhausted. His voice though carried a measure of confidence but the news was grave.

"Sorry Captain. I'm down in 2 India." The compartment next forward of the damaged 2 Juliet. "The starboard Steerpod directional control motor is useless for now we can't do anything until the compartment is dry again and we've replaced it or at least stripped it. The port pod might be recoverable soon, the blast just popped all the hydraulic leads but we can replace them." In his mind he added, then bleed the system and test it.

"Both Pods however are non-steerable at present, we can move but only in circles on a heading of starboard ten best guess is several hours work to get either Steerpod useable." They heard him shout something back into the compartment regarding shoring timber.

"There is damage to the hull and we have water entering 2 Juliet. It may be one of the welds has given under the pressure or simply that the double explosion was so powerful that it penetrated the armour. One of us needs to go over the side to see if we can get an umbrella into the hole if it isn't too wide or awkward, and then hold it until the pumps remove enough water so that external pressure keeps it in place." Jake raised his eyes to the deckhead and drew deep breath, another external foray, more people exposed on that splinter swept deck.

The metal umbrella was an ingenious invention, usually applied from the inside of the vessel though. The idea was that the metal umbrella was pushed through a hole with water gushing in and then forced to open by a lever. As soon as external water pressure began acting on it, the umbrella was then forced open fully and pressed against the hole stopping the ingress of water. It could then be secured in place until the ship reached a dockyard.

Scotnikov continued.

"As soon as the pressure comes on we can empty the whole compartment in minutes, then I can inspect the internal damage and see whether we can get the starboard pod back online. We're blowing high pressure air into the compartment now. With that and the pumps I don't think we'll have any problems containing the flooding and then inspecting the damage. I'm afraid the port pod hydraulics will take longer to replace and there's some unusual vibration, that's usually a drydock job, in fact anything to do with the pods is usually a drydock job." Scotnikov paused a second. "We may be able to do something if we can get back alongside in George Town though."

It was almost as if he were fishing for their chances of doing just that, thought Reiner.

"Mr Herring is down here supervising DC and has temporary shoring in place." You could hear the tiredness in his voice. "It would help if we weren't being shot at whilst we inspect the hole."

"We'll see what we can do. Carry on Chief and keep us informed please." Said Reiner.

There was a rumbling double thud in the background, the deck jumped and Kopf cut in quickly.

"Sirs we've lost Dora, hit on the barbette junction I think, it can only fire on its current bearing I'm afraid."

It reminded them all that they were still in a fight. Reiner nodded and turned to face the OPs room at large.

"Simon coordinate with McClean and Kent to get the ammunition re-stocked as much as possible, use any spare hands you need. We clearly aren't going anywhere for a while."

Jake chipped in. "Buller, use the bow thruster to turn us around so that the damaged area points to the shore. Scotty can we use the pods to turn further to starboard if we need?"

"Only if you have to Sir."

"OK. Julius, do your best to keep the bastards at long range, conserve ammunition now and coordinate re-loads with Simon."

Jake pondered. "I think our best bet is to waddle over to George Town as soon as we can move and turn, perhaps beach her south of the town to make a fixed battery. That is of course if Buller can get us going in the right direction and our friends don't finish us off in the interim."

Buller was having a bad day. Up on the main bridge there was just himself and 'Danny' Kay another seaman. For twenty minutes or so now they'd been trying to point *Bismarck* away from Grand Cayman some four miles distant using just the bow thruster with a bit of 'pod' to help the turn when it could but the current offshore here made it difficult to maintain the heading and they couldn't anchor. It was going to be difficult to keep the diver sheltered from the incoming shells.

Down aft, Roger Nightingale, a qualified navy clearance diver, checked his single tank and the mouthpiece a final time then with flippers in hand dropped over *Bismarck*'s side near the damaged section. He quickly donned the flippers and rapidly inspected the hole to ensure that any edges were bent in, otherwise the umbrella wouldn't seal well.

Having completed his inspection he signalled with one thumb raised above the water that he was ready to receive the umbrella which was quickly lowered on a lightweight line by Kipper.

The umbrella, like most of the ship was made of Titanium alloy and once in the water with him was light and easily manoeuvred towards the gaping hole about eighteen inches or so below normal waterline.

He activated the opening mechanism and began to fin gently towards the hole. When he judged he was close enough to the hole, he slipped the surface line, then pushed a second short and weighted line inside the hole and finally shoved the stem or umbrella handle, gently through the hole until it was nearly flush with the side.

Bismarck was still slowly rotating and a shell from an overshoot exploded in the water fifty yards away. The pressure wave slapped him against the hull with terrifying force and made his head ring. Unknown to him blood now ran freely from both ruptured ear drums and it would be a year or so before he could dive again.

Holding the umbrella in place with one hand he raised the other and made a circular motion.

On deck, ducking and hiding near a set of solid metal mooring cleats, Kipper kept checking for the signal. It wasn't easy working out which were outgoing bangs and which were impacting hits, well not as quickly as your reflexes caused you to duck for either he'd discovered.

He sure as hell couldn't detail anyone else to this duty and if they got out of it he was going to recommend Nightingale for a gong or a bonus or something. As soon as he saw the hand and its circular motion he spoke into his mike.

"Now!"

Nightingale waited a few seconds and then saw the umbrella suddenly clamp in place as the pumps inside sucked at high rate. He waited another few seconds to be sure it wasn't just going to fall off as it wasn't fastened on the inside yet, then he surfaced.

Ditching the flippers he climbed quickly up the alloy peg-style ladder Kipper was holding against the side and ran for the hatch.

Kipper stood and pulled up the ladder then he too ran for the hatch into the after superstructure. He nearly made it. He'd thumbed the button on the panel to open the hatch when the shell arrived in a whoosh and terminal scream.

Kipper never knew what hit him as he was dashed like a rag doll against turret Caesar's barbette. It was another five minutes before someone noticed he hadn't come back. Repeated calls on the intercom got no answer. Page went up to look for him and called it in over the comm.

"Medic." Click. "Bren, its Kipper, he's down. Blood every-fucking-where. Shit, shit, shit Turret Caesar, port side."

Bren arrived at the double and bit his lip as he saw the rash of bloody splinter holes across the back of Kipper's chest and the widening pool of blood beneath him.

"Stretcher party wait inside the airlock." He shouted into his mike as he worked at examining the downed Coxswain and good friend as more shells landed nearby. Too fucking dangerous, he decided as yet another brace of shells exploded near the stern.

He quickly grabbed Kipper under the arms and dragged him to the open hatch, over the coaming and into the after superstructure, punching the door close button before starting work on Kipper again.

05:30 Sunday 27th May 2018
Luda D class DDG *Gonaives*, North of Grand Cayman, new Haitian Flagship

Captain Pulon cursed as the medic swabbed the cuts on his face. Stupid, stupid, stupid. He winced again as the frightened medic pulled a glass shard from a cut just below his right eye.

All around him were dead and wounded sailors, some still waiting for treatment others lying in a morphia induced limbo, now uncaring of their surroundings, as the overwhelmed medical staff did their best amongst the human debris.

He'd wanted so desperately to see, to witness, to feel, the destruction of the mercenary ship that had killed so many of his friends and colleagues in the last few minutes.

His best friend on the Flagship, Captain Georges Guyon had almost certainly died when the cruiser had blown up, surely no one could survive that. He then tried to coordinate an attack with the other frigate nearby but had turned too early and in range of the enemy guns as they'd rounded the point. Their own guns had hammered out a response while they turned quickly away again.

But he'd gone to the main bridge so that he could personally give the missile firing order from there, overruling the protests of his own First Lieutenant and the Ukrainian advisor. This was to be his moment and he wanted to see it and imagine the terror of his enemy as the deadly missiles sped on their way towards him. They had accompanied him and now were dead, along with so many of their men.

Pulon struggled to recall the moments leading up to that fatal mistake but everything was still spinning around in his head like an endless tape. The ship had been considerably damaged even before the turn to allow all his missiles to fly. Speed had been reduced due to boiler damage, there had been a definite list to port caused by flooding forward but the missile launchers had remained intact.

He should have realized that his enemy would understand the significance of that sudden turn to starboard; he should have realized that they would then turn the full and terrible might of their guns upon them, desperate to stop the launch of any missiles.

Terrible might. A good choice of words. Until that moment he hadn't really understood the awful firepower that was condensed into that one vessel, smaller than his own in fact.

He had watched through his binoculars as the enemy had erupted from stem to stern in what had seemed a continuous blaze of yellow fire. So great was the rate of fire that it seemed to his mind's eye that there was no pause between each discharge, on and on it went a yellow flickering light like a silent movie.

Then with a terrifying suddenness the air about them was rent with the banshee shriek of arriving shells. The din was overpowering, he'd quickly tried to give the firing order even though they hadn't yet finished the turn.

The ship had staggered and shuddered under the multiple impacts, amazing how nearly four thousand tons of metal can be thrown around like that, he recalled thinking at the time.

His last conscious sight had been of successive impacts working forward along his own ship. Then his world had been filled by a flash of light followed by nothing.

The medic finished patching him and moved on. He staggered along the dimly lit corridor back towards his proper place of duty, the OPs room. Emergency lighting only, he thought and noticed also that the list was much more pronounced now.

Coherent thought slowly returned as he took his place and began to absorb the reports that flowed into the brain of his ship. A wave of remorse swept over him as he listened to the casualty toll, thirty five dead and fifty three injured so far, dear God! But the ship was still under way.

But most important of all, to him, was the report on the after missile tubes. Whilst they were damaged, it was thought that one, possibly two could be made to fire before long. That was very, very good news, having learned that his enemy, despite two hits from his presumably dead friends in the now sunken *Miragoane,* had indeed survived the missile attack.

No matter. He was now in command and the landings would go ahead just as scheduled but at Boatswains point now. What was left of the task force he wondered? He checked the reports on his lap. Gone were the flagship and the big DDG *Miragoane*. Gone were two of the *Ludas* and two of the Type 37 corvettes. All three Yunshan LSMs had gone but the two Ropuchas had survived. He wished the damned interlinks had worked. They had never been able to get the Chinese built ships to talk to the Russian ships and so had not bothered with the ship to ship network of discrete transmissions otherwise he'd know exactly the state of the remainder of the task force.

Dear Lord, nine ships gone. I am down to one destroyer, two frigates a corvette and two landing ships. But as he assessed he decided there was still the required force necessary to achieve the objectives and then have revenge on the damned enemy ship that had so far refused to die.

He confirmed the order to the Type 53 class *Jeremie*, returning from her attack on what had clearly been a decoy, to fire her missiles at the enemy when in range and then join the remaining ships as they closed around the two landing ships. And if the Navy couldn't see off this persistent irritant? Well then the Air Force would have to do it now it was light!

Jake had seen in the true dawn at 05:23 with a good deal of trepidation and not a little uncertainty. The horizon was fortunately clear all round and *Bismarck* continued its slow rotation as it slid southwards past George Town without the ability to alter the direction in which either Steerprop pointed.

The current was a lazy 1.5 knots offshore and less inshore and so she drifted in a slow circle with people manning viewers for the first hint of a renewal of battle. They'd shut down the thruster because they didn't want it stressed or burned out perhaps when they'd need it most.

The Airborne RPV pictures showed men at work on the missile bins of a *Luda* class destroyer to the north around the point but more worrying was the determined approach from the south of one of the frigates which had shot at the decoy last night.

He had no idea if they had reloads for their missile bins so it would either be another gun duel, which even though damaged they'd win, or a one sided missile attack.

Other problems had become visible at dawn, one of the last hits from the *General Farache*, before she sank, had struck the base of the foremast. The mast, whilst not completely severed, had just canted forward toward the surviving radar antenna, preventing its full sweep. Sods law, Jake had thought, that the bloody mast would do it when the antenna was facing the wrong damn way.

He shouldn't complain, at least it still worked. Now they had a radar which could be activated but which could only sector scan the port side and all the remaining AA weapons were on the starboard side. So they lost radar sight of the Haitian frigate coming in from the south and east for extended periods of time as the ship slowly revolved.

Rautsch, and three men, were up there trying to free it now. Jake had been reluctant to agree to another outside foray, having been informed of the earlier costly ones, but there was little choice in the matter.

Fortunately firing had died down as the remaining two assault ships, and their surviving escorts had rounded the top of the island. With no radar *Bismarck* wouldn't be able to detect a missile launch until it was over the horizon.

Unless, that is, they could get one of the Arado RPVs on task but they were running low on fuel as Kempfe had had to get them to climb with the coming dawn so they wouldn't be so obvious. The RPV covering that quarter was near enough gliding in the right direction and until the sun broke through the clouds its solar generation wouldn't give much power for the auxiliary propeller to use.

Jake sat with Simon and Reiner over a cup of strong coffee and a bacon sandwich pondering the new set of problems that dawn brought them. Seaborne attack was only one; with the coming of light he could expect air attacks on their crippled, un-manoeuvrable ship. Chief Kempfe interrupted to ask permission for the southern RPV to abort and return to the Caymans for later recovery. He informed them he was re-tasking one of the other two to try to cover that sector but it would be several minutes before it gave them a picture of that area again. Reiner nodded and the OPs room acknowledged the change.

Jake looked at the screen showing the low dark mass of Grand Cayman and wondered how things were going over there, time to communicate with all interested parties, he decided but he didn't get the chance.

On the bridge 'Danny' Kay, at a viewer, was just finishing another sweep of the southern horizon when he saw the first one. He gulped back a sudden rush of bile and yelled.

"Vampire bearing red one zero. Elevation zero!" The bow had just passed south as it rotated clockwise. Buller, without waiting for the command, instantly engaged the bow thruster to push the bow back around to port so the remaining anti-missile weapons on the starboard side were able to bear.

From the start everyone knew that the turn would be too slow. A visual sighting of an incoming missile gives only a few seconds warning before impact or miss, just enough time to bend down and kiss your ass goodbye, as the old saying went.

Rautsch, Stroder, Page and Reisler were still working high up on the forward superstructure when the first missile flew past them, almost down the length of the slowly turning ship, and detonated on the rear of turret Caesar's barbette.

A massive explosion followed that blew them flat against the radar antenna and near deafened them. The forward, starboard Ak630 managed to get a few rounds out before the second missile arrived.

It hit level with the main deck, mid-way down the starboard hangar, some thirty feet below and behind the working party. This time they were not so lucky. Poor Stroder, the victim of the attack on the dockside at Bermuda, was lifted and, already partially dismembered, thrown forward to land splayed over turret Bruno.

He was the closest to the blast. Page, the next, was hurled against the side of the superstructure collecting literally dozens of fragments, suffering six broken ribs, concussion and a potentially fatal rupture of his spleen.

Rautsch was thrown around the side of the mast platform and, as he flung his right arm up in a futile attempt to break his fall, it was caught by a fragment the size and shape of a meat cleaver providing an instant almost surgical amputation just above the right wrist.

Reisler was luckiest. He'd been shielded from most of the blast by the antenna mounting itself but still managed to collect thirty one fragments in his, unluckily trailing, left leg.

Ignoring the pain, fear and nausea, he lurched awkwardly around the protective mounting and found an unconscious Rautsch covering the deck with bright red jets of blood from the severed wrist. Reisler ripped out one of Rautsch's boot laces quickly tied it tightly round the stump and then rolled him into the recovery position before staggering around the next corner to find Page.

Seeing that Page although unconscious, was not obviously bleeding to death, he sat down, vomited, and then called for help on his mike whilst picking pieces of metal from his legs.

Meanwhile a third and fourth missile was arcing toward the ship. By now however, *Bismarck* had turned sufficiently for her last remaining 3 inch guns to join in as well as the twin barrelled Ak630 mount.

To add insult to injury, the survivors up on the superstructure were now subjected to the ear splitting racket of their own guns as they tried to bring the missiles down. Reisler could only groan with relief as they finally detonated in impressive explosions half a mile and a quarter of a mile from the ship respectively.

With Halshaw, Kipper, Rautsch and Nuttall down, the decimated damage control parties were now being led by the normally jovial Supply Officer, Lt Marchello Vitali. Despite his trade he was, like most modern naval officers, well versed in a variety of other duties on board ship including damage control and firefighting.

Jake listened without interruption as Vitali described the damage to turret Caesar. The turret, weighing in at around sixty five tons, was intact but no longer sitting centrally on its gyro stabilized circular gimbal on top of the barbette.

Engineroom artificer Chief Louis Braime a taciturn French Basque, reckoned with a crane they'd be able to re-seat it without damage. He was now 2 i/c of damage control which seemed to be a particularly unhealthy occupation on *Bismarck*.

The explosion had simply pushed it off its usual resting point with the ease of a man lifting off the cap of a beer bottle. So now it could neither train nor fire. The turret barbette itself, showed merely a dent and scorch mark. Penetration had been prevented by the Titanium Diboride composite sandwiched between the layers of Titanium alloy.

The second missile, apart from decimating the work party, had blown the starboard crane across the barrels of S3, the after starboard 76mm turret, rendering it useless, but no one had yet done a proper topside inspection to see what could be recovered, mainly of course because people kept shooting at them, thought Jake sarcastically.

God help us, we're gradually being whittled down and it isn't over yet. It soon became apparent that the missile attack was part of a coordinated effort to get rid of *Bismarck* once and for all.

Shortly after the missiles had struck, the remaining RPV's had picked up a force consisting of the *Luda* class DDG from the north and the Type53 frigate which had just fired its missiles, approaching from the south.

Bismarck had several major problems now. First of all, it wouldn't take the enemy long to realize that *Bismarck* had no main armament firing from aft and as soon as they did, they would try to manoeuvre into that shadow and attack from astern.

Secondly their lack of manoeuvrability would mean that more shells would hit than miss; no more high speed jinking to out-fox the enemy gunners.

The only plus on their side was that Scotnikov had managed to pump out the compartment and thought it likely that the starboard pod would be useable soon. But 'soon' was a variable quantity.

Kopf and Dettweiler up in the MGCC were busier than ever, with only partial radar coverage they had to take a more active part in the gunnery control using TV and laser ranging.

At least the ammunition problem was becoming less acute thought Kopf. With the knocking out of a number of guns, ammunition was being transferred to the remainder leaving them reasonably well off for now.

He concentrated for a second on the image dancing in the viewer under high magnification, he wanted the cross hairs lined up precisely on the bridge of that *Luda* to get the lock. He'd thought it was all over once they'd drifted out of range, how wrong could I get, he decided, locking the weapons and opening fire.

Dettweiler, sitting next to him, was already busy using the remaining starboard 76mm turret in an attempt to cripple or deter the frigate whenever *Bismarck* pointed in the right direction. It must have expended its missiles and had decided to use guns, foolish he thought, this one clearly hadn't seen what we can do.

He didn't fire at the *Luda* because the two remaining main bow gun turrets were already firing at it, for now. Of course since they were slowly rotating it would soon fall to the turret he controlled to attack it. But still, he was puzzled why it hadn't moved out of gun range before attempting to fire its own missiles a few minutes before, as *they* already knew what *Bismarck*'s guns could actually do.

Down in the OPs room, Jake thanked Vitali and Reiner dismissed him. He leaned forward and rubbed his tired eyes, as he picked the coffee cup up, gunfire crashed out once more. How much more damage can she take? He asked himself. How many more of my crew and friends shall I maim and kill?

He decided an update on the state of play was in order. He suddenly realized what he'd just thought 'the state of play'. Hell, he berated himself, what a ridiculous expression; this wasn't a damned game of cricket!

After five more minutes or so the new attack fizzled out under the highly accurate fire from *Bismarck*'s now super stable forward guns. The destroyer to the north had taken the brunt because OPs believed the *Luda* was one which hadn't fired its missiles yet, although it was difficult to work out which had done what in reality. It must have been an opportunity their Commander had felt was worth it now that *Bismarck* had again been struck by missiles.

Julius Kopf didn't think the *Luda* would get home. Having destroyed its bridge area with four beautifully placed shells he'd switched fire more to the stern and definitely taken out the aft missile silos with an impressive explosion which appeared to have started other sympathetic detonations. The ship had swerved further to starboard and trailing smoke, disappeared around the north point again.

The Type 53 to the south had ineffectually shelled *Bismarck* causing little damage, probably Dettweiler thought, because there was sod all left to damage on the upperdecks. With a mixture of frag rounds and HE on high rate he had caused major damage to it each time *Bismarck* had rotated so that he was able to use the starboard guns on it. Both ships had now retired out of range.

06:15 Sunday27th May 2018
Government House, Grand Cayman

"Bastards!" Roared Andy Evans in rage, as he saw the flash of the missiles exploding on the crippled *Bismarck*. He'd been watching her since just before dawn from the roof of government house, initially drawn by the flickering yellow flashes on the horizon and the thunder of gunfire.

Then the gunfire had died to a sporadic exchange as the Haitians steamed out of range. When the dawn had finally come he'd watched in anguish as the once graceful ship, crabbed and veered its painful way helplessly past the island.

Just a few minutes before, she'd signalled that one of the Steerpods should be manoeuvrable fairly soon and that they were hopeful that it could be used to get them back to George Town.

Now this. A killing rage filled him as he watched the smoke and flames billow up from the badly hurt ship and heard the belated thunder that followed it. It threatened to tear away his sanity completely; not bad enough that he wasn't out there with them, now he had to watch helplessly as they were torn apart in front of his eyes.

'Mr Cool' in action and out. He knew that's what everyone always said of him. Bloody ice water in his veins, never lost his rag didn't Andy. But enough was enough. Now his anger and frustration needed an outlet and the Haitians unwittingly provided one for him.

At that moment reports came into Government House of enemy landings near Boatswains Point at the north western tip of Grand Cayman.

Andy needed no urging and needed no permission either. Slipping the field glasses into the pocket of his combat jacket he grabbed his Heckler and Koch machine pistol and ran down the stairs.

With a curt nod and quick word to Miles Carlson and the Prime Minister, he excused himself and ran for the pick-up truck he'd borrowed. Lifting the tarpaulin in the back he grunted in satisfaction as he saw that his surprise packages were still lying there.

Jumping in he raced down the seafront stopping only to pick up a dozen or so MPP who were marching purposefully toward the north of the island having been manning the pillboxes on the beach.

The Haitian soldiers were advancing into Hell. Literally. The small settlement of Hell in north western Grand Cayman with its famous post office was right in their path.

Now it lived up to its name as the heavily outnumbered MPP defenders clashed viciously with the Haitian advanced units, sending them reeling back before themselves retreating down Reverend Blackman road to just beyond the junction with West Church Street and their next defensible position in the woods opposite West Bay Church. With another small party down West Church Street on the coast road they could hold a short while here, until flanked again.

Andy arrived as the MPP were settling into their new defensive line on the east side of the road but in view of the junction. He considered the illogical Haitian tactics. For some reason they seemed to be just following the 'opposition' rather than trying to pin them, flank them and destroy them in detail, which was fine by him. Just as long as there weren't some sneaky gits coming round the back. He asked one of the MPP officers if they could speak with their mates over by the wood and get them to cast around at their north and eastern flank just to be sure.

He checked the view to his front again. At this point there was about a hundred metre strip of clear ground in front of the main MPP line in the woods opposite the road junction.

The Haitians were cautious now and had deployed either side of the approach road through the house gardens which lined the road. Sporadic sniping was making them keep their heads down. Through his range finding field glasses Andy could make out a couple of heavy machine guns being brought up, one each side of the road they'd advanced down. A mortar further back started coughing out its deadly bombs even as he watched. They hit the tree line and houses at the junction opposite to the main force, he hoped the MPP boys had been quick to dig a shell scrape to soak up the splinters.

Grabbing a young MPP corporal he asked for two others to assist in setting up his gear. The surprise from his truck was a Spanish made automatic grenade launcher. Firing 40mm grenades about the size of a small shave foam tin out to 1500m, the SB40 was belt fed from a hopper to the side.

It looked just like a thick barrelled machine gun, he thought as he set it up, but is really like having a battery of light artillery on your side. Andy, assisted by a young constable, lifted the now assembled tripod and launcher and carried them to an upstairs room inside a house which formed the left of the defenders line. It neatly covered both the main junction and the one the Haitians would have to use when they eventually tried to flank the position, which was of course why he'd picked it.

The other two carried the boxes of grenades.

He gave instructions for the MPP to watch for flanking movements and with a grin of vengeful delight sighted up the road to the junction where he could hear the sound of approaching tracked vehicles as well as see squads of infantry moving parallel to the road. Rather than breaking the glass he opened the sash window to its full extent and kept the barrel at least a foot inside the room.

He used the laser rangefinder to check the exact distance and then dialled in the range on the launcher so his first rounds would be straight in, and then waited until the armoured vehicle arrived at the junction.

It was a BMMP he noted with professional interest, the naval infantry version of a BMP3 and he watched while its 30mm auto-cannon rotated left and right looking for targets. With their armour commanding the junction the Haitian foot sloggers began their advance toward Andy's position and the quickest route now to the coast road, leaving their flank exposed.

As its right track stopped and the left kept going, it turned towards him, then he heard a bang and just had time to see the dust puff as a 66mm LAW rocket fired by the MPP in the wood line, hit the side of the BMMP. The

HEAT round detonated on the thin side armour and blew a lethal stream of molten metal into the main compartment killing anyone inside.

As soon as it was hit Andy began firing grenades into the two areas occupied by the covering machine gunners. Within seconds of the first explosion most of the gunners lay dead around their weapons and the remainder ran for it. Quickly Andy re-located to another room and began slamming grenades down along behind the burning BMMP and at any flanking movement spotted by the others in the house, causing mayhem amongst the troops gathering at the junction; he just hoped everyone had fled the houses when they knew which way the Haitians were coming.

Down below, the MPP cheered as they watched the Haitians retreat further in confusion, dragging their wounded and dead with them. But Andy knew it was only a temporary respite and began packing up ready for the next move.

Buck Taylor studied the array of motion sensors which plotted the advance of the Haitian invaders. Occasionally he would flick his eyes up to the pictures coming in from his strategically placed low light cameras.

The 'pit', as he called his Command Centre, was quiet apart from the odd whispered voice from the teams' com-units, noting the enemy dispositions and movements.

The herald of this sudden attack had been just after dawn when a dreadful howling whoosh, audible for miles, had preceded earth trembling detonations as the sixty 122 mm rockets from the assault ship had impacted on and around Anchorage Bay. Then the escorts joined in with naval artillery HE rounds prepping the area surrounding the landing site.

That had been twenty minutes ago. The sudden barrage had been followed by sporadic bursts of naval gunfire from the escorts moving their fire to what he assumed were preselected points. He hoped they didn't manage to find any of his dug in and scattered men.

The overcast sky would keep the temperature down a few degrees for them but the humidity was nearly 100% and that made it tiring and uncomfortable to be lugging kit around and wearing heavy webbing and equipment.

The enemy had, as Buck predicted, chosen Anchorage Bay for their landings mainly because of the rapidly shelving beach with no reef; in fairness to them it was where Buck would have selected if asked. Deliberately he'd decided not to contest the actual beach landings with his small group of specialists, especially as naval gunfire support would be most effective in such a confined area.

Watching with his low light cameras he saw the assault ship beach, then open its bow doors and drop the ramp. Immediately a squad of soldiers had splashed through the last few feet of water and up the beach to the fringe of the mangroves to take up covering positions.

No sooner had they flattened into the undergrowth than the assault ship began disgorging its cargo of troops and personnel carriers. This was what he needed to observe.

Five Ukrainian made copies of Russian vehicles disembarked; four BTR80UPs, wheeled armoured personnel carriers, and a BMMP tracked mechanized naval infantry combat vehicle. The most dangerous of them being the heavier BMMP with its 30mm turreted auto-cannon and better armour. Two of the BTR's loaded their squads of seven and turned south along Olivine Drive with more troops doubling behind them. This led to the south coast and then either west or east, he had no idea of their plan. He watched them head off out of sight.

They clearly didn't think they had significant opposition because the commanders were allowing troops to ride on the outside of the vehicles. They looked like Indian buses, barely able to see the vehicle for the passengers; they clearly weren't expecting trouble.

Buck called the four man ambush team near Tarpon Lake on the south side of the island and informed them what might be coming their way shortly.

The first encounter though would be at 'Bloody Bay Point' on the north side. Very appropriate, thought Buck grimly. He sat back satisfied. He'd done all he could by way of preparation. Andy Evans had been impressed with the web-like series of ambushes leading always towards the east end of the island; it was now down to the guys at the sharp end.

As he knew well enough, a plan is only viable for the first few minutes of combat, after that it's a case of understanding what it was trying to achieve and moulding what was actually happening into that framework if possible.

The four men of the first northern ambush lying in wait in shallow scrapes at Bloody Bay Point, looked for all the world like part of the jungle floor. Their disruptive pattern camouflage smocks and helmets bedecked with strips of similar fabric enabled them to blend in among the shadows of the twisted mangroves totally.

It would have been very difficult to spot them even from just a few feet away as they lay motionless, but that would happen soon enough. They'd reckoned on fifteen minutes or so from landing, for the first vehicles to cover the six hundred yards from Anchorage Bay which gave time for the loading up of men and equipment and plenty of time for cock-ups.

Whilst they waited they checked their personal weapons again. All carried Heckler & Koch machine pistols with silencers, and Glock 17 automatics. Reliable, user friendly kit. Two carried Light Support Weapons (LSW), the light machine gun version of the SA-80 and the other two an automatic shotgun in case it got to close work, as well as a LAW each.

As the time wound down to confrontation each man prepared himself for the coming combat and mentally rehearsed his route of retreat. The road mines were laid and primed, the Claymores positioned and set and communication tested via the 'natty' little ear piece and skinny boom mike attachments of their helmets.

The ambush site was chosen because of Jackson's pond on one side and the sea on the other with no beach as such. That meant that the enemy vehicles would have no manoeuvring space, and neither would the infantry. They'd already checked that the half dozen or so houses and buildings closest on the sea side of the road were empty.

Andy Talbot, ex-trooper 22nd SAS, lay on the landward side of the lagoon at right angles to the IED they'd laid in the road. Next to him was his partner Arkady Zotov, ex-Soviet Spetsnaz officer and explosives expert.

Their position was ideal from the point of view of LAW rocket use. Camouflage, was provided by the crisscross roots of one of many large Mangrove trees, but the road was in clear sight and no 'dangly bits' as Andy put it, to get in the way. Still, it was damned uncomfortable because of the mud and God knows what crawling into their clothes, nipping and nibbling at them.

The rising sun was behind them or would be when the clouds cleared, and anyone coming along the road would even now only see darkened undergrowth topped by increasing light as the sun, although behind the clouds, rose higher.

Movement ceased completely as they heard the growl of powerful diesels accompanied by the distinctive squeal, clank and rattle of a tracked vehicle as the lead enemy unit arrived.

Both watched as the BMMP led the way down the road from Anchorage bay, it's turreted auto-cannon training menacingly from side to side as the gunner scanned the underbrush and mangroves that started less than ten yards away from the edge of the road Like the ones moving south these had men decorating the sides like weird cammo nets. In this case the lead vehicle had no one forward of the turret so at least it could fire.

Andy slowly trained his sound supressed HK-MP5 and let it rest gently in the crook of two crossed roots. Moving his eyes only, he watched his Russian partner prepare to detonate a mine underneath the first vehicle, the BMMP.

Arkady kept the transmitter pointed at the mine and waited till the front of the BMMP had passed over it before he squeezed gently on the transmit button. The resultant upward explosion of the 130mm HE shell buried in the road, was more of a 'whummp' muffled as it was by the BMMP, but it still lifted the eighteen ton vehicle with majestic ease and as it landed, flipped it on its side scattering the men who'd festooned it.

Smoke poured from the dying machine and its left track hung uselessly from the mangled drive wheels. Before anyone else could react, a LAW from the third ambusher Alex Pickthall, sited fifty yards back down the road towards Anchorage bay with his partner, flew into the rear of the last BTR, blowing a stream of liquid metal into the troop compartment and throwing everyone on the outside to the ground like soggy confetti.

The crewman manning the 14.5mm machine gun on the middle vehicle began frantically spraying the undergrowth as his driver desperately tried to turn the sandwiched APC in what became an eighty point turn, urged on by the bellowing of his Captain who'd taken cover beach-side of the vehicles.

Infantrymen poured from the rear of the still moving vehicle as they strove to avoid the fate of their colleagues behind and in front. As soon as they appeared, Andy, Arkady, Alex and 'Fingers' Morgan, started firing in short controlled bursts, their silenced weapons dropping the enemy as they attempted to take cover. The Haitians had no idea where the fire was coming from partly at least because of the noise from the burning vehicle as rounds began cooking off from the stored ammunition.

They hadn't a chance. They didn't know where their attackers were or how many and any who didn't move quickly did not live long enough to guess. The centre vehicle was halfway through the turn when it was hit by a LAW from Andy Talbot hiding in the bushes near the head of the convoy.

Lucky for this crew Andy fired a moment too soon as he gave an understandable jerk on the trigger when the heavy machine gun on top started spitting half inch heavy slugs in his direction; the missile deflected from the steeply sloped glacis plate and whizzed off into the sky. An explosion from the BMMP then blew it sideways on to the shoreline, thick smoke and flames spewing from the engine compartment effectively screening both defenders and attackers. Time to move back Andy decided or the ships will be joining in.

He toggled the com-unit and told Alex and Fingers to leg it back up to their position before they all moved back to the next line. Ten seconds later Pickthall and Morgan threw themselves behind the slight berm and they prepped to move out, as more heavy bullets thudded into wood and soil nearby.

The ambush team melted back into the mangroves towards their next ambush point with 'fingers' Morgan leading. The craggy ex Foreign legionnaire had picked up his nickname when he lost two fingers from his left hand, a scratch he picked up fighting the Tuareg rebels in Mali, he said.

The crackle of ammunition cooking off and the sound of flames consuming the two burning vehicles was all they left behind, no movement and no counterattack. Then came the naval gunfire, loads of it. Andy Talbot wondered how many fucking battleships they had, but the good news was that it was all landing behind them as they slogged through the mangroves.

Buck Taylor sighed with relief as the action fizzled out and the team retreated to their next ambush point. In just five and a half minutes they'd eliminated 40% of the enemy's transport and around 20% of his manpower. From his surviving low light camera near the landing site he could see the troops who were distantly following the APC's up the road scatter and take cover as the first ambush was sprung ahead of them.

Give them their due, they reacted properly, he mused. Men moved quickly into the bush inland and the others leap frogged forward in groups of two or three towards the sound of gunfire while someone produced a mine detector and began sweeping. Buck hoped it was one of those dodgy ones that Jimmy McCormick got banged up for flogging a few years ago.

But now, he thought, the real problems begin. Each subsequent ambush would be harder to effect on this side of the island especially with the enemy now on foot and aware that there was opposition.

The danger to the ambushers would increase greatly as the enemy became more wary and hungry for revenge, unless of course they quit and went home, which he didn't think likely.

The pilot quickly twisted the throttle grip and pulled on
the cyclic, feeling the lift power push him down in his seat
as the HM2A 'Merlin' leapt from the flightdeck and quickly
banked right.

Bouncing all over the place, Leading Aircrewman Simon
Jones wondered what the hell was going on. He was
feeling at the same time that it was probably a good thing
that he hadn't been plugged into the long mike lead or he
might have been strangled by the sodding thing.

Muttering to himself about 'ex-jungly' pilots and their
fucked-up sense of humour, he managed to get into his
seat and pushed his mike lead into the nearest jack plug.

He'd been making his way aft to get himself strapped in
when the Merlin had suddenly decided to launch. Settling
himself down and plugging in he tried to tune into what
was going on, they were still leaping around the sky like
nutters at an air show! Finally he got the gist of what was
going down and it sent a cold cramping feeling through his
gut. *Dorsetshire* was under missile attack hence the dodgy
take-off!

Jon Roby settled himself back into his oversized
captain's chair in the OPs room and watched the ship run
itself as the missiles raced towards them. Thank God he'd
ordered the radar on when he had.

In the kind of situation they'd been in up to the time of
attack, it was always a hard judgement call as to when to
go active with your sensors. Too early and you let
everybody and his dog know that you're about and awake
–but can't see them. Too late and you do a Sheffield.

The Type53H2G had been alert, it had to have been to
pick up *Dorsetshire* with its surface search radar at a range
of twenty six miles or so. But why had the buggers opened
fire? *Dorsetshire* had seen them half an hour ago on ESM,
with an accurate bearing and type identity.

Jon pondered while things happened automatically
around him. Just switching radar on wasn't considered to

be an aggressive move as such, hell if that were the case, the third world war would have started decades ago.

Also they had only three surface tracks on radar and ESM, so where was the fourth one that Jake had mentioned? Everyone was waiting for a response from him. Think man think, he ordered himself.

Well, as far as the rules of engagement went they certainly had the right to fire back didn't they? The wording of the signal echoed in his mind 'engage only after demonstrated hostile intent.'

Wasn't firing missiles at you pretty bloody hostile? Yes damn it, of course it was. The fact that I shouldn't have been within fifty miles means that I'll pay later but such is life.

He made his decision. Even if *Dorsetshire* didn't survive the incoming missile attack, then revenge would be taken by their helicopter.

"Order the Merlin to attack track Sierra zero two. Flash signal to MOD repeated to the E3 sentry, 'Am under attack from SSMs -my position- am engaging source -his position- with helo.' Now weapons free."

Dorsetshire was picking up speed and turning directly away from the incoming missiles in order to put some distance between her and them but also to offer her stern area as a target. He debated throwing a couple of Harpoons at the frigate but decided to reserve his long strike weapons for the moment, they had re-loads for the Merlin but not for his Harpoons.

Roby considered the Merlin skimming towards the enemy; about 5 feet above the water he decided, knowing that ex-jungly pilot. They were lucky to have a Merlin at all with the usual dates nailed in jelly and the efforts of the parsimonious pencil necks in the treasury and MOD.

The fact that they had one of the first Merlins modified to take the Marte-ER long range anti-ship missiles was a gift from heaven. Still, when good fortune smiles. He decided that was an inappropriate thought with four bloody cruise missiles zooming towards them.

The seconds passed slowly at first for those waiting in the circling helicopter. Then suddenly the order came to attack and everything was business; the approach to be worked out, preparation of the two Marte-ER anti-ship missiles and a good deal of 'puckering up'.

Almost before *Dorsetshire* settled on her new course, two Sea Ceptor missiles were up and arcing away from *Dorsetshire* towards the first of the incoming missiles.

Hayden sat in the OPs room thinking about his career, now in the toilet. He could hardly object to *Dorsetshire* defending itself now. I should have made my point before we crossed the fifty mile threshold, he cursed himself. It would have been in the log and I would be in the clear, now I'm in the shit with this old fart.

Well at least the new Sea Ceptor was performing well, he noted later as the final incoming missile was splashed but they'd used fourteen of their thirty two missiles. He rather hoped they were not going to be attacked again.

With great satisfaction Simon Jones observed the first Sea Ceptor do its job, eight miles from the ship. A brief yellow flash and a black puffball was all that remained of the once deadly threat, now let's see the others get whacked he thought as they skimmed the water preparing their own launch. Maybe Jungly pilots had their uses after all.

Shutting out the sounds of the damage control reports, the Captain tried to assess what had gone wrong. It was obvious now that he'd attacked, not the mercenary ship, but another naval vessel of some kind and it had retaliated using helicopter launched anti-ship missiles which had appeared literally out of nowhere.

When the radar had picked up the surface contact at twenty six miles steaming straight for them, he had assumed that it must be the mercenary ship.

He knew now his logic had been faulty and he shamefully admitted to himself that he had panicked.

From the fragmentary reports of the action off Grand Cayman he'd gathered that the enemy ship had attacked, caused much damage and then itself retired damaged, hit by missiles.

His mistake, he realized, had been in assuming that it had then turned north, and his fear for the troop landing, had led him to conclude that it was the mercenary ship approaching to attack his less well defended invasion force. That was why he'd fired his last six anti-ship cruise missiles at it.

His 30mm Gatlings had taken out one of the approaching missiles but the other had performed a terminal spiral movement and plunged into his ship just aft of the funnel exploding deep below decks.

The resultant fires and damage to the boiler rooms, he knew was extensive, and the ship was reduced to only seven knots for now. Worse he had no idea whether the other ship would try to complete the job.

The Senior Tactical controller waited until all eighteen of his station operators checked in. Now the immensely powerful air and surface search radar was active, it was picking up aerial targets as far away as three hundred miles and surface targets out to over two hundred.

The screens were quickly filled with all manner of both contact types. The operators went into their well drilled routine and quickly sorted the sky picture removing all civilian traffic whilst, saying a prayer of thanks to the inventor of IFF.

All friendly aircraft were 'squawking' their identity in response to interrogation by the Sentry, so too was the known friendly ship in the area, the frigate *Dorsetshire*.

He briefly considered the crew of the frigate. They'd just survived a missile attack, incredibly someone had just launched missiles at one of Her Majesty's very expensive frigates in a totally unprovoked assault.

What had it been like for those men? Waiting, waiting. There was however another ship down there considered to be friendly and he needed to know which one of the dozen or so contacts it was. Time to call them up on their sat-phone, that should give them a surprise, he decided.

"Bravo Kilo this is Overseer." A pause.

"Overseer this is Bravo Kilo, state your ID and reason for calling please." Answered Robby Robinson in *Bismarck*'s OPs room with a quizzical eyebrow raised.

Thank God for the briefing, the controller thought, imagine having to guess the bloody phone number.

"Bravo Kilo we are a Romeo Alpha Foxtrot, Echo 3 on station West of Grand Cayman. Please squawk I/P so we can tick you off as a good guy."

Robby hit the I/P button on their transponder. A moment later one of the E3 operators indicated that *Bismarck* had just come up and was now plotted.

"Bravo Kilo I see you now, we have you plotted. You have four friendly Charlie 130s closing, ten miles apart in trail, bearing 280. Number one is twelve miles out. They are inbound for Golf Charlie. Over."

"Overseer this is Bravo Kilo. Message understood. Caution! Be advised there are possibly Hotel Quebec seven Alpha systems in range of their final approach, tell Charlie to be careful and good luck. Out!"

"Roger that Bravo Kilo, and thanks for the warning, out"

At a nod from Reiner Robby continued.

"Overseer, we need to establish a datalink, broadcasting uplink details now."

"Err thanks Bravo Kilo, we have the uplink now, have made it two way, good luck."

The controller quickly relayed the threat information about the Chinese made anti-air missiles on the Type 51D destroyers and Type 53s to the four C-13OJ Hercules' and they prepared chaff canisters to deploy on the final approach.

He debated whether to call up Grand Cayman Air Traffic Control and tell them about their new traffic but, having checked for any civil aircraft in the area and found none, decided not to spoil their surprise or risk interception of the message.

His contemplation was interrupted by the not quite so calm voice of one of his operators.

"Multiple 'Bogies' bearing 084, range 295, course 270." She played the system and then continued.

"I have two groups, a low and a high. Refining now...." A note of tenseness appeared in her speech.

"Re-classifying. I now have multiple 'Bandits' at 084, range 290, course 270. High group has six tracks. Computer ID's them as Mig 29's. Low group is also six tracks ID'd as JF-17s. Speed of both groups is 530 knots."

Adrenalin surged in the Senior Tactical Controller. This is it. This is what it's all about. Over the next quarter hour or so he would justify his multi-million pound training at taxpayers' expense, or he would screw up.

He had two of the Typhoons fifty miles east of the island fitted for air to surface with AAMs for personal defence only and the other two air defence variants were close to him. Not much of an air force but so be it. Time to speak to the players.

Reiner thanked Robby Robinson for being on the ball. They had a sentry up there now so at least there shouldn't be any surprises from the air. Thank God they'd got the full radar suite back now.

Still it had been a hell of a surprise when the system had come back on line and the plot was covered with aerial contacts. The few seconds before the computer had identified them had been just a little nervy to say the least.

Once recognised though, it had been apparent that this was Jon Roby's airborne cavalry. He considered it a good bet that the transport aircraft were bringing in troops and that the others on the radar were there to send the Haitians a message like 'Sod Off', for instance.

Better get Jake to inform Andrew McTeal they're on their way, that should make him a bit happier, he decided, finally exiting the OPs room and heading back to the bridge.

*

In fact it did. McTeal stood out on the balcony to watch as the first transport flew in fast and low almost over the top of government house on its downwind leg, popping flares and chaff as it went before turning for finals on the single runway behind George Town. His personal protection officers chafed and chafed and eventually ushered him back inside now that they were in range of the attacking forces small arms fire.

Yes, he was relieved, but he was also annoyed that the British PM had not told him help was coming. He decided that it was the British Prime Ministers' way of hedging her bets. If the island had been already overrun then the aircraft would simply have aborted and flown back to Belize?

He wished it was all over, he wasn't a military man and felt lost now that the decision making for the island was almost completely out of his hands.

*

Down next to Salt Creek, six hundred yards or so from government house, Andy Evans and the tired and haggard

MPP survivors were forming yet another line, the final one this would be, he thought to himself. He would try and organise some water and food to be brought up if he could, they might have an hour so respite before the enemy made it this far. They'd be wary, weary and worn after the mauling they'd had and a bird farting would have them down on their bellies now.

There were less than a hundred MPP now out of the original two hundred or so sent to defend against the northern landing. They were running low on ammunition, morale and ideas.

The young Captain that had commanded, told him that rest of the defenders were either held as reserve near to George Town in case of other landings or were still scattered around the rest of the island looking for other intruders. Nice bloke the young lad was. Poor bugger. Had been a nice bloke that was until a sniper had taken the top of his head off as he'd checked on his men.

They were frantically digging scrapes into soil, sand in some places and sharp volcanic rocks in others, all along a line which was little more than 200 yards long. It may only be 200 yards but it ran the full 'dry' width of the island. This was because of a marina development built adjacent to Salt Creek which nearly split the island in two. To his right there was Salt Creek itself, a stretch of water deepened and dredged, which effectively led out into North Sound, the big shallow bay in the middle. You couldn't wade it, you needed boats to cross it.

To his left were two hundred yards of rough scrub and a beach bisected by the two main roads running north-south about parallel to the coast.

It's good that having fewer men coincided with a shorter line, he thought wryly, better than the opposite anyway. He kept all but a squad between the beach and this end of the creek, the others were spread out along the edge of the creek all the way to North Sound just to make sure the bad guys didn't cross behind the main line.

Now Andy was in command. It had not been a conscious decision on his part, it just sort of happened.

After the Captain's death, people just kept asking him what to do.

Many of them knew of him even if they'd never seen him, and of course he'd easily slipped back into the roll for which he had been trained and was well suited.

He settled down to wait for the next rush, knowing that they hadn't much chance at all anyway, rifle ammunition was low and the grenade launcher was completely out, the last had been used on a BMMP and two BTR's that had tried to force a way past a previous line they'd held.

He bent his head forward for a second to relieve the pain caused by staring forward whilst lying in a prone position. The relief was glorious and he let his head fall further forward onto the arm that supported his machine pistol. That was when he heard it.

All thoughts of his neck stiffness vanished as he slowly, carefully eased back from his firing point and sat up taking care not to expose himself above the level of the road embankment he sheltered against.

The noise faded and then came back more strongly, the instinctive part of his mind told him what it was but the controlling part perversely wouldn't let him believe it.

Louder. Now there was no question, he'd heard that sound so many times in his service career; it was a bloody Hercules! He turned to look out over the sea and saw a speck in the distance.

What the hell? He gave a short whistle and a sergeant nearby looked over. Andy beckoned him across.

"Send someone down to the airport with one of our tactical radios."

The man looked puzzled. Andy indicated the sky.

"I think we've got some help arriving; we need to talk with them as soon as they're down." He added.

"Also, tell them in George Town, that we need the reserves up here where they can do some fucking good and more ammunition NOW!"

The Sergeant belly crawled away, Andy turned back to his firing point and slowly eased himself forward again, his mind working through the possibilities. Who would they send? Paras? Booties? Or maybe Johnny Gurkha? How many would they send?

Earth kicked up in spurts near his face and bullets buzzed past him spanging off the flat stones of the opposite bank as voices to the front, rose in shouts of defiance. Then the stamp of heavy boots and stutter of weapons.

The Haitians were coming again.

"Stand to." He shouted almost unnecessarily. Fuck where was that respite? They must have used a fresh unit to leapfrog the others. The defenders stiffened, they gripped their weapons tighter, clamped down on their fear and they waited.

One last command.

"Fix bayonets!" He roared in his best parade ground voice.

Just has to be the scariest order ever given or received, he thought, as he expertly slotted his onto the borrowed SA-80. Fucking act of desperation sticking one of these on, was his musing as he sat back on one knee just at eye level with the road to his front and waited for the final charge.

They waited instead of running away, young men and some women too. They waited because of their training, because of each other, because of their newly independent islands and their families and because they'd no choice now after the kicking they'd given the Haitians earlier there wasn't anywhere to run.

They waited grimly determined, throats parched, sick with fear and the sheer inevitability of their end. But they didn't run. They were well trained and seriously motivated. They were good soldiers too. They died well.

06:55 Sunday 27ᵗʰ May 2018
Typhoon call sign Zero Two, twenty five miles South East of Grand Cayman

Up in the clear blue sky above, Flt Lieutenant Bob McKeith raced faster than the speed of sound towards his first aerial combat. Hours in a simulator, hours mock fighting colleagues, hours learning to kill in the clean cold skies.

Now it all came down to the next few minutes, the world compressed into the cockpit of his Typhoon fighter plane. Supercruise. Nine hundred plus miles per hour, supersonic without afterburners; nice.

Altitude two thousand feet, radar off. Course south-east, then east, then north east and then north. He and his wingman eating up the miles. Guided always by the calm voice of the controller as he led them around, behind and below the enemy. Stalking. The sun behind them now as they were vectored west on the final run in. External tanks dropped. Master arm on.

Radar silent. Stalking. Voice of the controller, calm, confident in his own ability and theirs, done it before, thousands of times it said subliminally. Time for the climb. Burners on and a kick in the back. Speed climbing up through eleven hundred knots. Nose up twenty degrees.

Listening to the growl of the ASRAAMs waking up as they sniffed the sky ahead for the heat signature of their prey in the cold blue aerial ocean.

Standby! Standby! Speed climbing through twelve hundred knots; incredible.

METEOR selected and confirmed on the multi-function display. Bandits eleven o'clock high. Range nineteen miles. All this from the datalink with the sentry and just as the man had said.

Chop the burners.

Three pairs of bandits in a rough 'V', no combat spread yet. Controller says optimal range. Squeezing the trigger, once, twice, three times.

Missiles flying under guidance of the E3. No one and nothing emitting except the E3, including the radar guided missiles. Counting down. Then there were eight not six. Shit.

A last second radar activation by the missiles for terminal homing was the only warning the enemy pilots got. Boom, he mouthed as three dropped in dirty smoke balls. Five survivors.

Then everything just compressed. His tactical screen went haywire. Some aircraft had reversed, his wingman still with him, got a tone, he thought as the ASRAAMs growled louder, got a shot he decided, as a Mig29 closed.

Nineteen miles is nothing with a combined closing speed of two thousand miles an hour, seconds only. Select ASRAAM. One trigger pull. Missile detaches from wingman at same time. Eyes sharper than ever. Time stretching. Adrenaline one-in-one with blood. Silver specks above and ahead. Slight left kick on the rudder. Closing at an incredible rate.

Explosion ahead and right. Vivid picture of a one winged jet fighter as it flashed past spinning out of control. Bank again, grunting hard listening to the controller, lining up for another ASRAAM. Trigger pull and away it goes, looking for the next target checking his MFDs straightening, a shout from his wingman.

Another explosion, two aircraft colliding, bits and pieces falling away. Turning away, turning south, levelling out at 23,000 feet. Going for separation. Speed climbing through a thousand knots. Looking behind, looking all round, talking to Dave Mcgee next door. No answer. Talking to the [fat?] controller, getting a new vector.

Listening to the radar warning receiver beeping, chaff and flares for good measure bank and turn -someone's trying for a lock. Turning harder! Loud bang the stick shudders master cautions on, no time to process which ones as green tracer zips by the cockpit. Bank and dive.

*

The senior controller watched the screen and bit his nails and watched, saw three bandits splashed, saw the two extra planes separate clearly flying very close together, and swore. He murmured calmly into his mike and talked to the two pilots and watched, as the gap between the two

Typhoons and the remaining Mig 29K's closed. He saw one bandit begin a spin and his rate of decent said it was uncontrolled, then one of his plots and one more bandit merged and disappeared. Then he slumped. Fuck. Lost one, two bad guys left and just one damaged Typhoon. Haven't got any spares for fuck's sake. He thanked the Lord that he was where he was and not out there playing Top Gun.

*

Jon Roby listened to the transmissions from the Sentry and the Typhoons, he heard the shout from a Hercules pilot and heard his own OPs people confirm the launch of an HQ-7 from one of the Haitian *Luda* D class destroyer near Grand Cayman.

The time for warnings was past, events led them now. They were involved, no time to wait for the dithering buggers in MOD. He heard himself speak to Berry Reeves ordering him to attack the damaged frigate and the corvette they had contact with near Little Cayman with *Dorsetshire*'s own anti-ship missiles and get the Merlin back on deck for a re-load.

He heard himself speak to the Senior Tactical Controller in the Sentry up above and order a strike against the remaining Haitian ships off Grand Cayman.

Commodore Jonathan Roby RN, Commodore Central America and Caribbean, had declared war. He saw his First Lieutenant approach then turn and walk away without saying anything. Odd. What the hell did Hayden want? Never mind, no time now.

*

Squadron Leader Nigel Greene received his instructions to attack almost with relief. He was most assuredly fed up with stooging around the tanker at twenty thousand feet with his colleague, whilst the fighter 'jocks' did their bit and missiles flew towards his mates in the Hercules.

Relief then as he detailed his wingman to follow, tipped his wings over and dived toward the sea. He wished for a navigator or backseater but the Typhoon didn't carry one and he found himself talking out loud as he ran through his check lists just as he had when he had a backseater.

He began his system checks again. They were armed with four ASRAAM missiles and two METEOR long range missiles for self-defence, and four 'SPEAR 3 missiles which could be targeted on practically anything. So he started the pre-firing checklist for the new Spear 3's.

Greene levelled out at ten thousand feet and locked up the targets north of the island using the datalink to the Sentry and ironically the datalink from *Bismarck*'s RPV's completed the targeting picture with perfect TV cameras shots of the targets and confirmed GPS positions.

The two Typhoon FGR4s now turned south east onto their final approach course with Nigel wishing the RAF still had an anti-radiation missile to take out the enemy search radars. He along with other pilots had fumed and raged when the RAF had retired its very effective ALARM missile without replacing it.

So now they had to do anti-shipping strikes knowing that at least some of the expensive SPEAR 3 missiles would be intercepted by the enemy defences. What was the frigging point of that he mused? The Americans and Italians for heaven's sake had a joint project to replace the American version, the HARM, with a new one but not the British, too busy giving our money away to all and sundry.

07:00 Sunday 27th May 2018
Luda D class DDG *Gonaives*, North of Grand Cayman, Haitian Flagship

Captain Pulon was confused and a little bewildered to say the least. The information coming to him was flawed in some way he was sure. So much he didn't know. He wondered if war was always this confusing.

His own air search radar linked with the surviving task force members showed new aircraft in the area, clearly military since they were travelling fast and had no transponders. His IFF had interrogated them with no ID returned.

His ESM told him that there was an AWACS to the west of Grand Cayman although his radar couldn't see that far, was it American? He didn't know.

Was it just observing or was it directing an unseen force of American aircraft? He didn't know.

Military transport aircraft were landing on Grand Cayman. Whose were they? They too failed to respond to IFF interrogation. The fool in the Type 53 had fired SAMs at them but no one knew whether they hit anything. They could have been anyone's.

What were they bringing in, for whom? He didn't know.

And what about the warship that the idiot Captain in the frigate *Petionville* had attacked near Little Cayman? What the hell was that doing there? He didn't know.

His ESM had tentatively identified it as a British Type 23 frigate. Was it a coincidental appearance or did it herald a more powerful force somewhere over the horizon? Would they now interfere because of that cretin firing on one of them? He didn't know.

He'd done his job hadn't he? He'd created a landing opportunity for the troops on the main island and one of the outer islands. But the cost had been so high. Three assault ships, two corvettes, two frigates, three destroyers and one cruiser sunk! He dreaded to think how many soldiers and sailors had died.

Two destroyers damaged, including his own ship which now had a pronounced list to port and was down at the bow, and one frigate and one corvette damaged.

All because of that bastard mercenary ship. What the fuck was it made of? So far it had been hit with four missiles, God knows how many shells, and it still floated and worse, fought on!

At least help was on the way. They'd received a signal that told them that air cover would be here soon and with it the ability to get rid of that mercenary ship once and for all. Still, he could feel his grip on the situation slipping. So many unanswered questions.

07:02 Sunday 27th May 2018
SqnLdr Green Typhoon Zero One

Green spoke briefly to the Sentry then pressed the trigger twice and waited for the missiles to detach, then twice more. Two missiles for each of the two ships at the north end task force. His wingman fired one at the corvette in the north and three at the frigate to the south.

The seekers on the warhead would remain passive until they were three miles from target leaving the enemy only twenty plus seconds to react; mid-course guidance having come from the Sentry leaving the milli-metric radar and semi-active laser for terminal guidance.

The Sentry controller counted down the range, issued the mid-course guidance corrections and waited for the sea skimming weapons to go active. Meanwhile a colleague had now vectored the two Typhoons on to the incoming JF-17 ground attack flight which was approaching the east coast of Grand Cayman.

*

Simon's voice calmly detailed the 'high' dog-fight twenty miles east of Grand Cayman and then switched to the RAF anti-shipping strike against the remaining ships near Grand Cayman.

Jake watched neither. On his screen he observed the third aerial duel as the two Typhoons launched missiles head on to the JF-17s which had their radar on now and so saw them, scattering as the missiles locked on.

*

Two hits reduced the odds and the others starburst to all points of the compass. Sqn Ldr Green pulled a canard enhanced turn and with his wingman headed back to re-engage.

Infra-red warning alarms screamed in his ears and he punched flares while using the Typhoon's extreme agility to put himself into a different patch of sky to the four heat seeking Chinese PL-5 missiles that headed towards him. His wingman parted company at that point in his own haste to avoid them.

*

The ground attack group were scattered and instead of re-grouping went for any available target. Two JF's had fallen in the first pass. Jake observed the Typhoons pull around sharply and prepare to engage the remaining aircraft again picking two to the north.

Nope, no way were they going to get them all. The enemy aircraft had split up and spread out, two of them now headed towards *Bismarck*.

Once more alarms shrilled through the ship, this time the speakers shouted 'Air Raid Warning Red'.

Jake knew, they all knew, that a hit from a bomb could prove fatal in the right place. On the upper deck, the frantic work to uncover the port aft AKM630M2 ceased momentarily as the meaning of the alarm sank in.

Barry Shaw, Gunter Henzel and a bandaged Scouse Smith looked at each other as the 3 inch turret on their left suddenly trained and elevated, clearly tracking an inbound target, and without another word they carried on working.

They knew that the extra gun could be decisive. They pulled away the last of the tangle of debris, pulling, levering, twisting and discarding, all the while aware of the thunder in the skies, any part of which could be heading towards them.

*

Green now minus his wingman focussed on a JF-17 that jinked and wriggled on the deck. He was desperately trying to get a gun shot before turning for his next target. Bright tracer drew a line from him to the left rear of the enemy jet and it immediately rolled straight into the sea just north of the Island.

Warnings in his ears, a frantic look over the shoulder. Gut squeezing, brain squashing, high G turn full canards and flares popped. Spine tingling breaking right! Climbing. Turning. Chaff....Flares....

Numbness in the right arm. Grunting against the G's. Leg won't fucking work either. Fear. Panic. Should have seen the Doc. Warning voices in his ears. SLAAAM!

*

Buller had his orders. He was to maintain the westerly course for as long as possible, then when he got the order, he was to turn the ship to starboard as rapidly as the crippled steering would allow. Not much of a defence really, but everything helped -he hoped.

Jake shook his head slowly as he watched the work party through the viewer. Was it bravery? Stubborn defiance? Or maybe simple self-preservation? They'd been ordered below but had carried on working.

You didn't ignore an 'Air raid warning Red', you just didn't. He punched a button on his console and the viewer swivelled quickly onto the bearing of the incoming aircraft. *Bismarck* was about four miles west south west of George Town now, still trying to reach the harbour when she wasn't being bombed.

The E3 had told them of the incoming raid, but they'd been tracking it anyway. What nobody but the pilots knew was whether *Bismarck* was the target or whether they'd hit ground targets on Grand Cayman.

The answer was seconds away. They were probably loaded for ground attack not anti-ship Simon mentally calculated. They would have taken off before dawn to be here now but they would have taken off after *Bismarck* had opened fire but re-arming isn't speedy so if they are here now, they must be loaded for ground attack he decided. Bombs and rockets much better for us than stand-off missiles.

The two JF-17s broke clear of the shore and rocketed towards *Bismarck* and that was the moment that Simon had been waiting for.

Bismarck's exploding shells would have caused damage and civilian casualties if they'd fired while the enemy was still over George Town but now they had no restrictions. The three inch guns of the S1 turret as well as the AK630M2 lashed out at the incoming jets.

The sky in front of the leading low flying jet was pocked with exploding shells but on he came ruddering left and right. At a range of only one mile, the lead aircraft suddenly pitched upwards tossing a pair of bombs at the slow moving target, the pilot didn't live to see the results.

Simon watching from OPs immediately shouted full ahead and *Bismarck* suddenly rotated to starboard as the

Steerpods did the only thing they could still do, accelerating the ship's motion rapidly enough to cause people to hold on to something.

Almost at the moment of release, a 3 inch shell exploded immediately in front and the aircraft disintegrated in a spectacular flash as his remaining ordnance exploded.

Swerving to avoid the debris, the second aircraft was now off line for his attack and flashed by *Bismarck*'s stern only to be caught by the first shells from the newly resurrected portside aft AK630M2 turret.

The stream of heavy shells walked up one side shearing the starboard wing like nothing anyone had ever seen, the fatally damaged aircraft immediately began to rotate at high speed until it ran out of sky plunging into the sea about half a mile away and before the pilot could eject.

The two bombs lobbed from the first aircraft fell into the sea no more than forty yards from *Bismarck*'s stern, exploding with a jarring crash and a tower of dirty white water that drenched the upper decks but did no more than shake the men inside the ship. Shaw, Henzel and a bandaged Scouse Smith climbed shakily to their feet near the wreckage of the after radar antenna.

Shaw had told the OPs room that the gun mount was clear of wreckage literally just seconds before the plane had arrived, then Dettweiler had pushed the online button and it had immediately opened up with devastating effect on the second JF-17.

The three tired and slightly stunned men picked their way back to the now passive twin multi-barrelled guns and grinned at each other. Scouse Smith put his fingers to his lips and gently patted the still smoking barrels before turning away.

Jake thanked the heavens that the JFs were loaded for ground attack not anti-shipping. He supposed that with the destruction of *Bismarck* last evening, so say, the Haitians had had ground support in mind.

*

The bayonet thrust from behind scraped agonizingly along his left ribs. Kicking forward at his frontal assailant and twisting round to the right away from the damaged side, thereby drawing the bayonet owner behind him, forward, Andy swung his short bladed entrenching tool in a vicious arc behind. He felt the jar along his arm as it struck flesh and bone, the owner's agonized scream was just confirmation.

Without pausing to check his handiwork Andy instinctively continued the swing through, angling it down. The blade clanged off the barrel of a bayonet tipped assault rifle, deflecting the forward thrust off to the side, whilst his left arm swept up and put two shells from his Glock automatic into the chest of the shocked Haitian soldier.

Still rotating, his right boot came up and smashed into the face of the doubled over enemy on his left. And again without pausing, he launched himself to the right and rolled once. A shaft of agony speared through him as his weight pressed down onto his damaged side. Blinking aside the sudden tears he lurched into a crouch and quickly scanned around for the nearest danger.

There were just too few of them left to stop this determined assault. Now the survivors of the initial onslaught, outnumbered and tired, fought vicious hand to hand struggles up and down the length of the line.

Andy selected his next fight and raced half the dozen yards towards three struggling soldiers. Two were Haitian and the other was the young corporal that had helped him set up the grenade launcher. The Corporal squirmed and struggled with one of his attackers on the stream bed whilst the other manoeuvred around them shouting at his comrade, looking for a gap to slip his bayonet through.

Andy raised the Glock and pulled the trigger from a range of five feet. Nothing. The Haitian spun round to face him and Andy barely had time to swing the entrenching tool at the rifle as it fired. The shots sprayed the bank as Andy continued forward, still pushing the rifle off to his left.

Dropping the spade shaped tool and the Glock, he grabbed for the rifle and the Haitian's jacket collar. He pulled the surprised man toward him and using that momentum, butted hard into the man's face twice.

The bridge of the Haitian's nose disintegrated and he let loose a scream, dropping the rifle and spraying blood everywhere from his shattered nose.

Andy swept the soldier's legs away with his left foot and grabbing the rifle, shoved the bayonet into its former owner's gut, wrenching upwards as he did so. Two steps forward and the heavy butt smashed down onto the neck of the second Haitian soldier. The Corporal rolled the unconscious man off him, climbed to his feet, put two rounds from his Glock into the attacker and snatching up his machine pistol joined Andy.

Andy noticed more Haitians running across the open ground towards the rough line and snapping a new magazine into the AK, he began to fire short bursts into them, the Corporal joined him and they slowly, tiredly scuttled towards the nearest struggling men.

They both knew it was hopeless, there wouldn't be enough MPP left to form another line even if they could extricate themselves from this close quarter fighting.

Still they persisted, Andy taking a bullet in his upper arm and the corporal a bayonet through the leg. They fought themselves to a standstill and panting heavily leaned against the road embankment for a second before launching themselves into the next fight.

Andy thought he was hearing things, again. Rising above the noise of sporadic shooting and the screams of desperate and dying men, a bugle sounded assembly.

The pure high notes impelled an urgency into those that heard, and almost everyone in the rough line friend and foe turned towards the sound.

Never as long as he lived would Andy Evans forget the sight and sound that greeted him. Rising from a fold in the ground some forty yards behind the MPP line was a formed line of soldiers.

The bugle now sounded the charge and screaming the strange sounding words 'Jaya Mahakali, Ayo Gorkhali', the newcomers charged. Andy found out later it means 'Glory to Great Kali, the Gorkhas are coming' but he didn't care at the time. Over and over at the tops of their voices the newcomers screamed their war cry as one mass they launched themselves toward the road embankment where Andy and the remaining MPP fought their losing battle.

About twenty yards out from them there was another sharp bugle command and alternate Gurkhas drew their famous Kukri knives, slinging their rifles behind them.

Screaming with manic glee, they launched themselves into the melee in the body strewn culvert.

The others ran on shooting and bayonetting as they went and took up firing positions against the embankment. The sight of the blades glinting as they rose and fell and the screams from the defile along with the carefully directed fire was enough to stop the enemy reinforcements in their tracks.

They turned and ran for cover. With a whoop of delight the rest of the fearsome little men from Nepal rose and began pursuit, firing their SA80s in short bursts on the run.

That was enough. Whatever resistance was left in the remaining Haitians, collapsed at that moment and the retreat turned into a rout.

Andy lay back against the bank, closed his eyes and smiled. Tears of relief made runnels through the grime on his cheeks and the morning sun gently warmed his face as it finally broke through the clouds. He luxuriated in the feeling, he hadn't thought he'd live to enjoy it again.

A polite cough, and a Michael Caine style voice above him.

"Err, are you in charge here old man?" Andy opened one eye, the smile still on his face. He looked up at a young man with wavy blond hair and Captain's pips just discernible at the front of his jungle fatigues.

Next to him stood an unsmiling older man, a Gurkha officer also wearing a Captain's pips. Andy opened his other eye and sat up wincing as his stiffening ribs and throbbing arm let him know he was still very much alive. He answered the young man.

"Yes I suppose I am." He reached out his hand.

"Andy Evans, late of her majesty's Royal Marines, now absolutely buggered and hurting."

The young man took the proffered hand, smiled again and pointed to his companion.

"This is Captain Ritu Limbu and I'm Captain David Jeffreys, both of the First Battalion Queen's own Gurkha Rifles. Pleased to meet you."

"Not as pleased as we poor buggers are son."

Andy held up his hand again, this time for a lift and groaned his way upright.

"Err, sorry about the dramatic bugle bit," said Captain Jeffreys. "but the men wanted to do it properly one last time."

Andy coughed and grimaced with pain.

"What do you mean one last time?"

"Aah the rumour mill is strongly suggesting that our lords and masters will finally disband the Gurkha brigade soon old son and Captain Limbu wanted, you know, to do the bizz with the Kukri charge, to charge to glory and all that, one last time."

Andy felt like laughing, he had no high ideas about death and glory in battle, but looking at the grim faced Gurkha Captain he knew it wasn't amateur dramatics the man had indulged in, it was in memory of the more than a century and a half of service the Gurkhas had given Britain and by proxy, Nepal.

He supposed it was their way of announcing that they still had what it takes. Andy wiped the smile out of his mind, you had to respect that kind of dedication and bravery, so he just said.

"Bloody pleased to meet you too Captain Limbu. Would you be so kind as to point this decrepit old 'Bootneck' to towards your company medic as I appear to be leaking a lot at the moment." He held up his hand covered in fresh blood.

"...and my friend here," he pointed to the Corporal "looks like he's leaking too." He sighed. "Then I have to check on my men, those that are left that is."

Bob McKeith shoved the throttle to idle, pulled back on the stick then moved it left bringing the nose of his Typhoon up and left wing down beginning a roll and suddenly slowing his passage through the sky. He swivelled his head to the left looking back and down as far as he could. The bucking gyrations of his damaged fighter made it difficult to focus on his assailant.

There he was, the bastard. Coming up fast, overshooting his easy kill, the overconfident son of a bitch. He shoved the stick forward and completed the roll to inversion and rammed the throttle to full military. Alarms in the cockpit. Noises telling him he hadn't long. The Mig 29 shot past under his starboard wing already beginning to bank right.

Parts of seconds stretching now as he struggled to lead the fast moving Mig with his gunsight pipper. There, you bastard. Slight pressure on the tit. A stream of bright tracer arcing out, 27mm cannon shells hosing through the sky and him, Mr Cocky bastard, flying right into it. Bits flying off.

One of the vertical stabilizers sheared away, the blue grey Mig spinning down and out of sight. Well me old son, just one more and we can go home, he said to himself scanning the sky, now where is he? Talk to me fat controller, then an image intruding. A Thomas the Tank engine book and his son asking why the controller was fat. Sort this bugger he said to himself and you can read it to him again, all you've got to do is get this crate of broken bits down in one piece.

The near miss from the R-73M air to air missile had damaged him but he didn't know how much. He eased the plane into level flight, called up Dave Mcgee and then remembered he wasn't there anymore, would never be again. He spoke to the controller and got a 'stand down'. Where was the last one then? He mentally shrugged and then began some very serious checking, cold sweat drying on his face as he concentrated and slowly turned back towards Grand Cayman gently descending as he did so.

07:15 Sunday 27th May 2018
Mig 29K FULCRUM, Co-Flight Leader of
Haitian Air Unit

Major Nikita Suvlov ex-Ukrainian Air Force now professional trainer to any third world air force who bought the stuff he could fly, which was how he saw himself, banked away from his rash and overconfident wingman. The man was the senior of the four Haitians to survive the surprise attack by the Typhoons.

He didn't like this situation at all. His instincts told him that they should break off contact and get out. His wingman ignored him and turned to engage the Typhoon flight coming up fast.

Then the fool had fallen to the short range in-the-face heat seeker that one of the two Typhoons had launched. The closure rate was incredible. Another Haitian had managed to get a kill all right, but ramming wasn't the best way as Suvlov watched him and his opponent fall in a fiery ball. He called to the last Haitian and told him to break off but the man ignored him and continued to pursue the damaged Typhoon fighter with the RAF markings. No doubt he wishes to claim a kill for himself, Suvlov snorted, and of course there'd be no mention of his Suvlov's own R73-M missile, the one that originally damaged the Typhoon which even now was limping south.

So what, he told himself, he didn't need the promotion points. His mind spun back a few minutes reliving the sudden commotion in the clear skies. What had gone wrong?

Where the fuck had those Typhoons come from? His instinct and logic told him that where there was one pair of RAF Typhoons in a war zone then there was likely to be at least another pair.

That was why he was still scanning the sky all around as he flew steadily north. 'Ignoring your instinct in the sky is like flying around in a rather expensive coffin', one of his old instructors, a veteran of the 73' Arab Israeli war had said.

Well he should have stayed on the ground. He hadn't liked the smell of this operation from the start and had only agreed to go along with it reluctantly and the big bonus had something to do with it, he confessed to himself wryly.

No airborne early warning aircraft, was his first objection.

Their answer had been that it was unnecessary because there were no hostile aircraft. Suppose they tell that to the widows of the pilots they've lost now, he grunted into his oxygen mask.

It was evident to him that one of the radars that was still busily keeping his radar warning receiver glowing, must be an E3 Sentry, given the RAF fighters and their perfect ambush.

Trust your own instincts, what a joke. There was no way they could have known what they were flying into, just that sudden shrill alarm in his cockpit as the missile radar had illuminated them before impact.

Thank God for good reflexes. As it sounded he'd shouted 'break', beginning an immediate steep down corkscrew left and punching his flare and chaff dispenser button.

History now. He noticed that he was still flying north instead of turning east for Haiti. Instinct again? Now he came to think about it, he wasn't sure of the reception he'd get back in Haiti, termination of contract might well be the least of his worries.

He was, however, absolutely certain of the reception he'd get if he turned up in Havana with a nearly new Mig 29K, the least they'd do would be to put him on the next plane to Kiev. Home.

*

Captain Pulon knew he didn't have a home to go back to now. He just sat in his command chair as his flagship and his future slowly sank. The sudden aerial dog-fight far to the east had been his first real indicator that the E3 Sentry was not alone.

The interception of his inbound air support had confirmed that there was now another major player in the area. With the losses sustained up until then he could have survived, would have even prospered if the army had been successful. Not now.

The last message from the northern group had been the beginning of the end for him. The 'idiot' Captain of the destroyer only just had time to let him know that his ship was about to be attacked by the warship he'd fired at earlier, then no further contact.

Nothing. Then came the air strike. The sudden arrival of the missiles, had been a body blow. He felt like a blind boxer groping in the dark, being hit from all directions.

With nothing to do but watch his ships defend themselves as best they could, he observed the whole thing with a kind of clinical detachment. Each of his remaining ships had been hit by at least one anti-ship missile and in some cases like his own ship, two.

There was nothing but debris to mark their passing now. His own ship and the frigate nearby had received hits and it and the *Jeremie* to the south had sunk now, leaving his vessel the only one in sight with smoke marking the last known location of the remaining Type 37 corvette.

He sat in the deserted OPs room, lit only by emergency lights, the water was lapping around his calves and the list to port was becoming acute. But he made no move to escape.

The news from ashore was every bit as bad and the Major General commanding, lucky to have been on the surviving LSTs, had been killed leading a final attack which had failed apparently when British troops had appeared. Presumably from the air transports they'd detected. The senior surviving officer was pulling back to the landing ships. He wondered if the young man had considered what his thanks will be for saving a part of the force. The attack on Little Cayman was still progressing but resistance had now been encountered.

07:35 Sunday 27th May 2018
Little Cayman, the last stand

After the ambush on the north road the advancing troops had unsurprisingly become wary. The decks of the remaining armoured vehicles had emptied and the troops advanced slowly, checking the ground and fanning out as much as was possible on either side of the roads. Every few minutes or so the waiting ambushers could hear a couple of short bursts of heavy machine gun fire as the cautious Haitians, now feeling exposed, advanced along both coast roads.

Buck watched them remotely from his command bunker and decided they were green. If he'd been in command, the vehicles would have taken up overwatch positions with their 30mm auto canons and an infantry squad would have advanced fanning out into the surrounding bush as well as along what passed for a beach at this point. They'd clear a stretch then move up, always covering the infantry squad with the heavy weapons.

He'd also have someone looking carefully at the road for any signs of disturbance.

Still, near Tarpon Lake, checking the road would have been a waste of time because the IEDs weren't in it. Right at the point the road turned sharply left, just on the bend, a shell was embedded at ground level pointing back down the road; it was set for instantaneous detonation when triggered, the base was backed on to a substantial rock to prevent it flying backwards when it fired. A second and third shell were embedded into the low bank on the landward side of the corner, one on each arm of the road both pointing out to sea and these too were instantaneous fused.

He kept his ambush team up to date as the Haitian unit slowly approached the corner. At that moment he got an alert from the Giraffe radar. Clever stuff this, he'd thought as the technicians had walked him through what the land based mobile radar unit could do. The system on *Bismarck* was basically the same but had clearly a different operations mode.

This one was on a wheeled vehicle for a start. They had carefully cleared a track for it from part way up Weary Hill heading west for about 500 yards. The work had involved no one but those who worked for König and was a closely guarded secret even then. A static radar would be destroyed very quickly so they had a very slightly rippled concrete track built in order that the radar could activate for a second or two at most, then scoot rapidly a random distance down the track before activating again a minute or so later. So it couldn't be spotted by overflight it was 'cammed up' to look like the surrounding forests.

The track wasn't a straight line either. There were little 'bud' points and zig zags to make its next appearance as unpredictable as possible. The system itself got the 'Giraffe' name from the way the radar deployed. The antenna was on an extending arm with an elbow half way along, like the platforms that clean lights and other elevated places. To deploy, the camouflaged head need only move high enough to clear the surrounding tree canopy, it then activated briefly with a couple of full sweeps taking about a second, then dropped quickly and the vehicle sped off to its next location before repeating the process.

The alert that had come in was telling him that one of the ships was now in range of the Dardo system on the harbour wall, and did he want to engage? He clicked on 'No' and went back to monitoring the upcoming ambush on the southern side. He should have noted he berated himself later, that the contact the Giraffe picked up, was heading towards the area of this first southern ambush position. He should have also noted that it was a *Luda* D class destroyer as identified by the system and these had retained their four big 130mm gun armament, the same that *Bismarck* used herself.

Much consternation was evident in the Haitian unit that approached the corner. They stopped fifty yards short and maps were produced. Andy felt a little sorry for them as they scanned inland at this point and could only see a small vertical ledge caused by the original construction of the road, backed by trees or mangrove pools of unknown depth and no vehicular access at all without risking damage or getting bogged down if they tried to push through. Contrary to popular belief light armoured vehicles avoided head butting trees and swimming if they could.

Clearly a consensus had been reached and the vehicles moved slowly toward the corner with a couple of soldiers carefully sweeping the road ahead, one with a mine detector, the other just looking, presumably for disturbed earth thought Buck. The two on the ground disappeared around the corner and came into Buck's view again as they started east. He gave another sitrep to the four man ambush party as the first BTR80 nosed around the corner into view and stopped while the machine gun waved side to side.

After fifty yards or so the trees briefly gave way to brackish mangrove pools before returning once more to forest and the Officer in the lead BTR waved forward four more soldiers who started heading toward the mangroves.

The second BTR nudged forward close behind the lead and its gunner trained aft to cover the rear of the group. The remaining dismounted troops took up position against the small cliff wall and shot worried glances over the top.

The Officer pointed up the road and the lead BTR let loose a burst at a promising hideaway fifty yards further along. Unfortunately it was actually a hideaway and the heavy bullets smashed into and through the concealed tree trunk partly dug into the ground. The two ambushers hiding behind it in shallow scrapes cursed into their mikes and Rolf Ungar the team leader holding the three labelled remote detonators and inland of the mangrove pools, pressed the first button to rescue half his team.

It was a shade too soon. Another half metre closer to the rock and it would have been perfect, but even so the 130mm shell exploded with devastating effect. The BTR80 was lifted and thrown first on its backend and then when it fell back forward, it landed awkward and slowly tilted right. As it encountered the slight down camber gravity took over and the tilt became severe. It then rolled right over and on to the narrow beach crushing the officer who'd been leaning out of the turret hatch and the gunner too.

Men began firing in all directions and the second BTR rolled forward a few feet in order to add its heavy weapon to the pandemonium. An officer at the rear of the company could be seen shouting into the radio on the back of one of his men while gesticulating wildly. Buck wondered whether this was time to pull back. The IEDs could be removed safely later, but despite all his experience he hesitated. He wasn't the commander on the ground.

This was when things started to unravel for the defenders. As Rolf lay flat, heavy bullets parted the air above with a sound like supersonic cloth tearing. He was waiting for the best possible moment to trigger the two remaining IEDs. Unknown to him the *Luda* that had passed the harbour wall a few minutes earlier was now in the perfect position to flay the area ahead of the stalled advance.

This it commenced doing with apparent relish as all four of its main guns and three of its lighter 37mm auto-cannon joined in, creating a deluge of high explosive along the line of advance and twenty yards or more inland.

The two men pinned by the machine gun fire from ahead were the first to be hit, in fact when Rolf looked quickly over the lip of his cover he could see only a smoking crater where they'd been. Fuck it, he thought as he quickly got flat again.

"Bravo One this is Two One. Two Three and Two Four are down. Am under intense naval gunfire. As soon as it lifts we're out of here over."

Buck listened, hearing the scream of incoming along with explosions in the background and a rash of different emotions played across his face. My fault he decided.

"Two One roger. Get out of there as soon as you can. Out"

Even through the thick walls of his command bunker he could hear the intense bombardment and the mute but continuous rumble of the ship firing in the distance.

"Four One did you copy my last? Out"

"Roger Bravo One. We'll be watching for Two One and Two Two. Four One out"

Another alert ping on the radar had him look round this time and check the read out. A vessel approaching the north harbour wall but weaving all over.

He switched to one of the cameras monitoring the harbour and moved it to pick up the incoming vessel. Small, fast ship. Zig zagging all over, range two miles and closing fast. A quick check of the silhouette sheet that Andy Evans had supplied showed it was a Type 37 corvette.

It must be under attack he deduced, but what from? Even as his mind arrived at the correct conclusion, *Dorsetshire*'s last harpoon missile popped up in its terminal phase. As he watched through the camera one of the twin 37mm automatic mounts got a lucky hit just as it began to pop up and the Harpoon disintegrated in an impressive yellow ball of flame. The corvette stopped its zig zagging and resumed its course which looked as if it was to join the destroyer causing havoc off the southern ambush site.

No fucking way.

He reached over and grabbed the controller for the north wall AK630M2.

He recalled the instructions he'd been given and switched it to automatic, quarter second bursts designating the image of the corvette. He paused it while he did the same for the Dardo 40mm auto canon.

Then when both were ready he selected commence and sat back to watch.

The barrels of the AK630 mount which looked like a lump of rock, suddenly elevated and the turret trained rapidly onto the corvette's heading. Through the viewer he could see a light stream of smoke leave the barrels but of course could not hear the sheet ripping sound as it fired quarter second bursts of thirty or so rounds, correcting aim all the time using its TV monitor to aim. At the same time the Dardo turret came to life and its barrels suddenly lurched upwards and the turret spun to train on its target.

With twin jets of flame the Dardo joined in.

Andy switched view to the ship and saw pieces being chewed off it by the heavy 30mm bullets as they marched up and down the starboard side of the craft. Then the

40mm Dardo shells started to arrive and the corvette was in real trouble straight away. Its two twin 37mm mounts began to train towards the source of the incoming fire and the bow gun actually got a few shots off before either the Dardo or the AK630 found its missile bins.

It simply disintegrated. A massive flash and a bang heard miles away and there was nothing left to shoot. Both gun mounts stopped firing and the units tracked back and forth with the barrels rising and falling slightly as they sought out their target. Then they reset. The turrets turned to their default position and the barrels lowered swiftly out of sight. Blink and they were gone, as was the corvette and quite a few men thought Buck. Shit, that was something else, poor buggers. At least it was quick.

He dragged his gaze and his mind back to the three remaining intact ambush parties.

Four One the leader of group four, otherwise known as Tufty Pullen was as unlikely a special forces soldier as you could find. From a visual perspective he was quite small, only five foot eight. Yes he was quite stocky but not massively so. He had a non-descript sort of face that someone would have difficulty recalling the detail of five minutes later, even my wife he'd once joked. But he was perfect for covert OPs and as tough as they came.

Tufty was pretty sure the last 'stonk' from the destroyer had got his mate Rolf, but there was no way he was going to go for a shufty. No answer on the net for three call attempts now. The naval guns had stopped for the moment but he could hear sporadic bursts from AKs and the thump, thump of a 30mm auto-cannon as the enemy company began advancing again just two hundred yards away from them now.

Rolf knew the risks and there wasn't the time left to do a covert approach and recce before the bad lads arrived on scene Tufty reckoned. He needn't call it in because Buck would be monitoring the net all the time. Shit happens, he decided and settled down to wait, reviewing again his own particular ambush and its retreat routes. The Haitians would have a three kilometre advance before the next ambush, plenty of time to get tired and start to relax.

The end of the struggle for Little Cayman was heralded by the sudden disintegration of the destroyer which had been plodding up and down the north coast dropping shells into likely ambush points. Buck Taylor had been monitoring its progress and was just about to pass out a warning to the ambush teams, as it turned once again to pass up along the Haitian line of advance.

He had tapped the transmit button on his earpiece ready to send when a massive explosion suddenly blotted out his view of the ship. All the ambush teams heard was Buck's.

"What the fuck? Someone's just malletted the destroyer in the north"

He panned the camera back and forth where he'd last seen the destroyer and all that could be seen was a boiling cloud of smoke from which debris rained into the sea. Slowly the bows of a ship poked through the thick black smoke, clearly listing heavily and swinging around. He tapped his earpiece once more to transmit again.

"Listen up everybody. It seems like we've still got allies out there somewhere, either that or God's pissed off with the Haitians. Someone's just taken out another chunk of Haitian naval support."

He was cut off as Jan Helders suddenly spoke.

"Buck it's Jan, they're pulling back. We're down by Sparrowhawk Hill and we can see the burning ship too and so can they. I reckon they've had enough, they're all trotting back down the road now, leaving gear everywhere; it's not organized they're just legging it."

Another voice cut in.

"Buck it's Piet Viermark, down on the south road. The last BTR has just turned round and is heading back West."

Buck made a decision. "OK. Everyone listen up. I don't know what the fuck is going on, but I'm going to find out, I want everyone to stay put except Andy and Arkady. Listening you two?"

"Listening." Came the twin reply.

"OK. I want you two to work your way towards Anchorage Bay and then let us know what's going down. OK?"

"No problem Buck." Andy Talbot answered. "We're on our way now."

Buck Taylor sat back in his swivel chair and thought for a moment. Best get in touch with *Bismarck*, he decided, I'm pretty sure they'd want to know the good news.

09:15 Sunday 27th May 2018
Bismarck alongside George Town, Grand Cayman

Most of them were too weary to acknowledge the cheers from the crowds lining the jetty. They were genuine too, it wasn't necessary to 'big up' *Bismarck*'s part in the Haitian defeat, it was crucial. Not just the ships sunk and battered but the fact that 60% of the men and equipment never got ashore.

The dog-tired sailors sent lines through the air towards willing hands and the battle scarred ship limped on one Steerpod the last few yards before tying up alongside. A frantic blaring of horns and police sirens heralded the arrival of the Prime Minister's car and entourage on the jetty. Reiner stood on the splintered, blackened quarterdeck to receive the guests.

Laid out in a row beside turret Dora were the body bagged remains of *Bismarck*'s four dead, ready and waiting to be taken ashore for refrigeration until their next of kin decided on burial details. One of the MPP officers who'd served as ammunition handlers, now proudly stood guard over them in full uniform; proud because he was the one chosen to pay that final respect. Ambulances already on the jetty were taking away stretcher borne wounded, some groaning in deep pain others stoically quiet and calm and in some distant place. Some of the casualties were for local treatment and some for onward medevac flights to the States.

McTeal and Roche both solemnly turned towards the dead and stood head bowed for a minute of respect. They were both thinking, but unable to say, that it could have been worse, so much worse. If they were wondering where Jake was, neither expressed it nor looked discomfited by his absence.

Since the final shots had been fired Reiner explained, Jake had sat in the bridge chair staring forward at the rising pall of smoke that rose above Grand Cayman as they closed with the island, now under power from the repaired starboard Steerpod.

He had given only monosyllabic replies to reports or attempts at conversation. He'd clearly been lost in a private torment which constantly revolved around the mayhem his ship had caused and the losses suffered themselves.

Reiner thought he'd been in between a rock and a hard place. At the end of the day, he decided, Jake was still short of one wife and through the bravery of his own men, had very probably condemned her to death.

A discrete cough broke into Jake's misery and he turned, coming face to face with Sandiford Roche and Andrew McTeal.

"Sorry Prime Minister, I should have met you at the...."

"Never mind Jake, I'm still able to climb a gangway unaided and you have every reason to spare the ceremonies." McTeal replied sadly, recalling the anonymous almost de-humanised corpses in their bags.

McTeal paused a second, unsure whether to change the subject and apparently dismiss the dead so lightly.

"Jake, are you getting all the help you need with your wounded? Do you need any more? We're a bit stretched, I gather, but I'm sure I could rustle up some extra assistance if it's needed."

Jake suddenly realized that McTeal had a great deal more on his mind than just *Bismarck*'s problems.

"Thank you Andrew but we should be OK for now, I gather our doctor wants three of them transferred to the hospital, he's busy organizing a company medical evacuation flight now for the others who are stable but need further treatment."

"What's the state of play here?" He corrected himself angrily. "What's our status here on the island?" McTeal took a deep breath and looked over towards the north of the island.

"They landed at Boatswain's Point and began advancing down towards here. It was apparently looking quite bleak at one point; we lost a hundred and five officers of the MPP all told with thirty five wounded out of the two hundred that took the brunt of the attack." Jake looked even more pained, they hadn't got the last two assault ships and look at what that caused.

McTeal continued not seeing Jake's pain.

"Oh by the way, your Mr Evans took command after our own commander was killed. Did a splendid job as I understand it, but picked up several wounds during the fighting. Not serious I'm told." He added quickly as Jake made to rise.

McTeal drew another deep breath before continuing.

"As I said it was looking quite bleak, then the British arrived with a company of Gurkha soldiers from Belize, God bless them. They got stuck in quickly, and according to my sources, in the nick of time, and suddenly the Haitians had had enough. Last I heard was that they were being allowed to re-embark on their transports, they lost many killed and so did we unfortunately."

Their conversation was interrupted by the scream of powerful jets as an RAF Typhoon turned in on its final approach to the runway, the survivor of the anti-shipping strike Reiner thought, the other remaining aircraft had landed earlier with a thin wisp of smoke trailing from its fuselage.

McTeal frowned at the sight and when the noise level had dropped again, continued.

"The British Prime Minister rang me just after the soldiers arrived, she apologized for the delay etcetera. I didn't care Jake, I just knew then that all the sacrifices weren't in vain."

He saw Jake stiffen slightly and turn away.

"Damn. I'm so sorry Jake. That was really insensitive of me, I hadn't forgotten about Sophie and your men. I'm just so pleased that Farache failed and it's largely due to you and your brave men."

McTeal turned to face forward and studied the damage visible along the length of the ship.

"It looks like you've suffered a terrible battering, what will you do now?" Up until that point Jake hadn't really thought past the next moment but there was only one answer he could give.

"I was hoping to get some help out to Little Cayman from the Gurkhas and one of those Hercules transports that dropped in but it seems the Haitians have packed up and are re-embarking their troopship. It's over it seems, they have three dead and one badly wounded needing evacuation to Cayman Brac."

McTeal nodded to Roche who stepped away and took out his phone.

"Anyway to answer your question, we shall be leaving here tomorrow morning at about this time if I can swing it. By then all the weapons we can repair locally will be fixed. We will sail to Haiti and I will have my wife returned to me." He paused and faced McTeal.

"Otherwise General Farache will quickly realize that today's losses are just the beginning of his misery." He finished grimly.

McTeal didn't argue, and he knew that Jake's commitment to defend these islands had perhaps cost him his wife. He had no illusions about the sentence that would be passed by a vengeful Farache on Mrs Sophia König once she was re-captured, if she was re-captured, he corrected himself guiltily.

He also knew the sentence that Jonathan Henry König would pass on General Farache if that event came to pass. You didn't mess lightly with people like Jake, he never made promises he didn't keep. He would use the law where he could, but as McTeal knew, where the law didn't provide an answer, Jake would make his own and the ship he stood on was a clear example of that.

McTeal faced Jake again and stuck his hand out.

"Anything you need Jake, anything. Just ask and Sandy here will see that you get it, but now we'll leave you to get on. As you'd expect I have some stuff to sort with the Americans, the UN and the Association of Caribbean States, otherwise I'd be personally looking after things for you and your men."

Jake retained the grip on McTeal's hand.

"Just one thing Andrew. I want one of the prisoners we brought back from the battle of the 24th. I want Lieutenant Francois Carcin please."

McTeal was truly puzzled, Roche however, was not.

"Prime Minister, the Lieutenant is the nephew of General Farache, I believe Mr König wishes to effect a private exchange of prisoners with Haiti."

Roche smiled broadly and Jake chuckled, a smile breaking out for the first time since the battle's end.

"I didn't really expect anything to slip by you Sandy." He faced McTeal. "Is that OK Andrew? I have to have some kind of leverage otherwise the bastard will just kill them."

"Sandy will see to it Jake and just let me know if there's anything else."

Jake and Reiner escorted them off the ship and went below to the nearly normal wardroom. The deck coverings and instruments had all been cleared away and the lightly wounded who were staying were in their own cabins being spoiled by two volunteers from the local Red Cross one of whom reminded Jake of the old lady who was in the Tom & Jerry cartoons decades ago, she even sounded like her.

They grabbed a coffee and sat down opposite each other on the big comfortable Balmoral chairs. 'Granny' Smith appeared from nowhere wearing a frown and a large sticking plaster on his forehead.

"Hello 'Granny'. I didn't realize you'd been injured? Jake noted. "Doc Crib didn't mention you in his casualty report." Jake raised a querying eyebrow waiting for an explanation.

"No Sir," said the gangly steward, "I don't suppose he would Sir, since I only did it twenty minutes ago. Is there anything you'd like Sirs." He said, stiffly formal.

"Just an explanation of your injury Granny please, I hope it's been logged in the ship's accident book."

Said Jake, sensing something funny.

Granny groaned audibly, at this bloody rate he'd have to get the explanation printed on a card. This was the fifth time he'd explained what had happened.

"Well Sir, I went to the upperdeck, just for some fresh air like." Reiner broke in.

"You mean you went to have a goof at all the damage." Granny ignored his Captain frowning even more.

"Like I said Sir, I went up for a bit of freshers and I was walking along the starboard side next to the forward 3 inchers, when all of a sudden I gets hit in the head with it and down I goes, blood and bits everywhere there was."

Jake interrupted.

"Slow down Granny, I missed something there I think. What hit you in the head?"

"I already told you Sir. The bloody 3 inchers did it didn't they. Mr Kopf was testing them y'see and the Tannoy on that side o' the deck is kaput y'see so no warning. I hears something and starts to turn then round they comes like a bloody great baseball bat and smack! I was wearing the starboard barrel Sir."

Jake couldn't stop laughing, every time he visualized what Granny had described he burst out afresh and so did Reiner. They sat there laughing like children, tears running down their faces as a disgruntled and muttering Granny exited the wardroom into his little pantry. Finally they quietened.

"I'd better go see Scotty and have a chat Reiner to see if he needs anything flown in or whatever, we may not be able to move as soon as I hope and I expect you'll be wanting to get busy as well, there's a thousand and one things to do before we're fit to sail."

Reiner stood up to leave but hesitated.

"It was a hell of a coincidence Jake wasn't it? All those dates and times, even the steering jamming was what happened all those years ago. Makes you wonder eh?"

Jake swirled the coffee grounds in the bottom of his cup before replying.

"It frightened me witless Reiner." Then he looked up smiling. "But couldn't you have waited for the battle to finish before you told me?"

Jon Roby sat in the armchair of his cabin and contemplated the report in his lap, it was just a first draft but already he found himself creating sentences in a defensive manner. Nothing official had happened yet, but he knew it would.

He had just closed the door on Berry Reeves, a good man that, it appeared that John Hayden, his First Lieutenant, was already saying that Roby had overstepped his mark. Officers like Hayden always seemed to prosper and often at someone else's expense, but Reeves, as the Advanced Warfare Officer, however, did not agree with him.

According to Reeves' reading of the situation, the timing of the strike orders was appropriate tactically and he would state so in his report and our range from Grand Cayman was irrelevant since the attack came from the Little Cayman area.

The problem was that if *Dorsetshire* had been where it should have, then he, Jon Roby, would not have been in the position of making 'the correct tactical judgement'.

That's how MOD would see it anyway. He sighed and dumped the draft on his desk. He'd just returned from a visit to Grand Cayman in the ship's helicopter, and he could clearly see *Bismarck* in his mind's eye, leaning against the harbour wall like an old man needing a prop whilst they fitted a patch at the stern.

His first duty had been to visit the Prime Minister in the company of a rather bewildered British Consul. The man had known nothing of his government's intentions and yet there he was accepting the grateful thanks of the Prime Minister on behalf of his people.

Mr McTeal of course knew nothing of how Roby had exceeded his orders, damn it! He swore at his memory, I did not exceed them. I merely carried out what I presumed were the intentions of Her Majesty's government.

God, he thought, that sounds very much like a courts martial defence. After the rather awkward meeting was over, Roby had dashed down to the harbour.

The crowds were still there ogling the ship he'd come to see. Finally managing to push, plead and elbow himself through, he approached the midships gangway and just stood and stared.

Christ, he'd thought, it looks like someone's been at it with a wrecking ball. Smoke charred, splintered decking everywhere and the wetted down post-fire smell pungent in the warm air. His meeting with Jake had been a curious mixture of sadness at the loss of life on both sides coupled with mutual satisfaction at the outcome, then tempered with gloom over Sophie's prospects of survival.

Roby had left Jake with the promise of help from *Dorsetshire's* engineers and technical staff. He picked up the sheaf of signals that had come in since the action that morning. He really had put the cat amongst the pigeons when he'd sent the signal that informed MOD of the attacks he'd authorized. He'd just got that one off when they replied to his earlier notification of 'weapons free', the service jargon for no restrictions on firing. The RS had delayed the delivery of that until after the action started. Roby knew he had an old shipmate on *Bismarck* but said nothing since the signal sic had not been 'Flash' anyway. He expected someone to get their backside roasted in the UK Comcen for that.

Now where was it? He scrabbled through the stack and found the sheet he wanted. '...actions must be limited to self-defence. You are not, repeat, not authorized to conduct any offensive operations against Haitian surface, ground or air forces. Maintain 50 mile minimum range to islands'. The rest of it was drivel. That paragraph would be enough to condemn him in their eyes anyway.

He picked up another stack of papers. Press reaction this one, culled from the internet and representatives of the press corps on the islands, and passed to him by the Mr McTeal's office this morning.

On the face of it he had come through as a hero, arriving in the nick of time. Odd when you thought about it really, since seventy seven years ago at this time the last *Dorsetshire* was probably fishing the original *Bismarck*'s survivors out of the water having just torpedoed and sank it.

Jake's press was even more heroic, phrases from the British and American press like- '...selflessly threw themselves into battle against enormous odds...' '...ranks with the 300 Spartans and Rorke's Drift...' and headlines screaming, 'Thunder at Dawn - Naval battle in the Caribbean' from the Telegraph or 'Caymans 1 - Haiti 0' or 'Bish, Bash, Bosh, Pocket Battleship cleans up again' from the tabloids, and the Times' staid 'Invasion Halted by New Merchant Protector Warship and Gurkha steel.'

Roby smiled as he read some of the accounts, most of them were pure speculation married to the few known facts, situation normal. At least his own censuring would be private because they couldn't publicly condemn a winner, could they?

He threw them all back on the desk. Just one thing left to do. Just one little thing for Jake. Something that he knew would condemn him in MOD's eyes even if the rest didn't. To help at all, he had to remain COMCENTAMCARIB for the next two or three days.

Winston once more wiped the sweat from his face and pressed his eye back to the Dragunov's sniper scope. Shit! No doubt about it, they were being followed.

He felt a weary resignation and a curious kind of futility swamping his mind. The thing they'd strived most to avoid the last three days had happened. Somehow they'd been spotted, not exactly pinpointed, but someone knew they were in the area. Those men down there were following their trail, no doubt about it.

How had they been sussed? They'd not spoken to, nor met with anyone at all during their trek. He shifted the scope slightly and focussed on one of the pursuers. He was different to the others, he wore a uniform designed for jungle work and kept separate from the blue uniformed paramilitary security police. This was the man that was tracking them he decided.

Winston speculated that he was one of the soldiers from the units along the Dominican-Haiti border, experienced in tracking insurgents through rough terrain. If that was the case then their options had narrowed considerably. He turned slowly and carefully to look back at his companions. Tetsunari looked as he always did, a figure of stone carved from the hardest granite. Old Marc was OK. He'd had a rough life until the past three years with Louis and Francesca, but he hadn't gone soft.

Sophie however had severe problems with her feet. It wasn't that she was unfit in the traditional sense, she ran several miles a day and played squash twice weekly to a high standard, it was just that she wasn't hardened. Her feet were used to comfortable trainers certainly not palm leaves folded and woven and tied on. He turned back to observe their pursuers and considered his options and the terrain. At least it had stopped raining for now and steam rose from the ground like fog but only thigh deep. Might slow them a bit, thought Winston.

At the moment the escapees were contouring along the middle slopes of a mountain, just inside the poorly defined treeline. Truth be told there wasn't much of a treeline at all, clumps of bamboo and the odd old tree was all that remained of the once lush tropical rain forest. Old Marc had told them of the perennial deforestation of his country, some by logging but others by ordinary people. He'd shrugged and asked what else the poor were to burn for cooking fires or for smoking fish?

Sophie had added that one of the key projects she had wanted to get going here was re-forestation; you only had to look next door at Dominican Republic to see the difference it made if you had a sensible management policy.

The ground they were moving over was fairly even with stony scree breaking through and patches of bare ochre coloured earth which Mark explained were usually caused by rains washing everything down the hillsides, including anything that was growing. Shallow rooted knee-high grass covered the rest.

What trees there were mainly looked young and Mark said most were mangoes planted the year before and pointed to the nearly covered sunken bamboo barrier in front of the tree to stop the soil erosion and the stones at the trunk's base.

Winston looked further ahead, lots of the hillsides appeared bare; soon they'd have to move just at night if they wished to avoid detection. Their pursuers were slightly lower down and about a mile and a half away. Choices. There wasn't much hope of throwing an experienced tracker off their trail for very long, the best they could hope for would be to decoy him occasionally.

The simple fact was, it was more than likely that they'd be overtaken and killed before they reached the coast behind the next ridge, about ten miles away according to Marc.

At present their tracker, unless he was really good, could not be certain that he was following the correct people. Boot prints might suggest it but they hadn't been sighted yet he thought.

If they began decoy tactics he would know for sure after the first decoy he spotted or fell for. There was another option available to them, the direct one. Given Sophie's slow rate of advance he was certain they'd be caught before nightfall.

What if he took out the tracker? What if he took out the tracker from above and the side? The remaining searchers would be unable to pinpoint them and might possibly be lured higher up the mountain in pursuit of the shooter. He moved away from the rock he'd knelt behind and walked back to the others, his face grim.

"Right everyone, I'm pretty sure we've an experienced tracker on our trail with a dozen or so security police in tow. They are in radio contact with a base somewhere and are about a mile and a half behind us and closing the gap. That's the situation."

He paused waiting for questions but none came and he continued.

"What I am proposing to do is this, I will climb up above and ahead of us, pick a suitable spot. Wait until you pass below and then kill the tracker sometime late this afternoon before the light goes. What I want you to do is keep going as hard as you can, trying to maintain the distance and stay out of direct line of sight.

At about four o'clock I want you to emerge from the trees, if you're in them, and set the trap. That should give me plenty of time to set up and be ready." He looked at what was left of Sophie's boots and noted the yellow and black striped laces.

"Tettas, when you come out into the open, or its four o'clock, I want you to cut off an inch or so of Sophie's lace then fray it to look like it's snapped. Then pick a place not too far from the track, maybe a yard uphill and sit down preferably on grass, and place the lace so that it's in plain sight from the track.

You'll have to use your judgement about that. I'll be watching from above so just wave your hand and point to it. Is that clear for everyone?"

Sophie sighed heavily.

"No it's not Winston, what's all this business with my laces etcetera?" Her tone was irritated and Winston knew already how volatile her temper could be so he was cautious.

"Sophie, I've got to take this fella out, to do that I need him to be stationary for a few seconds. This man's a tracker, he'll notice things that most people wouldn't.

He'll notice your lace and move over to pick it up, then he'll study it for a few seconds spot the place that someone recently sat in the grass, probably to adjust and do up the bootlace that just snapped.

It will make a picture in his head as he thinks it through. I'll get him before he starts off again. Ok?"

"How do you know all that Winston? What are you? Part Sioux?" Winston forced down his irritation, she was just hurting, tired and frightened.

"Just trust me Sophie, but just to make sure, why don't you do the same thing a few yards further on, but this time leave the lace tag right on the path. Then he can't miss it can he?"

He smiled his most winning smile at her. She capitulated. She hadn't really been that interested, it was just that Winston had sounded so sure and she couldn't work out how he could be. Never mind. The pain from her feet was more than enough to occupy her mind but she'd be damned before everyone had to slow down for her. So she just stood up and started walking.

Winston nodded to Tettas and a meaningful look passed between them before they parted and Winston began looking for somewhere to leave the track without giving away that he had.

15:45 Sunday 27th May 2018
Bismarck, George Town Harbour

"Belay!"   Shouted Reiner.   Turret Caesar swung ponderously as the crane stopped lowering it.   Scotnikov and three of his men ran restraints around the nearest cleats and hauled against the swing, finally managing to still the sixty five ton lump of metal.

Scotnikov looked up at Reiner standing on Dora's turret roof and indicated that the crane could start lowering again.   Another ten minutes of stop-go, left a bit, right a bit, then Caesar was finally back in place.

The turret's guns would not fire again until after a visit to a proper repair facility but to any observer there would appear to be four working main gun turrets.   They were still testing Dora to see if it could turn freely now that the burr of metal had been trimmed off the join between the turret and barbette at the front of the mount.   One of the 3 inch turrets was back in working order with debris cleared from the area and another of the AK630M2s' too.

Bismarck had some of her teeth back now.   The biggest problems had been the replacing the hydraulic lines from the port Steerpod, and of course the hole in the hull.   The Steerpod blades had been checked out with no obvious damage but it had been difficult and time consuming since it would usually be a dry dock job.   Scotnikov had dived most of the forenoon to check the hull damage and the alignment of the starboard pod blades and was now pretty confident they were OK.

Then he'd had to carefully counter flood for'ard and port to get a list which exposed the hole again.   It would have been nice to have Nightingale, the professional clearance diver, down with him but the poor lad was turned in his own bunk with such pain in his ears that he needed morphine to keep it under control, the doc was also bothered about the concussive effect of the explosion on other parts of his body, like liver and kidneys, they were going to medevac him before they sailed.

So it had been down to him and Chief Braime to fabricate a patch, but they couldn't weld it because

Titanium was such a bitch to weld so they had just managed a temporary seal to the hole. They'd come up with a kind of fibre glass and mastic paste around the umbrella plug, and had finished by lunch time. Now the previously flooded compartment had been inspected and driers had removed lingering dampness and once more the ship sat on an even keel.

That being done, Reiner had come up to rest before starting on the turret. At least the ship should be able to move at twenty knots now, Scotnikov wouldn't countenance any faster until they'd spent time in a dockyard.

With the control motors the damage hadn't been as bad as it could have been. The breakers had activated as soon as water splashed on them and Chief Braime had stripped them and replaced the winding where needed. The good news was that the seal into the hydraulic motor and the electrical motor that sat on it had held so with the replacement of the control motor they were back in business. They only had time to get one working though so there was no redundancy as would usually be the case. Bleeding the hydraulic system after replacing the leads had been and was being a pain in the arse as Kent had succinctly summed up.

All in all Reiner was content with the progress they were making. He looked over at the piles of deck planking on the jetty that had been ripped up from the upper decks and would need replacing another time. Simon had posed an interesting question about it, he wondered whether it had acted like a pre-detonator for HE rounds and an early detonator for SAP rounds? They'd have to spend some time reviewing that possibility when they were out of this mess, it certainly seemed plausible but did it make any difference?

Others were busy re-stocking the vastly depleted ammunition stocks and had managed to get them back up to just normal peacetime levels. Another team was recalibrating the remaining Saab Radar array; it wasn't expected that they'd have to face much in the way of surface opposition because most of it was at the bottom of the Caribbean now but the air threat was unknown.

Reiner and Jake had personally thanked each of the MPP ammunition loaders for their work and Jake had asked Roche for their details in order to reward them properly for their exhausting work. Brave men and volunteers all with some more shaken than others, an experience none of them would forget.

He checked his watch. In another hour or so they could expect a call and position report from Winston which should reassure Jake, he thought. Jake had gone with the five wounded men to the airport to see them off on the company sponsored medivac flight, they'd all wanted to stay aboard and see things through to the end but Jake would have none of it.

Rautsch's hand had been recovered and packed in ice by a quick thinking Bren; it was just possible it could be re-attached Lawrence Crib thought. Kipper and Pete Nuttall were stable now thanks to the heroic efforts of Lawrence and Granny Smith, his trusty instrument passer.

Miles Carlson had provided the destination for the wounded men. He'd been in touch with his friends and managed to pull some favours in to get everyone into the Bethesda Naval hospital in Washington, Jake was paying of course. There was no doubt they'd get the best possible care there.

The only wounded person who hadn't gone was Andy Evans, he'd walked back to the ship having discharged himself from the George Town hospital. Bruised and battered with a massive dressing on his side and another across his debrided and plugged arm he wouldn't take no from anyone.

On arrival at the jetty he had stared in horror at the mess that had been made of the ship he'd last seen the day before, and wondered how the hell any had survived what must have been a storm of shot and shell.

On arrival he'd gone straight to see the doc and enlisted his support for staying on board in order to co-ordinate Sophie's eventual retrieval.

Jake had finally relented and Andy with half a dozen of his security people from Little Cayman, including Arkady Zotov, were busy down below reviewing the day's action and talking about what had already been dubbed in the press as 'The Last Charge of the Gurkha Rifles'.

Right, he decided, time for a 'stand easy', the men had been on the go for hours and they would be dead on their feet, again.

*

Jake waited with the five men as the converted Aero-med VC10 rolled to a halt then began to turn back up the runway towards the airport buildings.

The usually fairly quiet airport was a hive of frenzied activity now. At each end of the runway was a Rapier FSC battery with its attendant radar and defence unit, manned by soldiers of the Royal Artillery. Off to one side was a temporary hard standing for the surviving Typhoon fighters. Ominously, on one side and near the end of the single runway, was a smaller newly laid steel mat on which sat the 'Alert 5' duty Typhoon. Two more were flying out from the UK today.

The Typhoon's pilot was sitting under a jury rigged awning in a folding chair next to his aircraft fully dressed in his pressure suit and all the paraphernalia reading a magazine and the ground crew lounged nearby.

Kipper was saying something and Jake turned back towards him.

"Sorry Kipper I didn't catch that."

"It was nothing boss, I was just burbling about this and that and pissed off that I won't be part of the gang that fetches Sophie back."

Jake caught the depressed tone, Kipper still looked as pale a sheet and the pain killers were enough to require straps on the stretcher to hold him down so the doc had said.

He bent down next to his friend.

"That's not all. What's the matter Kipper?" He felt instantly stupid and added, "Apart from being on a stretcher covered in bandages and full of holes."

"Come on Kipper what's bothering you?" Kipper looked away embarrassed.

"I was just wondering what I was going to do once I'm out of Jake's Navy'."

His voice trailed off sadly and Jake knew intuitively what was going through his mind.

"Kipper, you can leave any time you want." He said with a smile. "But I'd really rather have you back here as soon as you're fit again, there's a shedload of stuff to do now; there'll always be a place for you with me old friend."

The smile was enough, Kipper relaxed and let the morphine do its thing, he still had somewhere to come back to. Ten minutes later Jake stood and watched as the VC-10 taxied on to the main runway and began its take off roll. He'd given each of them a card with a Washington number on it.

The König Industries office in Washington had already been told to check daily and supply anything that the five men wanted. Anything at all. They would drop into Bermuda first to pick up Liz Halshaw of course before flying onwards, he'd never hear the last of it if she didn't get a lift poor woman. Daughter lost and husband badly injured. All down to me too, he added sourly.

Now to finish it. He turned and walked back to the government car.

17:15 Sunday 27ᵗʰ May 2018
West of Anse-d'Hainault Western Haiti

Winston checked to make sure that the ground in front of the long barrel of the Dragunov was still wet. He wanted no tell-tale puff of dust to give his exact position away when he fired; he just wanted them to be aware that he was above them.

Of course it hadn't helped that the clouds had parted and the bloody sun was busy lifting the moisture from the ground at a prodigious rate. His position was about as ideal as it gets for a sniper he decided.

He was located behind a newly planted pair of mango trees kept in place by their bamboo bastion. With little effort he had banked the earth up some more at the front and re positioned some decent sized rocks to line his 'crawl' exit route into a narrow gully heading back towards the others. So from below he'd be on a small rocky knoll with a few small trees and a bit of long grass which was one of a dozen similar places within a stone's throw of him.

Once he'd fired, his escape route would lead him around the mountain for a while before descending back to the track some two hundred feet below and four hundred yards in actual distance.

He had three major problems as he saw it. Firstly, whilst he was an excellent shot, he was not a dedicated sniper and he therefore had to think hard to remember such things as, how much a bullet will fall for every hundred yards it travels, when fired downhill?

Secondly, he'd never fired the rifle he was going to use and that was a big problem. Finally he wasn't so much worried about what range it was zeroed to, he wouldn't be more than a couple of inches above or below at 400 yards anyway, what bothered him was whether the bloke it was zeroed for, was for instance cross-eyed or had a squint or something.

Even within those with what's considered normal sight there are slight differences so, if the gun's owner had unusual sight of any kind he might as well just 'leg it' now.

Well it was going to be shit or bust in about two minutes or so he reckoned, as he watched the tracker carefully but quickly make his way along the line that Tettas and the others had taken, but much faster than them.

The security police were just meandering along behind the expert, they had their rifles slung and most were casually smoking as they walked. He eased the sling around the back of his elbow and then tightened his grip again. Carefully he sighted down to the left of where Tettas had signalled that the first piece of lace had been dropped, and waited.

All too quickly the tracker arrived in the scope's view and Winston waited for the sudden change of attitude that would betray the finding of the lace. There it was. Now a faintly heard shout and everyone came to a halt except the tracker who quickly took two steps to the side of the goat path like a dancer, and crouched suddenly.

Winston saw him pick something up to examine. The security police stood back in a relaxed manner and watched the expert in a bored sort of way. Winston saw one light a cigarette and as the smoke bloomed, he checked the wind strength and direction.

He'd noted all this in the two seconds or so since the tracker had stooped to pick up the lace. Sighting on the man's head he took a deep breath and let it slowly pass through his lips.

As the breath came out, the cross hairs of the telescopic sight dropped slowly, when they had dropped to the top of his sternum Winston stopped breathing and gently but firmly took up the slack on the trigger, past the first pull and continued pulling until the rifle fired.

Without pause to watch the strike, he breathed out a little more to drop the sights further and fired again.

As he fired the second time, the first bullet struck the tracker a hand width above his belly button bending him double and he crumpled in the path. The second bullet puffed dust off the track. Winston stayed long enough to make sure that his target didn't move and then eased back from his firing position.

By the time the security police had hauled themselves off the ground, decided where the shots had come from and begun to point their assault rifles up the hill, Winston was already seventy yards from his firing point and moving, in his own words later, like 'greased weasel shit'.

A mile away, further round the shoulder of the mountain, Tetsunari, Marc and Sophie all halted abruptly as the rifle shot echoed off the sides of the mountains again and again.

They weren't sure if there was a second shot or whether it was just part of the echoing. The small party moved off once more to the accompaniment of periodic short bursts of automatic fire to their rear. Tetsunari was thinking 'fire and advance' as he recalled his time as a marine; ten minutes later they all stopped again as the firing rose to a sudden crescendo before returning to an ominous silence.

Sophie looked askance at Tetsunari, the terror evident in her eyes and posture. He just shrugged slightly, commenting that the pursuers had probably just assaulted Winston's firing position and that he'd be long gone. They were all too tired to think beyond that and the talking ceased. Fifteen minutes later, to Sophie's great relief, Winston could be seen jogging up from behind and Tetsunari declared a halt.

15:00 Monday 28th May 2018
Bismarck 200 miles East of Grand Cayman

Jake sat alone in his cabin and wrestled with the dilemma facing him. He casually, automatically in fact, noted the ship's course and speed displayed on the bridge repeater screen fitted into his desk. They'd sailed that morning about an hour before dawn and in complete contrast to the last time they left George Town, there were just the 'dockies' to handle the ship's lines and the two MPP on duty who'd put thumbs up as the ship backed quietly away.

Reiner reported that, surprisingly, the crew were still in good spirits. The usual matelot banter, ribald comments and laughter had been evident in every compartment he'd visited, with juniors stepping up to replace the lost men and wounded, in the most professional manner.

The morning had been almost completely dominated by a series of system checks as the men got down to the business of testing things to make sure that *Bismarck* could fight again if she had to. Just to be on the safe side, Jake had ordered one of the recovered Arado RPV's launched to scout ahead. Three of the four RPV's had survived the battle to land in North Sound and were towed by a borrowed rigid inflatable to the gap in the outer reefs so that *Bismarck* could winch them up one by one.

At the close of battle Kempfe had had to put the last one of the incredibly expensive machines down on a small patch of stagnant water adjacent to the runway on Grand Cayman, after an enthusiastic Royal Artillery sentry had started banging away at it with his rifle when it ghosted overhead at around 09:00   before the Rapier batteries were active.

A lucky hit had severed something and Kempfe had no choice but to land it immediately hoping there were no obstructions. It had been hauled out that morning covered in green slime and foul smelling mud. The Battery Sergeant Major had set the 'enthusiastic' sentry to work swabbing the muck off and had congratulated him on his accuracy in shooting down one of the only friendly aircraft for miles around.

The newly launched RPV had almost immediately picked up four vessels forty five miles ahead steaming slowly eastward. Kempfe had taken direct control and vectored it in towards them. A few minutes later they had a clear picture of the surviving *Luda* D destroyer and the three remaining landing ships, two badly knocked about, the other apparently unharmed.

The four ships would probably have been picked long before, had *Bismarck* any working ESM, because the unscathed *Luda* clearly had its main search radar working.

Once more *Bismarck* cleared for action but unlike before, there was now a 'gung ho' kind of attitude in the men as they prepared for battle.

Jake and Reiner, both on the bridge exchanged looks at the banter as the duty helmsman was relieved by Buller with evidence in his beard that he'd just dropped by the galley to see if there were any cakes or nutty.

There is something about a winning team that shows in the way they behave, whether it be in sport, business or even war. What Jake and Reiner were seeing, was a ship's company that had beaten the enemy against all the odds, and were now ready to confront him again, but with things a little more in their favour.

Jake, however, had no desire to start another battle regardless of how confident he was of winning, he just wanted to get to Haiti and get Sophie back.

He decided on a compromise. It was a calculated risk but given that no shot or shell had penetrated *Bismarck*'s hide throughout the last battle, he didn't think it was too great a risk.

The opportunity to further reinforce ones superiority over a still potentially dangerous opponent should never be overlooked. He recalled an instructor saying at Dartmouth 'never mind the don't kick 'em when they're down philosophers', it isn't a game, just keep kicking until they stop moving. As far as Jake was concerned, whether it be in business or in war, you should never leave your opponent in any doubt that if they came back for more, they'd get it!

Closing the Haitian ships, they increased speed gradually to thirty knots, overriding Scotnikov's protests, a great rooster tail of water flaring out behind. Another poke in the eye, since the last time the Haitians had seen the *Bismarck* she was a slow moving cripple with hardly a bow wave. Now she moved to a parallel course that would pass the Haitians at a range of three miles, if they didn't react violently.

They didn't. As soon as it picked them up closing fast from astern, the Haitian destroyer had merely began to weave across the stern of its charges in a protective manner.

As its silhouette changed it became clear that it was indeed undamaged, but the missile launchers were set fore and aft rather than deployed for firing. The RPV zoomed in and further proof of its health was evidenced by the guns in the two twin 5.1" gun turrets moving slightly to check elevation and rotation. I can fight it, was saying.

Jake spoke to them over the maritime emergency channel, VHF channel 16.

"Haitian destroyer this is Cayman Islands warship *Bismarck*, please respond, over."

Jake paused for twenty seconds before repeating.

"Haitian destroyer this is *Bismarck* please respond, over."

This time a heavily accent voice replied in evident annoyance.

"This is the *Cap Haitien*, *Bismarck*. What do you want?"

Jake smiled to himself as he prepared to reply, but to those watching it was a cruel smile, without mirth.

"*Cap Haitien* this is *Bismarck*. Do you wish to re-commence hostilities?" A momentary pause.

"Say again *Bismarck*. Do we what?" Came back an incredulous voice. Jake shouted.

"I said, do you wish to continue the fight. You know, shoot at each other, that sort of thing. We wish to continue yesterdays' battle, don't you?"

Startled looks filled the faces of all those present on *Bismarck*'s bridge, never had they heard their Commodore speak to anyone with such cold contempt dripping from his voice. Without waiting for a reply Jake imperiously added a deadline.

"You have one minute to make a satisfactory reply before I destroy you, over." Everyone noticed the 'I' not we. This was the voice of domination, the playground bully even.

Then suddenly Jake's mask slipped and he smiled to the others.

"That should give the buggers something to think about. I expect they're well used to being dictated to though."

It took about ten seconds for anyone to get the weak joke then Jake had to shout above the laughter for quiet, as he waited for a reply. He spoke into his mike.

"Gunnery." Click.

"Lt Kopf you may train your guns on the enemy."

Kopf acknowledged and everyone watched as turrets Anton, Bruno, Caesar and Dora trained round to track the damaged Haitian destroyer.

The heavily accented voice came back over the radio.

"*Bismarck* this is *Cap Haitien*. We have no wish to engage. What do you want us to do?" Jake noted the hesitancy and reverted to his imperious tone as he answered.

"Sensible answer. Now turn immediately to course 180 and stay on that course for at least twelve hours otherwise I'll be back and next time we meet I will shoot first. We have surveillance on you all the time as you may have guessed, the slightest deviation and we'll meet again. Is that understood?"

The Haitian meekly accepted the order and they watched as the four ships immediately turned south.

Reiner turned to him.

"I suppose you've considered that they'll report our course and position?"

"Yes." Said Jake simply.

That had been an hour or so before Winston's message had arrived telling them of his encounter with the tracker and security police. Jake, Reiner, Andy Evans and Buck Taylor had crowded around the RS's work station in the OPs room to listen to Winston's message.

Though none had said as much, all had been thinking that Winston & Co must have been re-taken or were dead, since they were well past the arranged communication time.

As usual, reality proved a lot simpler than all their wild imaginings. After the contact with the police detachment, Winston had kept everyone going throughout the night in order to put as much distance between them and their now nervous pursuers.

They'd collapsed into a small cave just before dawn and huddled together, had all fallen into a coma-like sleep, hence the very late transmission. After a few moments of information exchange, Winston informed Jake that he'd decided to rest up for the remainder of the day since Sophie's feet were literally a bloody mess.

From now on they would only move at night due to the increasing sparsity of the cover. They expected to be in sight of the coast by dawn the next day and were hopeful that the place they'd picked, north of Anse-D'Hainault was as deserted as Old Marc thought it would be. He would report in then.

Jake desperately wanted to speak to his wife and decided to do so despite his aversion to public emotional displays. Winston wouldn't let him. He sat back aghast as Winston explained that she was still asleep and she'd need all her strength for the night's trek. Even Andy Evans had the good sense to look shamefaced as Jake looked incredulously at the receiver as if it were to blame for the answer.

Before his outrage found voice, common sense prevailed and he realised it would be selfish to wake Sophie just for the reassurance that would give him. So he wished them luck and left Andy and Buck to discuss matters military with Winston.

Now an hour later he sat in his cabin unable to decide on the best course of action. It was the 'what if' list that bothered Jake.

What if they were caught before *Bismarck* could reach them? Would Farache simply order their immediate execution?

What if Farache gave them to his pet torturers for another session? The very thought brought a surge of mixed anger, fear and frustration.

What if Sophie was unable to walk the remaining distance to the coast? *Bismarck* certainly couldn't hang around for any length of time before the Haitian authorities concentrated their search in that area.

What if the Haitians had more aircraft than the intelligence reports indicated? *Bismarck* might well sail in but would she get out again?

The questions spun round and round in his mind until he could stand it no longer. He got up and made his way down to the quarterdeck and stood staring out to sea and let his mind be washed clear, bathed by the peaceful constancy of the sea.

After a little less than an hour he made his way back to the stateroom, which he'd only once managed to share with Sophie. He put out a call for Reiner.

"Hi, we need a meeting. Bring yourself, Simon and Andy Evans and let's sort this."

A few minutes later everyone was gathered and seated and Jake told them of his dilemma. He had a large scale map of western Haiti 'blue-tacked' to the bulkhead.

"At present Sophie and the others are still free, but, I don't think you'd need to be a genius to figure out that they must be heading for the coast and given the contact with the police, it narrows the search area considerably. That being the case, the job of those wishing to intercept them becomes so much easier. Anyone Disagree?"

No one did.

"The coastline to choose from is enormous, but they can narrow down Winston's options quite a lot too." He elaborated for them with a laser pointer.

"Winston has many problems to solve but two of the biggest are Sophie with her white skin and red hair and Tetsunari with his Japanese features. With limited resources and absolutely no safe contact with any locals, I think his only real option would be to find a stretch of uninhabited coast from which to be picked up." He paused to let that sink in.

"This of course narrows his options further still. Now, he killed a tracker yesterday afternoon, but would that stop the pursuit? No is my guess. I expect they'll just bring another one or two or a dozen in to replace him given they now have a scent to follow."

He turned away from the map of Haiti and addressed Andy directly.

"That is no criticism of Winston by the way Andy, I think he's done an incredible job to get this far especially given his limited options."

Jake moved to the side and sat on his desk leaving the others a clear view of the map on the bulkhead.

"If I'm right, I expect that they'll very shortly be able to pin down Winston's options even further simply by extrapolating his route. Eventually they'll end up with a very narrow slice of coast and be able to saturate it with troops and police or whatever."

He looked around again as if seeking arguments from anyone. He got none.

"Finally, based on what I've said and deduced, I think their chances of reaching any rendezvous with us are minimal."

No one spoke, all realizing that Jake had just presented one likely scenario, all too likely unfortunately to be correct.

"Right. That brings me to my dilemma. I'm torn between doing nothing and betting that Winston and Tettas can pull it off or interceding directly with Farache and hoping that he values his only nephew more than getting revenge on us for spoiling his grandiose scheme of conquest."

Andy Evans broke the silence that followed Jake's statement. He knew that Jake wanted to do the 'intercede' option, he felt it. What he believed that Jake wanted was either constructive support or outright opposition in order that he could make the decision.

"What did you have in mind for your intercession Jake?"

Jake took a deep breath and stood up again, the strain of the past few days clearly etched on his normally relaxed features.

"Just suppose I manage to get in touch with the General and explain that I'm holding his nephew hostage against the unopposed return of our people, that I want to make a private deal with him, nothing to do with the Caymans at all. Does anyone think he wouldn't do it?"

Andy was first in again.

"So you'll ask him to pull out all his troops from the area and allow Sophie, Winston, Tettas and that gardener just to bimble down to a beach and be picked up by us. And in return for that you'll drop off his nephew somewhere?

Jake was silent for a second or two.

"I suppose when you put it like that, it does sound a like a bit of a one sided deal."

His shoulders slumped slightly and he turned away looking more dejected than anyone Andy had ever seen.

"I'm not trying to destroy your hopes Jake, I'm just trying to work my way through this minefield. Somehow, a deal like the one you suggested has got to come about, given that both major players have something that the other wants. And I can understand why you want to wave Farache's nephew under his nose, just to say hey! I've got something that you want, so don't let your boys get over enthusiastic if they do manage to catch my wife and Co."

Andy shook his head slowly as he tried to see a way through it.

"The problem as I see it, is this. You tell Farache that you've got his nephew and he's going to tear Haiti apart to find his own bargaining chip and in doing so however severe his orders are, his men may kill the very people you're trying to save."

He looked askance at the faces around him.

"Is that about right?" A grim row of nods confirmed Jake's worst fears, everyone seemed to have the problems in perspective but nobody had come up with a viable, safe solution.

Simon McClelland had said nothing so far, he'd just imbibed the raw information and begun digestion. Now his tactician's brain began to assimilate, order and process the mass of information and the implications of various stratagems.

He let the desultory conversation flow about him whilst his mind examined the problem from all angles. There must be a solution. Suddenly he had it, there was a solution! But he didn't jump up and shout eureka!

He examined his answer from all angles again and again, projected possible results and potential problems.

Finally he was ready.

"Jake." He asked for attention in his normal voice.

Reiner, Jake and Andy were busy in a heated discussion which seemed to involve levelling half of Port Au Prince.

"Jake." He said louder than before, finally getting some attention.

"I have a possible solution. It's probably going to be hard for you all to swallow but I think it's the only one which gives both sides a measure of security."

He had their full and undivided attention now.

"Sophie, Winston and Tetsunari must surrender to Farache's men."

Simon waited calmly whilst Andy Evans went supernova and Jake and Reiner just stared at him speechlessly. At last, when Andy had finished his first-line repertoire of abuse, Simon managed to continue.

"Our problem is that our opponent has no bargaining counter on his side of the table. His desperation to obtain one could lead to both sides being disappointed. If we provide him with one, his responses will then be predictable and controlled, given his desire to have his nephew returned. The way things are, there is a high probability that one or more of our people will be killed before extraction."

He could see Andy was still livid and wanting to interrupt.

"Just think about it without building in the emotion of knowing the people involved. Remember our objective is to have our people returned and avert a bloodbath. Farache isn't stupid, he'll see the sense of the arrangement and if he gives the order, no one would dare harm them."

Andy sucked in his breath to ready to speak several times, he raised his finger to point and put it down, finally he sat still and thought it through.

Jake stood up and went to his liquor cabinet, extracting four crystal tumblers he poured a good measure of Lagavulin into each, not noticing that Simon shook his head at the offer.

Without a word he handed them round and waited until everyone had sipped.

"Gentlemen, as unsavoury as it might first seem, I think our Warfare Officer has supplied us a solution.

Now down to details, I need to speak to General Farache soonest.

18:00 Monday 28th May 2018
Presidential Palace, Port Au Prince, Haiti

General Farache sat back and disconnected the radio link with his nemesis. His hands trembled and his thoughts veered and swung in several directions at once and he could make no sense of them, partly he decided, because of the infernal chatter of his ministerial cronies.

"Silence!" He banged a large meaty hand on the wooden table for emphasis and the noise abated as if someone had switched off a TV. As the silence grew around him he tried to bring his thoughts into focus.

His nephew was alive. This was the young man he'd chosen to rule after himself. Was anything more important than getting him back?

What König had said was true in large measure, the security police were on the trail of his wife and her pet guard dogs and yes, the target area was flooded with personnel.

Unaccountably he felt a certain empathy with König, yes he hated him for interfering but he also admired him for his courage, and both of them were missing a person very dear to them.

He considered König's offer of a truce, at least until both men had back what they wanted, and then he considered König's reply to his own question of what would happen then?

He chuckled, causing eyebrows to be raised and glances exchanged around the table, König's answer had simply been 'I don't care what you do Mr President, but I suggest you leave me out of it. I'm not very forgiving at the best of times, so I suggest that you stay out of my way and I promise I'll stay out of yours.'

He chuckled again, the sound like a rumble of distant thunder, causing expressions of alarm to be seen around the table. He has balls that König, he told himself, perhaps it would be a good idea to leave him alone at least for now. He himself had other problems involving some rather nasty characters from Columbia.

Looking up quickly he caught some of the glances exchanged around the table, and filed them for future use.

"We will agree to this König's terms for exchange."

He noted a smile on the Interior Minister's face and quickly wiped it away.

"No Ricard, there is to be no messing with the prisoners, I mean that. They will be exchanged intact for my nephew or I will have someone's head."

Everyone studiously looked away from the Interior Minister who suddenly didn't feel that secure anymore. Farache continued.

"Set up the call and we'll make the arrangements now."

It was dark enough now to be able to stand in the open and use the satellite phone without one of the thousands of soldiers and police seeing him, thought Winston. He could see lights from roving search parties along their line of advance, and to the left and right of it. There were also dogs with the searchers, he could hear them occasionally barking at something interesting.

He positioned himself just to the left of the entrance of the small cave they were hiding in and slowly rotated until he was getting a good satellite return.

Further back in the cave Tetsunari, aided by the last of the chemical light sticks, was bathing Sophie's feet prior to dressing them. She winced but kept quiet.

Tetsunari had long ago decided that she was an honourable woman and was pleased to see this confirmed again and again in the past few days as she'd struggled across the mountains with her feet getting worse by the hour.

She had born her pain with the kind of stoicism he expected from Japanese women of high breeding, not from western women who were usually soft and pathetic, in his experience.

Despite their best efforts to prevent it, Sophie's feet were infected and even in the unnatural chemical light he could see the 'tracking' lines climbing her legs and showing the progress of the infection.

Unless they obtained proper medical care soon, he determined, the infection could prove fatal. Even old Marc was starting to show the ravages of the journey now, his normally cheerful countenance replaced by a kind of hollow faced numbness and whilst Tetsunari still considered him a barbarian, he had come to respect the man's stamina.

Climbing stiffly to his feet, he made his way back towards the entrance and Winston. Winston looked up and announced.

"They want to speak to us all, for some reason."

Up until then, Winston had been usually the one to talk to the outside world. Tetsunari simply nodded and went back to get Sophie and, as an afterthought, old Marc too. They all sat around to listen as Winston switched to speakerphone and set the volume so they could all hear. Jake's voice came clearly over the speaker surprising them.

"Good evening Sophie my love, and you Winston, Tetsunari and of course Mr Bellard. I shan't waste time as Winston informs me that power is getting low and there's a great deal to tell you all. At present, *Bismarck* is about a hundred and sixty miles from your part of the coast and we'll be off there by four in the morning." He paused to let that sink in.

"Now the bad news, as you have probably noticed, there's a lot of military activity in the area, we believe that they've narrowed their search area considerably and I understand Winston is of the same opinion. We also believe that it's only a matter of time before you fall foul of Farache's patrols and are possibly injured or killed. I want no heroic last ditch defences people, I want you out alive. Winston and Tetsunari alone could possibly do it but Winston tells me your feet are in a bad way Sophie."

Sophie looked daggers at Winston and all he could do was shrug apologetically.

"And I don't think Mr Bellard should be any further involved. Do you think Mr Bellard, that you could slip away unnoticed?"

Old Marc looked stunned at being addressed and asked his opinion.

"Well yes Sir, I could. But my boss, the Minister, told me to look after your lady an' I haven't finished that job yet Sir."

Jake chuckled. "I'm sure the Minister would have been proud of the way you've helped out and I hereby relieve you of that obligation Mr Bellard. I also thank you from the bottom of my heart for your kind assistance and will ensure that, one way or another, you'll be rewarded." He became all business-like again.

"Now, the rest of you. On board *Bismarck* is a young Haitian officer, one of the survivors from our first battle, and he just happens to be General Farache's nephew."

Winston felt an impending sense of doom, he even stopped wanting to ask about the battles that had been fought, as the feeling took hold. Dutifully he tuned back into what was being said.

"...now what I need you three to do is to give yourselves up to the nearest patrol."

Sophie shouted over the next few remarks.

"Jake you can't be serious. You want us to just walk down and give ourselves over to their tender mercies?" She paused a second to gather herself as the memories re-surfaced.

"Do you know what they've already done to me? I, I bloody...."

Jake interrupted harshly. "Sophie listen to me for Christ's sake. Do you really think that I would want you, or the others, back in Farache's hands if there was another viable way? You have only two choices." He laid it out for them.

"You can either try to fight your way down to the coast, risking your own lives and the lives of the boats crews that will have to come in through a storm of fire to pick you up, or you can give yourselves up to the nearest patrol and be back with me just after dawn. That's it Sophie." He knew he was being harsh but the battery level was low and they had to sort this now.

"Until a few hours ago you only had the first choice now you've got a second, take it. I've spoken to him. For what it's worth I have Farache's personal guarantee that you will not be harmed, he wants his nephew back badly, ask Mr Bellard he'll tell you, Farache's love of his nephew is well known."

He added briefly.

"Switch off now and talk it over, then come back to us as soon as you can. OK?"

They retreated inside the cave and in the dim light the four looked at each other and weighed options. Old Marc believed the man on the phone. The general doted on the only male in his bloodline he told them, it was well known.

It didn't really matter to him now anyway, he'd done his job, the man on the phone had said so, all he had to do was say goodbye and disappear into the night.

Tetsunari fought down the urge to rush out into the night and kill and kill again. The past few days had been one long series of humiliations without the expurgation of killing those responsible.

He didn't want to surrender. But, whatever his personal feelings, he had his duty, his *Giri*, the highest part of which at present was the safety and protection of Mrs König, so no matter what was decided, he would follow her. He had to.

Winston sat staring out into the night. For four days he'd kept them all together and now, just in sight of their destination, if it were daylight, they had to throw in the towel and give up.

He had no illusions as to what awaited himself and Tettas at least. Farache knew that Jake wanted Sophie back badly, he would also guess that Jake would sacrifice the rest of this little party to get her back.

So that meant that Farache's boys could at the very least have a little fun with Mrs König's bodyguards. And what if one of them accidently died? Would the exchange go ahead still? You bet your ass it would.

Logically then. If the cover, the protection, doesn't apply to me and Tettas that leaves us with a couple stark choices doesn't it? He was tired, more tired than he'd ever been, and he was sick at heart.

If his number was up, then he wanted to go out with a bang rather than whimper, what was that Queen song? Something out of Highlander wasn't it? How did it go now 'It's better to burn out than fade away' his resolve hardened.

Then he turned slightly and looked at Sophie. She looked small and vulnerable. Could he let her just walk down the hill alone? Towards those bastards? After what they did to her? What kind of person was he to even think that? Just so that he could jump off this mortal coil like one of Tettas' Samurai heroes.

Sophie shuddered inwardly at the thought of simply walking out and handing herself over. The physical signs of her rape and confinement had all but disappeared, but the mental damage was still raw and real.

But she was being selfish, she realized. Winston and Tettas' only chance of survival lay in her giving up. Jake had painted a stark picture of the next twelve hours or so in her mind, a sort of Dunkirk scene in which everyone died trying to lift her off a beach.

She couldn't permit that, no way, especially when there was an alternative on offer.

In the brief discussion that followed they were all surprised to learn that the decision was unanimous they would give themselves up at first light. Marc decided to head out there and then and when the goodbyes had been said, he'd finally disappeared into the night. Winston completed the return call and signed off. He told them to get some sleep, but no one could.

06:30 Tuesday 29th May 2018
Bismarck Half a Mile Offshore,
Western Coast of Haiti

Tension on the bridge and in the OPs room, at its peak with the coming of dawn, had stepped down a couple of notches from iron bar tautness to a nervous silence in which any noise or movement caused all heads to turn in the direction of the offender.

Dawn had seen the highest state of hair-trigger alertness, as the 'enemy' coast had become slowly visible. *Bismarck* had gone to action stations at a little before 05:00 and when the sun had finally put in an appearance at 05:47, everyone had been glued to viewers in spite of the protection offered by the revolving search radar up above and the RPV out there scanning the coast.

At 05:50 'Overseer' reported in and the RAF E3 sentry had brought along two little friends and a 'Texaco' so they could refuel on station if needed.

So thanks to Jon Roby they now had air cover for the next six hours or so, plenty of time for it all to go right, or wrong.

Just after 05:55 everyone had jumped when Robby Robinson acting as RS, had suddenly announced over the bridge repeater that the Haitians had taken possession of the escapees.

Movement along the shoreline could be plainly seen as armoured vehicles and troop transports manoeuvred on the coastal road running parallel to the shore. A truck appeared and parked up. The people ashore seemed to be split into two distinct groups and as the light grew and they closed to half a mile, it was possible to discern that the soldiers were not mixing with the blue uniformed security police. Now they waited.

Most people scanned the shore looking for the light signal that would indicate that the Haitians were ready to effect the exchange. Reiner kept his viewer locked onto the large inflatable hauled up on the beach, which he presumed would be the transport for the Haitian end of the exchange.

There were three soldiers and two sailors standing around it smoking in a relaxed, easy manner. He switched to another viewer and checked out their own readiness. Near the single surviving crane located next to the catapult track on the port side, the prisoner stood with hands bound behind his back, looking small between Jan Helders and Buck Taylor who were each carrying their Heckler and Koch's.

Next to them was a borrowed Gemini inflatable, *Bismarck*'s own boats had been obliterated during the action on the 27th. Manning it were Trev Kent the engineer and Scouse Smith an AB.

Both were armed with holstered automatics and the boat was ready to be swung outboard by the crane. Jake was in his stateroom using the viewer there and Kopf up in the gunnery control centre had all turrets trained shoreward even though only Anton & Bruno for'ard were fully functional.

Jake tried to remain calm as the exchange drew near and he waited to see if his judgement had been correct or if he'd just asked his wife and two brave men to commit suicide.

His emotions ran the full gamut from a chilly fear to barely controllable rage, and all stations in between. The seconds passed with agonizing slowness, the minutes never seemed to pass at all.

He thought of all the things he'd ever wanted to say to his wife but hadn't and resolved to remedy that if he could. But he may never be able to say them now. Why? Because of one man's ambition. This one man had caused all the death and misery of the last week, just one man.

His callous disregard for anything but his own ambitions had caused an estimated two thousand killed and seven hundred wounded of his own soldiers, sailors and airmen alone, bodies were still washing up on the beach when they'd left Grand Cayman.

Maybe not just one man. Somewhere out there also, was a filthy, manipulative cocaine baron who had co-opted the General into his warped plan for revenge.

It was intolerable. Accounts would have to be settled and he was damn sure governments wouldn't do it.

But he'd made a deal and he couldn't go back on it, no way. A movement caught his eye and he trained the viewer round a little to the right.

A procession was now making its way down the beach; it had started just as just a large black limousine arrived. The three tonner further back with Interior ministry police insignia had its tailboard down and blue uniformed thugs lounging around smoking.

He ignored the procession for a second and panned back to the limmo. Calling up the highest magnification, he focussed on a man standing beside the black car, there was no mistaking the gaudy uniform and large paunchy figure. General Farache, President of Haiti had come to see his dear nephew returned to the fold.

Jake's vision blurred momentarily, a muscle 'ticked' in his right cheek and blood pounded in his ears. Never had he felt such an overwhelming desire to kill, but at the same time optimism rose in him that Farache's presence meant he was going to keep his word and he would get his wife back along with her minders.

He swung his eyes away from the viewer and sat shakily at his desk, he voice linked to Reiner.

"Reiner, take overall command until further notice please, I'm not... I'm too close to it old friend, I'll be up when they get near us."

Without waiting for a reply he terminated the link and sat staring at the photograph of his wife and children both of whom had been in touch repeatedly wanting to come along at least back to Grand Cayman, to which Jake had relented.

On the other side of his stateroom his music system selected its next album. Jake listened for a second and thought how appropriate, as Mozart's Magic Flute commenced. The soaring perfection of the music never failed to raise his spirits and it was one of Sophie's favourites too.

*

Reiner was bothered. Not because Jake had just handed him overall command, something else made him feel uncomfortable. He spoke quietly into his mike.

"Drone control." Click. "Kempfe, scan the area behind the beach along that treeline with the thermal imager will you, I think I caught a movement over there."

Kempfe dutifully activated the thermal imager in the drone and commenced scanning the undergrowth and treeline behind the beach. His breath caught suddenly as he picked up a series of shapes and lots of human movement all around them.

"There's something there Sir, human movement, lots but I think it's artillery of some kind they're looking after but I'm no artilleryman, can you get Arkady or Andy Evans to look at them Sir?"

Reiner acknowledged and checked the images. Yes he needed Zotov or Evans to tell him what was hiding there and called them up.

He thought for a few seconds.

"Julius, have S1 and S3 loaded with PFDHEC and fused for airburst at 5m, program them to start each end and walk shells along the treeline finishing in the centre, twenty rounds a minute set. OK? "Load now."

"Yes Sir. What about the main battery Sir?"

"Load HE and train them towards the beach, no targets yet and lastly Kopf, have one of the AK630's lock on to their inflatable wherever it goes."

"Aye Sir". Returned Kopf.

Reiner went back to the viewer that was zoomed onto the beached inflatable. A gaggle of personnel were approaching it now, carrying what looked like three stretchers. Three stretchers? Reiner was now thoroughly alarmed.

Winston had only mentioned Sophie's bad feet, nothing about any other injuries! The light signal flashed out from somewhere to the right of the armoured vehicles grouped near the beach.

Reiner linked to Kent near the crane, telling him to get the Gemini in the water and have Bren the 'Doc' join them with his medical bag. He ordered Buller onto the bridge wing to answer the signal with the lamp. Things were starting to move.

*

Sophie cried quietly as she was carried down the beach on the stretcher. She looked across at Winston and Tetsunari on their stretchers, the sight causing a fresh flood of tears.

Both men were unconscious. Winston, despite his black skin, had somehow managed to look pale, his face was puffy and there were open cuts along his eyebrows and cheeks.

She looked along the blanket that was carelessly thrown over him and shuddered, she could only see one arm and that had a new joint in it between wrist and elbow. The blanket was dark with blood near his feet. They'd beaten both his and Tetsunari's bare soles with wooden staves.

Tetsunari looked even worse. God why do men have to be so macho! Tetsunari hadn't much of his face left, skin hung in tatters from both sides where they'd cut him to try to stop him smiling at them. That was after they'd ruined his mouth beyond the point where he could tell them that he thought they were motherless monkeys with no honour and no courage.

No one had touched her. She was very definitely Taboo. She had screamed at them and fought the two men holding her; she'd tried everything to stop the beatings that had commenced as soon as they stopped near the beach.

For a good twenty minutes, the men in the pale blue uniforms who claimed to be policemen, had taken turns methodically laying about both men and they'd only stopped when buckets of water failed to bring their victims around.

At least, she thought, while they were both unconscious they'd feel no pain. She looked up to her right as she sensed someone watching her. She saw a big man in a flashy uniform with lots of medals and gold braid; she looked him in the eye from a range of about ten feet and spat at him.

He simply looked away and focussed his binoculars on the ship lying off the beach. Sophie turned to look too and felt a surge of hope. She could see a sleek, powerful looking warship with a thin stream of smoke climbing vertically from its single funnel.

Jake was out there watching, she knew, and controlled her sobbing. She wiped her face on the sleeve of her jacket; she didn't want him to see her looking like a ragamuffin. General Farache turned away from his study of König's ship and spoke to the Colonel behind him. "You have a question?"

The Colonel of artillery swallowed quickly.

"Yes Sir. I wish to know what your orders are regarding the enemy ship once the exchange is made Sir?"

Farache turned and stared out to sea at the ship that had caused him so much grief.

"You may do what you wish my dear Colonel, if our fleet and Airforce failed to sink it, do you think your little field guns can? Still if you wish, you may try, but not until I'm far enough away so that when Mr König squashes you, I won't even hear it."

The Colonel saluted and left the group.

Farache turned to the Security Police Lieutenant who commanded the detachment.

"I trust the prisoners are fit for exchange Lieutenant?"

The dapper officer in the blue uniform gulped twice before he could speak.

"Yes Sir, as per your instructions."

He knew it was a lie, he'd looked away while his men beat the bodyguards to a pulp, the message he'd got from the Interior Minister was to have them all alive, not alive and undamaged. It sounded like there had been a communication problem.

*

Reiner carefully kept the viewer centred on the incoming inflatable; the two boats were only a matter of yards apart now as they manoeuvred close enough to make the swap.

Thank God it's calm, he thought as the delicate job of moving the injured took place. He could see that Sophie was basically OK because she had been the first to cross the between the lashed together boats. He listened carefully for a report from Bren on the condition of Winston and Tetsunari.

*

Bren crossed to the Haitian boat, lifted the covers off both Tetsunari and Winston and shook his head in disbelief as he took in the injuries that they had suffered. Lying unconscious on carrying sheets in the Haitian boat they were in a bad way; not even on a stretcher, the bastards. He couldn't even begin to catalogue their injuries here he needed them aboard *Bismarck* quick.

Everyone was tense, Buck and Jan had their weapons cocked and were casually covering the three soldiers in the other boat.

Big Trev Kent had hold of the scrawny looking Haitian officer by the back of his shirt collar, waiting to pass him across. Mrs König looked bloody awful, he thought, as her stretcher was helped across the gunnels into their own boat.

He turned back to see the two Haitian sailors take a grip on the carrying sheet with Tetsunari in it, one of them dropped his end and Tetsunari's bloody feet came into view.

Fucking bastards have tortured them, he realized. The mood shifted starkly and both Buck Taylor and Jan Helders cocked their weapons noisily and if looks could kill the Haitians would have died on the spot. The Haitians in the boat made shrugging gestures.

"Bren check they're alive. If not get down and cover Mrs K. Got it."

"Yeah I'm in."

"Kent, keep hold of that scrawny bastard and if Winston and Tettas are dead, let him go over the side."

"Gotcha." Said Kent, dangling the prisoner like a bad smelling sock.

Shit it's going to kick off in a sec, thought Bren as he checked for pulses! With relief he signalled both were alive and spoke quietly into his mike. "Doctor." Followed by the inevitable click of connection.

"This is Bren, Lawrence. Mrs K looks OK but Tettas and Winston have had the shit kicked out of them and I mean that almost literally."

He paused a second as he tried to straighten the unconscious Japanese in the bottom of the boat.

"Aw shit Lawrence, stand by for some surgery, we're looking at multiple lower leg fractures, arms as well and major facial damage to Tetsunari, I'm checking Winston now, standby." He manoeuvred to Winston's carrying sheet.

"Fuck, Winston may have internal damage; he's certainly got multiple open fractures. It looks like the bastards have really worked them over."

Kent dropped the General's nephew in the other boat and ostentatiously put a large wicked looking knife through the ropes holding the boats together.

Both Buck and Jan had seen what had happened to their two colleagues and seethed. The slightest excuse and they would have opened fire on the receding Haitian craft. It was clear that the Haitian soldiers knew it too; they appeared disgusted by what their fellows in the Security police had done.

Bren turned to Kent now manning the outboard engine.

"Best get us back as quick as you can matey, but don't bump the fuck out of them." He turned quickly to Sophie. "Sorry Ma'am I forgot you was here."

Jake stood by on the catapult deck as the loaded Gemini neared *Bismarck*, he didn't need binoculars to see his wife now, she leant against the boat's small steering position looking straight at him as it curved in towards the crane derrick hanging over the water.

The boat was quickly hooked on and the crane rapidly and smoothly lifted the Gemini out of the water and set it down gently next to the wrecked portside hangar.

Jake walked quickly over and lifted Sophie out of the bow of the boat, he held her tight against his chest and just murmured into her hair. All around them there was frenetic activity as Doc Roberts and Bren supervised the removal of the two injured men from the boat.

Sophie stiffened as she watched them over Jake's shoulder, she lifted an arm from Jake's waist and tapped him on the shoulder.

"Jake, just look what they did to Winston and Tetsunari. As soon as we got to the beach they started beating them and didn't stop until that bastard in the Limmo showed up."

She pushed herself away from his chest and moved to watch as first Winston then Tetsunari was lowered onto a stretcher with Bren putting an IV in one and Doc Cribb the other.

Jake tore his eyes from his wife and looked down at the two men who had helped and guided her through the misery of past four days. Blood from one of Winston's feet was slowly pooling on the deck, he looked at Tetsunari's shattered face and broken legs. It was enough. More than enough. Sophie saw the change in his face and put her head on his shoulder. He turned to Lt Marchello Vitali.

"Marchello please take my wife to our cabin and stay with her until I get back."

Passing Sophie gently to the Lieutenant he kissed her on the nose and said.

"Shan't be long darling, I've just got something to attend to on the bridge."

Then he turned and walked purposefully towards the nearest hatch in the forward superstructure.

Reiner was surprised to see him as he bundled in and sat in the command chair. Jake grabbed at a viewer and stared intently through it for a few seconds then he stabbed the 'lock on' button on his chair console.

He pushed the viewer away and ordered Buller to go to full ahead, then he spoke to Kopf in the gunnery control centre.

"Mr Kopf what is the main battery loaded with please?" Kopf although surprised at the question immediately replied.

"HE sir."

"Right. Orders. Anton, Bruno. Target is locked in on viewer six. The jeep and the three tonner behind the

Limmo are to be destroyed. Five rounds mixed air and ground burst. Maximum rate..."

"Wait!" Shouted Reiner.

"What is it Reiner?" The anger in Jake's voice was almost physical.

"Sir there are six D30 122mm howitzers hidden in the tree line."

"What have you got covering them." Jake knew Reiner would not have left them uncovered.

"S1 and S3 are set to sweep in to the centre using PFDHEC sir."

"OK. Kopf commence firing as ordered and keep a careful eye on the treeline, if someone even lights a fag over there shoot."

"Aye Sir. Commencing now."

"Sir can I have a word please. Reiner led Jake on to the starboard bridge wing as Anton and Bruno began shooting.

"Why Sir? You have your wife, Winston and Tetsunari."

"The Ton Ton Macoutes in that three tonner spent twenty minutes systematically beating Winston and Tetsunari's feet with poles. They broke their arms and legs and they smashed their faces Reiner. Winston probably has internal bleeding and Tetsunari is going to need plastic surgery to put his face back together. Now from what Sophie has told me, they stopped when the general arrived. Since he's not noted for squeamishness I can only conclude, lucky for him, that he didn't order it. Therefore the man in the jeep allowed or ordered it and the bastards in the three tonner did it. Therefore in my opinion he didn't keep all of his bargain. OK?"

The guns crashed out, the sound deafening on the bridge wing.

Reiner went back into the bridge and took over the nearest viewer. He braced himself slightly as *Bismarck* quickly responded to the thrust of the gas turbines.

Fitting his eyes into the rubber cups again he was just in time to see the first shells arriving above and on the Jeep and the three tonner. After a few seconds and ten or so shells, Reiner looked away sickened, it was just murder.

He looked at Jake and it must have shown on his face. Jake looked back calmly.

"There's an old saying. It goes something like this, 'All that is required for the triumph of evil is that good men do nothing'. Well it has lots of variations and this is my take on its meaning. Don't judge too quickly Reiner, if I make an agreement I keep it. I expect others to do the same especially when it is concerning the health of my family or employees. If they don't there are consequences; and the deal was to get everyone back unharmed. I kept my side of the bargain, they didn't."

"Who decides the price Jake?"

"I do." Was the quiet reply. Then more loudly.

"Damn it Reiner, go and look at Winston and Tetsunari, go and ask Sophie what they did to her. Ask Liz Halshaw how she feels about Farache's global political ambitions or Rautsch what it feels like to have one hand. Go and ask the Haitian widows, the mothers and sisters of the dead. Go and ask our wounded and the next of kin of our dead."

The bridge crew studiously scanned the horizon and Jake drew a big breath.

"Go and ask them whether they approved of the General's ambitions and the consequences for them."

Jake raised his arm and pointed out through the bridge windows at the now spiralling smoke where the convoy burned. Jake was coldly calm.

"He was responsible for this, the rest of us danced to his tune, all along led by the nose, but I didn't kill him. The main reason for that is that I expect a certain 'Drug Lord' to do that sometime in the next few months because he hasn't got what he paid for and when it happens I will be pleased. Haiti deserves better than that trash but regime change isn't something I want to get into. Look what happens when that is brought on in a poorly planned way."

He was referring to the mess in North Africa and the Middle East brought about by America and Europe's poorly thought out foreign policy. He moderated his tone a little.

"I did however kill the bastards who tortured my employees because I care about people who put themselves in harm's way because of my orders. They have to know that when I say 'All back unharmed' that I will not accept any less because, although I couldn't claim to value them as much as my wife, I will not stand idly by while the animals who tortured them happily drive off to repeat it with someone else." He looked a last time to the spiralling smoke in the distance.

"I don't take pleasure from killing Reiner but I will do it when I deem it necessary, and what's more I won't be spending the rest of my life replaying or regretting the decision."

He made to leave the bridge but stopped before going down the stairs.

"I hope that when regime change comes to Haiti that it will be someone like Louis D'Orville who takes over, in fact I may well bankroll him myself if Sophie thinks he's good enough."

Reiner just looked stunned but the rest of the bridge crew clearly approved of his actions.

Jake made his way briskly to his stateroom leaving a deeply perturbed Reiner on the bridge. Buller and Scouse Smith kept their eyes on their tasks and no one looked at Reiner as he fought through the idea that men could be killed legitimately outside of actual combat.

Jake opened the door and as he walked in, she rushed into his arms on her newly bandaged feet courtesy of Bren, and a sore buttock courtesy of Doc Cribb with an antibiotic injection.

"What was all that Jake? Why the gunfire?"

"Just something that needed doing, for Tetsunari and Winston, I'll tell you about it later. Come on let's get you cleaned up, you smell!" He pulled a face and she batted at him with a seat cushion.

"You bastard!" She smiled for the first time in four days.

*

President for life General Farache continued looking back over his shoulder as the Limmo bounced along the poor road. He'd very nearly wet himself when the first shells had arrived but quickly realised they were targeted at the Interior Ministry police unit following a hundred yards behind. He pondered that for a second or two and then turned to face front nodding to himself.

The two body guards had been beaten. He had meant to say something at the time but his nephew's return was more important. Clearly König had somehow not held him to blame for their treatment or he'd be dead now. That was something to file away for the time when he would take his revenge on the man who had been almost single handed responsible for the failure of his attempt on the Caymans

Artillery Colonel Sutern put down his binoculars and considered his President's last words before he'd driven away. Something about being squashed by Mr König's ship wasn't it?

He looked over at the plume of smoke rising from the wreckage of the Jeep and the three tonner, some of his men raced toward it even now. God but it had been quick, the detonations had been so close together too. He shielded his eyes and looked out to sea at the squat menacing shape of the ship. Still he couldn't find it in his heart to disagree with such instant justice.

The cocky Lieutenant had been disrespectful of his rank at the very least, borderline insubordinate at worst. He had ignored him, a Colonel, when he had ordered the police to stop beating the bodyguards citing the General's orders, but the cocky shit simply said his orders came from the Interior minister.

The Colonel had been about to round up some of his own troops and go back to enforce his orders when the President had arrived.

There had still not been any communication from the President's car, no orders, no questions.

Using his binoculars again, he observed the rising bow wave and the frothing water under her counter. Lastly, he observed that the guns on the ship were now pointing his way and not towards the Interior Ministry funeral pyre or the limmo.

They know I'm here, he decided. He unslung the heavy binoculars and jumped off the bonnet of the command car, leaning against it he casually lit up a cigarette.

His gaze travelled over towards the row of D30 howitzers hiding behind the treeline. He decided that maybe the President had been right about his little guns after all.

Epilogue

Gulf of Aden September 2018.

Hood sliced through the dazzling azure sea as she approached the mouth of the notorious pirate riddled waterway and entrance to the Red Sea, but had nothing to fear from such as them, armed as she was.

They were however hunting a ship, one in particular.

"Are you sure it's him Andy?"

"Absolutely boss. He was filmed going on board this morning and we've tracked the boat all the time, the drone hasn't lost it once, a continuous record."

He looked down at his notes.

"Are we sure the people with him are the same ones that took the *Kristina*?" Asked Captain Jonathan Henry König, commanding König Industries newest Merchant Protector vessel.

"Again yes boss, all bar two who are new crewmembers. They are however known Al-Qaeda in the Arabian Peninsula operatives."

Andy Evans had tracked down Reza al Aboudi self-styled Commander of the AQAP navy, the week before.

It had taken some time and a considerable amount of *Baksheesh*, or bribes to anyone else, to get the pictures and background which positively identified him as the man who stole a Yemeni patrol boat and then massacred the crew of the König Marine survey ship *Kristina* in 2016.

Jake König spoke into his mike.

"Drone control. Click. "What is its exact position now?"

"Fifteen miles from the nearest piece of Yemeni territory and nine miles north east of us Sir. Satellite verified, substantiated, recorded and uploaded Sir."

The drone chief responded knowing exactly why his Captain was asking.

Next he checked the other crewmen important to the upcoming action.

"OPs, Guns. Have you a positive ID?

A chorus of 'Aye, Ayes'.

Have the drone move closer to film the event Chief, and zoom as much as possible."

"Aye Sir."

"Dusty." He spoke to his OPs room RS Petty Officer.

"Aye Sir."

"Dial him up then please."

*

Reza al Aboudi felt the sat phone vibrate in his pocket. Most unusual, very few people knew the number and none outside AQAP. He answered in Arabic.

"Hello who is calling?"

"This is Jonathan Henry König. You don't know me but it was my ship you stole and my people you killed back in 2016. I have waited what seems a long time for this moment."

Reza was on the bridge of his stolen vessel and he frantically scanned the horizon finally looking south west and seeing a rapidly growing shape.

"What do you want to say before I request a *Fatwa* against you and your people." Reza replied, wondering whether the ship rapidly approaching, and the only other vessel in sight, was related somehow to this conversation. There was a chilling laugh before the voice continued.

"Really, you threaten me? You clearly haven't become a better person or shown any remorse at all for killing all those people in such a barbaric fashion. No matter, I am here to tell you that I have found you guilty of piracy on the high seas and since you are not actually part of the recognized Yemeni navy, then I have decided that summary punishment is in order.

I'm sure if I took you prisoner your friends would probably do what you say, and the liberal progressives would somehow get you off the charges. But they'll never know."

"You're crazy, you'll be dead before the week is out König, you and your family." He spoke in accented English. He put the phone against his chest while he looked at the ship, a warship he could see now, looming ever larger.

"Achmed, get on the radio to our brothers and tell them we are being threatened by a man named König, owner of that survey ship we took a couple of years ago."

Then he continued his conversation.

"You are a fool König, even as we speak the order is going out for your death."

Then Achmed shouted.

"I cannot, there is nothing but static. I have tried all frequencies and bands. Nothing."

In Reza al Aboudi there was a dawning realisation that the ship, which was only a mile away now and slowly moving parallel, had something to do with the conversation and the radio not working.

He looked across at the vessel and noted the elegant sweep of the bows and streamlined shear of her hull, but most of all he noted the four twin gunned turrets now trained towards him.

The voice continued.

"My guess is that you have now looked out of your windows and seen your destruction approaching, oh and don't bother with the radios, they won't work. Sentence is to be carried out immediately."

*

On *Hood's* bridge, Jonathan Henry König kept his promise to the wife of a gentle giant of a man, brutally murdered two years before.

"Shoot!" He said into his mike.

All four turrets began shooting at the same time and after ten seconds they stopped. Briefly in the air together, were twenty four high explosive 5.1 inch shells, targeted and directed by a Saab radar and fire control system. The last four slammed into the water where previously had been a 37 metre fast attack boat.

"Job done. R.I.P Willy." Said Jake.

"Amen." Answered the bridge crew.

*

Malacca Straits night time, September 2018.

Using his CIA and DIA contacts, and pulling in every single favour he could, Senator Paulus, Chair of the Senate Armed Services Committee, had put together a comprehensive dossier on the pirate group which had attacked the MV Pacific Olympian on which his nephew had been serving.

When he'd asked for help eradicating the group all he'd got was sympathetic 'palm offs'.

Then he recalled reading about that new kind of ship, the Merchant Protector. He dug out the info on the company which owned them and re-read of their exploits earlier that year. Sounds like my kind of enforcer, he concluded having read a CIA report of an incident off Yemen earlier in the same month.

It seemed that in a series of coincidences a new Merchant Protector vessel just happened to be in the same place as a certain stolen Yemeni patrol vessel whose crew was known to have been responsible for some dreadful murders a couple of years ago. The coincidences didn't stop there. The new Merchant Protector vessel just happened to be from the same company which had lost a ship and crew to these self-same terrorists.

CIA concluded that there was no connection and that it was a purely serendipitous occurrence that that put them in the same place, and even more amazing it had foolishly opened fire on the Merchant Protector vessel before being predictably utterly destroyed. He looked at the signature of the CIA officer who'd compiled the report, Miles Carlson, now where had he heard that name before?

He recalled when the Caymans incident had been debated in the house he had reminded everyone that there was a great tradition of privateering in the US too and the reasons it has come back to us now are same as before. Governments now are as reluctant as ever they were to spend money on navy ships that will be a cost to the government until they go to scrap.

Senator Paulus had had himself introduced to the CEO of the company which owned the Merchant Protectors.

Then, over an excellent lunch he'd explained his problem to someone he decided he liked from the get-go.

He was pleased to hear that the company were being proactive and like any other privateer they had agreed a price with Lloyds in London for each proven pirate group they attacked and destroyed. They'd also decided to be pro-active in regard to generating opportunities to expose pirate groups by way of an intriguing new 'Q' ship they'd just commissioned.

König had been more than happy to explain how the superstructure of the vessel could be moved, changed in shape and in effect made to look very much like a wide variety of vulnerable vessels in order to lure in pirates.

They had even gone as far as planning to advertise for pirates from a certain hotel in Manilla bay and lure them in by creating false cargoes to be hijacked. Mr König accepted the folder with all the data and promised that if possible his Q ship would make this particular group their first sting.

*

In the South China Sea over towards the Malacca straights the new König Q ship, *Ocean Guard* readied herself for a night of low speed turns with its especially low midships freeboard. The perfect bait according to the International Maritime Organisation.

An external inspection from one of their four high powered RIBs had satisfied their stickler of a Captain that all was as ready as it could be.

The false trail had been set in Manilla and this would soon be the closest point to the suspected base for the pirates.

Captain Simon McClelland gave the orders to go to Q stations and set the ship's lighting as per plan. Three hours later their advanced Saab Radar, a smaller version of the ones on *Hood* and *Bismarck*, had detected two small vessels approaching at speed. The drone launched earlier confirmed that the vessels were full of armed men and duly took near perfect images showing the weapons which appeared to include several RPGs.

As the two fast boats manoeuvred to come in, one on the starboard quarter, the other at the portside midships, preparations were made for their welcome.

The pirates waited until both boats were in place then they made their move. As soon as the first grapnel landed on deck, the angled panel on the starboard quarter of the rear superstructure rolled up and in the darkened recess the six barrels of an AK630 Gatling type gun began winding up. At the midships entry point the deck plate rose so there was no low level entry point any more, a plate in the hull then slid back and the high pitched whine of a motor could be heard from the dark hole now present.

Before the pirates at the stern could begin to haul their boat alongside there was a brief ripping sound as a hundred or so 30mm heavy rounds utterly destroyed the vessel and all in her. The startled pirates waiting at the midships point turned back towards the black hole and the whining noise where before there'd been a boarding point. They didn't have long to wait, a brief *BRrrr* sound heralded their destruction as another hidden AK630 tore them and their boat apart. The screens and plates rolled seamlessly back into place and the *Ocean Guard* continued on its way leaving little to show where the pirates had met their end.

Senator Paulus said thank you and put the phone down when Mr König finished his call. He thought it was both kind and typical of the man to do the notification himself. He'd also offered to speak to and if satisfied, employ a certain former Third Officer of the Pacific and Olympia Line when she was ready to re-start her life.

Senator Paulus said he's pass the message on; he'd been impressed by the young woman's courage and desire to get well quickly, and he thought a job with König, even if not in the Merchant Protector program, would be a real plum posting to have. Did he have any regrets about having the pirates killed? He gave it serious consideration for a moment before answering himself. Nope, not a one, like stepping on a scorpion in your kitchen.

*

As for a certain Drug Lord and his former dictator partner, things went more or less as König had predicted.

The DEA got wind of several attempts on General Farache's life and left Andino on the back burner whilst he eventually got around to sending General Farache to hell, ironically together with his nephew as they attended a cabinet meeting together, since he was now a junior member without portfolio.

New elections in the spring of 2019 had given a runaway victory to one Louis D'Orville, the former minister of Farache's regime had mounted a very successful campaign and his first command had been to disband the Security police force, the resurrected Ton Ton Macoutes. The new Chief Gardener at the presidential palace, a Monsieur Bellard had begun his work immediately, pleased to have a dozen or so helpers for the task.

After Carlos Andino had settled his bill in the customary Cartel way the DEA had put into operation one of their better organised pot-stirring stings, a certain DEA agent by the name of Nathan King and a veteran NSA colleague were attributed with the plan which ended in a shootout at Andino's fortified headquarters and resulted in the deaths of at least forty senior cartel members and many more of their minions from several groups, including Andino himself.

If you enjoyed the books, please take a moment to review them on Amazon, many thanks.

22243557R00161

Printed in Great Britain
by Amazon